The Predicament

Signed edition

WILLIAM BOYD

PENGUIN
VIKING

The Predicament

A Novel

WILLIAM BOYD

PENGUIN
VIKING

VIKING

UK | USA | Canada | Ireland | Australia
India | New Zealand | South Africa

Viking is part of the Penguin Random House group of companies
whose addresses can be found at global.penguinrandomhouse.com.

Penguin Random House UK,
One Embassy Gardens, 8 Viaduct Gardens, London sw11 7bw

penguin.co.uk

Penguin
Random House
UK

First published 2025
001

Set in 12/14.75pt Dante MT Std
Typeset by Six Red Marbles UK, Thetford, Norfolk
Printed and bound in Great Britain by Clays Ltd, Elcograf S.p.A.

The authorized representative in the EEA is Penguin Random House Ireland,
Morrison Chambers, 32 Nassau Street, Dublin D02 YH68

A CIP catalogue record for this book is available from the British Library

HARDBACK ISBN: 978−0−241−76113−7
TRADE PAPERBACK ISBN: 978−0−241−76114−4

Penguin Random House is committed to a sustainable future
for our business, our readers and our planet. This book is made from
Forest Stewardship Council® certified paper.

MIX
Paper | Supporting
responsible forestry
FSC
www.fsc.org   FSC® C018179

For Susan

Il y a d'abord l'histoire, puis l'histoire dans l'histoire, et ensuite une autre histoire, enfouie, à laquelle n'ont accès que de rares privilégiés.

Jean-Baptiste Charbonneau, *Avis de passage* (1957)

[There is the story – and then there is the story within the story. And then there is another story, buried, that only a select few are able to read.]

PROLOGUE

Claverleigh, East Sussex, England

March 1963

Gabriel Dax looked out of his kitchen window over his back garden and saw the fox slink along the foot of the beech hedge. It was moving almost daintily, its dense brush holding a steady horizontal line. He noted the rich amber of its fur offset by the dark brown of the near-leafless hedge. The fox paused for a moment, as if to allow Gabriel to register the perfect juxtaposition, and turned its sharp head to stare directly at him, with animal clarity, or so it seemed. Then it slipped through a gap and disappeared into the small oak wood that lay beyond the garden's border.

Gabriel felt a sudden whelm of apprehension, and shivered. Was that a good omen – or an evil one? he wondered. He was still troubled by last night's unwelcome phone call that he had received from his 'contact' at the Russian embassy, Natalia Arkadina. She had requested a meeting, today, at the familiar place, the Café Matisse on the King's Road in Chelsea. He could hardly say no, given that the money Natalia and the KGB supplied him with had, to a large degree, allowed him to purchase his new home, this solid old Victorian cottage on the outskirts of Claverleigh, in East Sussex.

He knew Claverleigh, having visited the place twice during his long investigation into the cause of the fire at his childhood home that had killed his mother – a trauma that had haunted him for most of his life. It was a fair-sized village, also, with an architecturally handsome high street, and well served with shops and amenities. When he decided to leave London, East Sussex had seemed almost a natural choice – and Claverleigh, after some property-sleuthing, duly delivered the ideal house.

Rose Cottage was uninspiringly named after a large rambler that had once covered its facade, so he had been told, now long gone, replaced by a clematis over the front door. It was a two-storey square-built ashlar house with a steeply pitched slate roof. It was unpretentious and unadorned, apart from a stone ledge under the front eave with arched openings for doves (now blocked). He rather liked its simplicity and functionality. He had hoped that moving out of London might have put a symbolic distance between him and his various handlers and the complications they brought to his life. No such luck.

He stepped out through the kitchen door and wandered moodily into his garden. It was early and chilly but there had been no frost. A heavy dew spangled on the lawn and there was a blear, sulphurous morning light in the air, almost as if it were about to snow. He knew why he felt troubled, jangled somewhat. Natalia Arkadina's telephone call reminded him of his other, unsought-for, parallel existence, his life in the shadowy fringes of the espionage world. Try as he might, he couldn't pretend it didn't exist. What had Faith Green said to him when he'd tried to quit, tried to tell her that his connection with MI6 and the Institute of Developmental Studies was terminated? 'Nobody quits in this business, Gabriel. You know that.' Yes, he thought bitterly, and now the fucking Russians are on board.

He fished in his pocket for his pack of Gitanes and lit a cigarette, making his way over to the chest-high rubble wall that bounded the side of the garden that was next to the lane. His cottage was at the very edge of the village, on the single-track B-road that led to Offham, near Lewes. He had one neighbour on the west, the village side, a widower and retired colonel from the Sherwood Foresters, Royston Mitchell-Moore. To the east was open Sussex country – distance-hazed gentle hills, woods and copses, fields and pasture. It was very private, his cottage, any comings and goings were noticeable, easily logged.

Looking over the wall, Gabriel immediately registered that the black Ford Popular was still parked on the verge opposite Royston's rather elegant house, Barley Court. It was much grander than Rose Cottage, so much so that it merited a few lines in *The Buildings of England*: 'Late C18, two storeys, five windows. The interior has good doorcases. Central first-floor Venetian window. Quietly charming.' Royston lived there alone. He had never remarried.

Gabriel stared at the Popular. It wasn't Royston's car, he knew. Royston drove an Armstrong Siddeley Star Sapphire. Maybe a friend was staying with him, Gabriel thought – and therefore it was not necessarily something to ponder or worry about. Worry, yes, Gabriel recognized – his new companion, dogging his heels, always by his side, at his elbow. He strolled back into the cottage. He'd bike to Lewes, he thought, catch a London train well before noon.

He had arranged to meet Natalia Arkadina at 2 p.m. He intended to capitalize on the encounter in London by visiting his editor, Inigo Marcher, and delivering the latest chapter of *Rivers*. The book was almost finished, he reckoned – two more rivers would be enough, three at a pinch. He already had an idea for his next travel book – he'd suggest it to Inigo, see what he thought. Considering his real life, as opposed to his secret life, cheered him up, to a degree.

And as if to emphasize the normality of his existence he put out a saucer of milk for the creature he had dubbed the Cat. Shortly after he'd moved into Rose Cottage a large tomcat adopted him. He had seen it prowling about the garden, black with white paws. One day, when he had momentarily left the kitchen door open, it had come inside. He gave it some milk and it – he always referred to the Cat as 'it' in his mind – decided to stay. Gabriel had a cat-flap fitted in the kitchen door and the Cat came and went as it pleased. Gabriel bought catfood in Claverleigh's small supermarket. The Cat deigned to eat it. Sometimes the Cat disappeared for a day or two but it always came back. Mice were caught, terminated and left as trophies on the kitchen floor, along with a small butcher's bill of songbirds. Gabriel never stroked or petted the Cat. He had tried once and the Cat hissed at him, baring its thin sharp teeth. It slept on an armchair in the sitting room. Sometimes, rarely, he heard it purring. After a month the arrangement seemed established and natural: Gabriel now had a relationship with an aloof domestic animal; the Cat had shelter, warmth and nourishment. There was no rodent problem in Rose Cottage – and that was the reasonable quid pro quo as far as Gabriel was concerned.

He squared off the carbon copy of his Mississippi chapter and placed it in a wallet file. He was thinking of doing the Nile, next, then perhaps the Mekong or the Yangtse. The Indus? The book's concept was, he thought, rather brilliant: great and minor rivers analysed through one specific locus – a city, town or village situated somewhere on the river's journey to the sea with no attempt at a wider view: the part would be greater than the whole, or as great, was the theory. However, he was aware that there were no South American rivers amongst his tally – no Amazon, no Orinoco. He'd talk it over with Inigo, see what he thought.

He pulled on his black leather coat – his grandfather's – and put on his cream Bakelite crash helmet and goggles. Outside, he wheeled his motorbike, a new Norton Navigator – a lightweight, four-stroke twin, another instance of Russian largesse – from the woodshed next to the cottage. He put his briefcase in the pannier and kick-started the machine. He straddled it, revved the engine – and immediately noticed that the Ford Popular had gone.

He drove slowly out of his driveway, thinking. The car had been there, minutes ago, and had been parked across the lane for two days. Strange. He saw Royston Mitchell-Moore in his front garden, clipping away at the decorative round box balls that flanked his front door. Gabriel throttled back and gave Royston a wave. He put down his secateurs and wandered over.

Royston was a handsome, lean sixty-year-old, Gabriel noted once again. Even in his gardening clothes he seemed faultlessly smart: the many-pocketed olive-green jacket; crimson corduroy trousers, a French brand of wellington boot in an unusual mud-brown colour; his thick, wavy grey hair oiled back like metal from his large forehead; his regimental tie with a knot the size of a hazelnut. In his two months as his neighbour at Rose Cottage Gabriel had never seen Royston tie-less. His face was seamed and his voice was a bass, nicotined rumble. He was a sixty-a-day man.

'Gabriel, good morrow, old fellow, what can I do for you?' he said.

'That car that was parked opposite your house the last couple of days,' Gabriel said. 'Did it belong to a friend of yours?'

'No. I thought it belonged to somebody staying with you, actually. Why?'

'It just seemed odd. A car parked there, all this while.'

'I did see a chap with a rucksack come and go. Walking the Downs, I suppose.'

Gabriel thought that was the logical interpretation. But he knew all too well that it could sometimes be foolish to trust logical interpretations.

'You didn't happen to note the number plate, did you?'

'What? Why on earth should I do that?' Royston said, trying not to look too bemused.

'Silly question. I'll be on my way.' Gabriel waved goodbye and accelerated down Offham Lane on the Navigator, heading for Lewes. Stupid bloody idiot Gabriel Dax, he said to himself, angrily. Why hadn't he noted the licence plate himself and jotted it down? He realized that he had to start thinking like a spy again.

PART ONE

London
East Sussex
Guatemala City

March 1963

I.

The Café Matisse

Gabriel strolled up the King's Road towards the Café Matisse, pleased to be back in London, in Chelsea, his old stamping ground, and simultaneously wondering, somewhat ruefully, if he had made the right decision in moving to the countryside. As time had gone by he had become less and less sure. He was essentially an urban person, he felt, and village life, however comfortable Rose Cottage was, had confirmed that. Claverleigh couldn't offer the same quotidian pleasures that living in a big vibrant city did. By simply walking up the King's Road from Sloane Square Tube to the Café Matisse he had already seen at least two dozen interesting-looking people, and some very attractive young women, not to mention the intriguing variety of shops available and the different marques of cars in the passing traffic. Sleepy Claverleigh couldn't compete – inevitably, of course. Still, he had made his bed and he must lie in it, he supposed, at least for a while. He was thirty-three and now a home-owner – that was a plus. He was free to sell Rose Cottage and move back to town, if he fancied. Everything in life is temporary, he reminded himself – who had said that? Henri Bergson? Samuel Beckett? Ludwig Wittgenstein . . . ?

Outside the Matisse, Gabriel checked his watch: 1.50 p.m. He was early. He thought he should just go in and order a glass of wine – steady the nerves before his meeting with Natalia Arkadina.

He stepped into the Matisse and looked around, almost with a kind of sob of recognition in his throat, greeted by its warm fug of cigarette smoke and fried and spicy food, the enthusiastic susurrus of conversation, the stony-faced waitresses, the eponymous large blue-period Matisse poster on the back wall between the ladies' and gents' toilets. Nothing had changed in his brief absence: how reassuring. He found a booth at the rear and ordered a carafe of Chianti. Why had he left Chelsea? he asked himself, again. Was he insane? No. He knew the answer: after his fraught and complicated experiences with MI6 and Faith Green and the suicide of his brother, Sefton, he needed distance, a new set of circumstances, new surroundings that would reflect the change he was determined to introduce into his life – that was why. Chelsea would always be here; he could return whenever the mood took him. No, Claverleigh actually suited him at the moment. He shouldn't complain about living in—

A shadow fell across the table and he looked up to see Natalia Arkadina standing in front of him. At her shoulder was another woman, older, with short greying hair.

'Mr Dax, how are you?' Natalia said as he stood up and shook her hand, very aware of the fist-thud increase in his heartbeat. His parallel life reclaiming him.

'I'm very well, thank you, Natalia.'

'May I introduce my colleague, Varvara Sergeevna Suvorina.'

Gabriel shook her hand. She had a square, mannish face, accentuated by the cropped hairstyle, a firm jaw and a gently hooked nose. Older than Natalia, in her forties, he reckoned. She was staring at him intently. She had very dark brown eyes, he noticed, suddenly feeling a bit uncomfortable being faced by these two Russian women. What did this extra person portend, this Varvara Suvorina? He had only met Natalia twice before, always alone, and on each occasion she had given him the present of a book, the pages interleaved with money, £10 notes. The first book, a selection of Chekhov short stories, had contained £1,000. The second, Gogol's *Dead Souls*, £500. His stipend from the KGB. Money that had gone towards his purchase of Rose Cottage.

He smiled. He had a sudden urge to see Faith Green again. Faith had told him to spend the Russian money, conspicuously. Show them you're happily using it. That will let them see you're properly hooked, properly suborned. Gabriel Dax, a suborned man. It was both typical and annoying of Faith to use that word, he thought.

The two women sat down opposite him, both ordered tea, both refused the offer of his French cigarettes and lit their own – American ones, he noted. They spoke about the weather, his state of health, the problems of London transport.

'How is your cottage in Claverleigh?' Natalia asked.

How does she know where I live? he asked himself.

'Very comfortable, thank you. A quiet life. Hard at work.'

'And your new book? The *Rivers*?'

'Nearly finished.' He was aware of Varvara Suvorina's continued scrutiny. He smiled at Natalia. Blonde, cheerful Natalia. She was wearing very bright lipstick today, he noticed. Cherry red.

'I am going back to Moscow,' Natalia said, lowering her voice. 'Varvara here will take over my liaison with you. The same telephone numbers will apply.'

Gabriel glanced at Varvara Suvorina and smiled. Always smiling, compliant Gabriel Dax, he thought, with some discomfort, playing his double-agent game as best he could. She smiled back and the sternness in her suddenly vanished. She was wearing a black coat, with an aquamarine polo-neck sweater beneath it. She had a small gold cross at her throat, dangling from a fine chain. What you'd call a 'handsome' woman, he supposed. Now this enigmatic Varvara would be his go-between. He'd miss Natalia. A bit.

Varvara took a brown paper parcel from her handbag and pushed it across the table to him.

'It's my favourite book,' she said. 'A good translation, I'm told.' She stubbed out her Peter Stuyvesant.

Gabriel tore off the wrapping. Lermontov, he saw: *A Hero of Our Time.* How very apt. He put the book in his briefcase, vaguely wondering how much money it contained and what he should conspicuously purchase with it.

'Mr Caldwell sends his greetings,' Varvara said. 'I saw him last week.'

Gabriel swallowed. Kit Caldwell, notorious defector, Soviet double agent – except he wasn't. He was an MI6 triple agent. Our man in Moscow and the very reason I'm sitting here with these two Russian women, Gabriel said to himself, the bitterness rising in him, as if he had a sump of bile somewhere in his body and from time to time, when agitated, it surged inexorably to the surface.

'How is he?'

'He's a happy man. A hero.'

'A hero of our time, perhaps,' Gabriel said, thinking back to their last meeting in Warsaw – aeons ago, it seemed, another life. What was it Caldwell had said to him? 'You don't know how important you are.' A nice compliment but he didn't want to be 'important', thank you very much.

'Are you all right, Mr Dax?' Varvara asked.

'Yes. Absolutely. Just remembered something – about Lermontov. Didn't he die in a duel?'

'Precisely. Twenty-six years old.'

Natalia leant forward and lowered her voice again.

'We would like you to try to get some information for us.'

'Oh, yes?' This was the first time he had been asked to perform a task – the unspoken leverage of the money-gifts finally being applied.

Natalia took a small piece of folded paper out of her handbag and presented it to him.

'We would like to know more about this person,' she said. 'The area of responsibility. Anything you can provide will be most helpful.' Natalia inclined her head Varvara's way. 'Anything, even triviality, will be useful for Varvara.'

Gabriel nodded and unfolded the piece of paper.

There was a name written in capital letters: 'FAITH GREEN'.

2.

The Plagiarist

Striding up Long Acre, heading for Covent Garden on his way to meet Inigo Marcher, his editor, Gabriel deliberately walked past the unassuming door of the Institute of Developmental Studies – with its permanently tarnished brass plate – Faith Green's MI6 fiefdom, the source of almost all the complications and frustrations in his life. He thought about ringing the doorbell but held back. She had to know that the KGB were suddenly curious about her and he wondered if there was any connection with Kit Caldwell. Caldwell's 'defection' had been meticulously, brilliantly planned by Faith Green and the Institute. He didn't think it was a coincidence that the Russians were suddenly interested in her – there were no coincidences in the espionage world, Faith had once said to him. He would drop her a line, Gabriel thought – all in due course. Now his own, old, proper life had priority.

'Ah-ha, the Mississippi,' Inigo Marcher said, accepting the manuscript with enthusiasm. 'I can't wait to read about Hattiesburg.' Hattiesburg was the town Gabriel had chosen as his *point de repère* on Old Man River. 'How many is it now?' Inigo asked, crossing his large, shambolic office in Mulholland & Melhuish Ltd to his well-stocked drinks table and his fridge.

'Thames, Tweed, Liffey, Danube, the Blyth at Southwold, Vistula, Mississippi. I think another two should do it. I'm close to seventy thousand words already.'

Inigo poured them both a large Scotch.

'Water? Soda?'

'Water, please.'

Inigo sat down and lit up one of his noisome Indian cheroots.

'I think we need something exotic – African, Brazilian, Asian.

Or some small river, unknown, that you effortlessly put on the map for ever, like the Blyth.'

'I agree,' Gabriel said, enjoying the warm hit of Inigo's quadruple Scotch. 'I'm working on it.'

'By the way, I was going to write to you but I knew you were coming in today. We've just sold *Rivers* in the States. Wheelwright, Russell and Duprée.'

'WRD! Bloody hell.' Gabriel was genuinely thrilled. 'How much?'

'Three thousand dollars.'

Gabriel did a swift calculation. There was Mulholland & Melhuish's commission, then tax on that income to be set aside, and, no doubt, tax to be paid in the USA. He suddenly didn't feel quite so thrilled. Still, Wheelwright, Russell & Duprée was an elite publisher. All manner of advantages lay ahead.

'Bound to be a Book Club deal soon,' Inigo added, as if reading his mind.

Gabriel allowed his pleasure at the news to register.

'And I've got an idea for the next book.'

'Spit it out, *mon frère, mon semblable*,' Inigo said, topping up their whiskies.

'It's to be called *On the Beaten Path*,' Gabriel said, enunciating the title clearly, emphasizing the 'On'. 'I'm going to go to very, very familiar places and make them unfamiliar.' He paused. 'You know – the Pyramids of Giza, the Eiffel Tower, Rock of Gibraltar, Machu Picchu, Angkor Wat, the Houses of Parliament, the Empire State Building, the Great Wall of China. Et cetera.'

'Astonishingly good idea,' Inigo said, genuinely, admiringly. Gabriel could see he was thinking fast. 'Yah, listen. We could announce it when we publish *Rivers*, don't you think?' He paused. 'Love that title. Clever bastard.'

Gabriel felt his enthusiasm rise. This was his true, real life he realized: a life of writing that was fairly well remunerated and appreciated; a kind of rich literary conversation with like-minded folk. And yet he had just come from a meeting with two Russian spooks who assumed he was a British double agent within the ranks of MI6 who had very usefully facilitated the defection of the Soviet

'Super Spy', Kit Caldwell. It couldn't go on, this schizophrenic life that he was leading, he said to himself for the hundredth time. One life full of pleasure and intellectual satisfaction; the other full of tension and darkness. It had to end, as soon as possible, if only to preserve his sanity.

Inigo was paying no attention.

'Write up the proposal,' he said. 'Get, whatshisname, your agent, to submit it—'

'Jeff Lockhart.'

'Good old Jeff, yes – and we'll make you an offer.'

He should remember these moments in life, Gabriel thought, when you're on a roll, when everything you do seems to meet with instant approval, and people pay you serious money for your ideas.

However, Inigo was now frowning.

'Why are you frowning?'

'There's another, more delicate matter. An, ah, awkwardness. We should discuss it.'

'My God, what?'

Inigo looked at his watch.

'Pubs are just opening. Let's repair to an adjacent hostelry.'

There was a pub Inigo frequented just off Kingsway called the Prince Regent that had a gloomy basement room with an unused dartboard and red leather banquettes. There was a certain tackiness, a mulch in the nap of the patterned carpet beneath their feet, Gabriel noticed, as they sat down with their beers, and in the still airlessness of the room there was a faint redolence of astringent disinfectant from the nearby gents' lavatory. Nothing remotely 'Regency' about its ambience, he thought. Not surprisingly they were alone. A good environment to hear of this 'awkwardness', as Inigo put it.

'You're being sued for plagiarism,' he said matter-of-factly. 'We've had a lawyer's letter.'

'What the fuck are you—'

'So are we, by the way. Being sued, I mean – as your publishers.'

'Who's suing me and what am I meant to have plagiarized?'

'We're being sued by a writer called Lucian Applegate and he claims your first book, *The Wine-Dark Sea*, is a blatant steal from his book, *Ioniana*.'

'That is the biggest load of grade-A horseshit I have ever heard,' Gabriel said, registering a degree of pure fury in him that he hadn't experienced since he was a schoolboy. He felt himself blush. A blush of shock.

'What's his evidence?'

'That you visited the same Greek islands – or, rather, four of the same islands – that he wrote about in his book.'

'What islands?'

Inigo fished a notebook from his pocket and opened it.

'Rhodes, Crete, Skios, Hydra.'

'Well, he should advise his lawyers to sue every writer who has ever written about the Greek archipelago.' Gabriel began to relax – it was a scam, clearly. 'It's malicious. Malicious nonsense. Stirring things up. What damages is he claiming?'

'Five thousand pounds. If we pay him the case goes away.'

Gabriel laughed out loud.

'Tell him to fuck off. Tell him we'll see him in court.'

'It's not as simple as that,' Inigo said. 'Have you ever read Applegate?'

'I love Applegate. I've read everything he's written. Including *Ioniana*.'

'That could be evidence.'

'But I didn't copy out what he'd written about these islands,' Gabriel said, trying not to let his voice become shrill. 'I just visited them, myself, like countless other writers, and recorded my impressions. He doesn't *own* those islands. He can't stop people writing about their reaction to them, just because he's done so himself at some stage in his writing life. There were writers before him who went to those islands. Lawrence Durrell, to name but one. Homer, to name another. Henry Miller. Maybe Durrell should sue Applegate for daring to set foot on Corfu.'

'Fair point.'

'Applegate's clearly broke, I'll bet you. It's a desperate attempt to screw money out of you – and me.'

'Mmmmm,' Inigo mumbled, thinking. 'You're right. Let me talk to the big boss. We don't want it to get in the papers, whatever happens. These journalists love a spat between writers.'

Gabriel felt cast down, after his moment of elation. Maybe he'd just experienced the fundamental pattern of life – good luck, then inevitable bad luck. He felt a shiver of – of what? – of panic run through him. The Lords of Misrule seemed to be visiting him in the shape of Varvara Suvorina and, now, Lucian Applegate, both banishing happiness, stability and calm.

He looked at his watch. It was time to catch the train back to Lewes, return to the placid safety of Rose Cottage.

'I'd better go.'

'Sorry to cast a cloud,' Inigo said.

'It's all a nonsense,' Gabriel said, standing, draining his glass. 'An act of vindictive desperation by a penniless old writer.'

'We'll make it go away, don't worry,' Inigo said, rising to his feet, also, with an uncertain smile on his face. 'But maybe – just to be on the safe side, *amigo* – you should brief a lawyer. These things can get nasty.'

Gabriel brooded darkly on the train back to Lewes. He was in a sour, angry mood, he realized, despite the good news he'd received about his American publication. What was he meant to tell the Russians about Faith Green? And how to find a lawyer to challenge Applegate's ludicrous claim? He didn't know any lawyers. He'd ask his uncle, Aldous, he suddenly thought – inspiration coming to him. Paradoxically, that cheered him up: he'd enlist Aldous in the fight. Little did Lucian Applegate – the vengeful old bastard – know what he'd let himself in for.

He motored back to Claverleigh on the Navigator in a calmer frame of mind. He'd cook himself a meal, drink a lot of red wine, listen to wonderful music on his Hi-Fi and let his cares take care of themselves. Fretting, worrying, solved nothing; practical, swift action was required, he told himself, turning into Offham Lane. He braked sharply. Parked on the verge opposite his house was a sports car – a silver Mercedes-Benz 190 SL. Faith Green had found him.

3.

The Return of Raymond Queneau

'Of course I know where you live,' Faith Green said, wandering around his living room, idly picking up books and bowls, candlesticks and framed photographs, and putting them down after swift scrutiny. 'Why would I not?'

It had been a day of piled-on emotions, Gabriel recognized. Pelion heaped on Ossa, all right – or was it the other way around? Who had said that? Samuel Butler? Virgil? Elizabeth Barrett Browning . . .? Anyway, he had run the gamut of apprehension, alarm, confusion, pleasure, self-satisfaction, outrage, panic, fury, calm and now . . . Lust.

He hadn't seen Faith for many weeks – well over two months. They had last met in early January on a platform of Covent Garden Tube station when she had seized his hand as he hurried out heading for the lifts. They had shared a cup of coffee in a coffee bar and reluctantly recognized that their affair, such as it was, brief though it was, had no future. They had experienced an intense moment, true, they had been lovers, but now she was engaged to be married. So – *finito, fini, fertig*. They could still be friends, she hoped. But her life as his handler – his puppet-mistress, as he termed her – had to continue, she said, regardless of our feelings, or of what had happened between us. There was no stepping away from that – this is too big, too much at stake. The facade of the Caldwell/Dax collusion had to be perfectly maintained. Keep seeing the Russians whenever they ask for a meeting, she told him; take their money, spend it extravagantly. All this will ensure and enhance Kit Caldwell's security in Moscow, make his story wholly valid, rock solid.

And here she was in his sitting room in Rose Cottage prowling around, curious, oddly excited beneath the calm surface, he thought, knowing her subtly shifting moods now, as he did. She was wearing a fur coat – the colour of wet sand shot with umber – to the mid-calf. She had her usual Alice band, holding back her tousled, girlish hair. Her long, still, enigmatic face was pale, with just a touch of make-up – a glossy pink lipstick, her eyebrows dark and strong. He felt a pang of longing for her – his Faith-pang that he recognized. That ache she provoked in him . . .

'Is that coat mink?' he asked, wanting to say something chattily bland, trying to seem unperturbed by her presence, though his mind was already noisy with unanswered questions.

'I wish,' she said. 'Shaved rabbit. Very warm, though. Warm as mink, they say.'

He had lit the fire in his wide brick fireplace and it had caught quickly as there was a great mound of warm ash beneath the kindling and the dry logs. It crackled and spat a bit, throwing random orange light-beams around the room, the new pale flames writhing high in that strange kind of autonomous fire-ecstasy that happens, he had noticed, when a well-laid fire is first lit.

'What a lovely cottage,' she said. 'A writer's cottage. Like a rural variant of your old Chelsea flat.'

'All this furniture is from the flat,' he said, dully.

'Yes. It's the same, I can see that, but different, being here. That great wall of books there. You didn't have that in Chelsea.'

'I did, actually. I wanted a replica. I had those shelves built when I moved in.'

'And I haven't seen that picture before. Lovely.'

She pointed at a big still life above the mantel. A bowl of green figs in a blue-patterned dish set on a cream tablecloth.

'It's by Vanessa Bell. Sister of Virginia Woolf, as it happens,' he added.

'How interesting. I have heard of Virginia Woolf, you'll be pleased to know – but not her sister, I admit.'

'One of my presents to myself from the Russian fund. A hundred and fifty pounds.'

'Excellent. The more the merrier.'

Gabriel stood there looking at her, remembering their lovemaking.

It seemed as if it had happened in another historical era, on another planet, even.

'Why are you staring at me like that?' she asked.

'I was wondering if you'd like something to drink.'

She put down the framed photograph in her hand, crossed the room and stood with her back to the fire, now it had taken.

'I'd love a dram of that malt whisky you have, Glenfeshan. Just a tiny one. One ice cube. Thank you, barman.'

Gabriel went into the kitchen to fetch the ice, sensing a slow erection buckling behind his fly, wondering how it was she got to him, how she insinuated herself into his mind, erotically, how the most innocuous remark seemed to have reverberations that were not so much unexpected as improbable. He was smitten, he had to admit. Perhaps that was too mild. In thrall, might be more accurate. He told himself to be more distant, more amused and insouciant if he possibly could. He had to stand his ground when faced with Faith Green. He had to put up a fight.

He served her drink. She stirred the ice cube in the glass with a finger and took a sip. She looked at him.

'You must wonder why I'm here,' she said.

'Perfect timing. I have information to relay to you also.'

'You go first.'

'I had a meeting with the Russians today.'

'I know. There's a new contact. What's her name?'

He closed his eyes for a second. How did she know? Who else had been in the Café Matisse?

'Varvara Suvorina.'

'Recent arrival. We logged her. Age?'

'Early forties, I suppose.'

'Did they give you money?'

'Five hundred. Again.'

The Lermontov had duly yielded up its bounty of fifty crisp £10 notes.

'What did they want?'

'This is where it gets interesting,' Gabriel said. 'They want me to investigate you.'

To his astonishment she didn't seem to react. Not a hint of surprise.

'They must know who I am,' she said, with a shrug. 'I suspect it's more likely a test of you.'

'Me? Really?' He felt a little spasm of alarm.

'Yes. What has all their money bought? You can tell them about the Institute, my role there. Nothing about Caldwell, of course. Let them think I'm a termite-hunter, pure and simple.'

'Right . . . I will. I'll try to be as vague as possible.' Again, he felt the fog of confusion descend. And its corollary of resentment. Why was he being tested by the Russians? He was a travel writer. But as he labelled himself he knew the pretence was futile. Of course, he *was* a travel writer, but since he had become embroiled with Faith Green and her Institute he was now in another category, with another label, and one much harder to slough off.

He sat down opposite her and sipped his whisky. He glanced at Faith's left hand and noticed she wasn't wearing her engagement ring.

'How's Vivian?' he asked. Vivian was her fiancé, a chartered surveyor.

'We've broken off the engagement. It was never going to work.' She showed him her ringless finger.

He felt a sudden heart-swell and tried quickly to subdue the instant, stupid smile that spread on his face.

'Commiserations. Poor old Vivian. He must be bereft. I'm sorry to hear that,' he said, hypocritically.

'No, you're not.'

'No, I'm not.'

'Don't get any fancy ideas, Gabriel.'

'Why would I do that? I know you too well by now.'

'You do, I suppose. We both know each other well, very well, come to think of it. After everything we've been through.' She smiled, then frowned, thoughtfully. 'That can only be a good thing.'

What is that meant to mean? he asked himself. What game is being played here?

'So, what brought you to Claverleigh?' he asked, changing the subject and the mood. 'I assume you weren't just passing by.'

'Could I have just another little splash of whisky?'

He topped up their drinks and threw another couple of logs on the fire. He watched the flames rise for a second, lambent, richly orange, and then turned to face her.

'A body has been discovered,' she said, flatly. 'Washed up on a beach in Scotland.' Now she smiled at him knowingly, disconcertingly. 'Very badly decomposed. Many weeks in the North Sea. Half-consumed by sea creatures.'

'And what does that have to do with me – us – this encounter?' he asked.

'We think it's the body of John Hillcrest.' She spread her hands. 'Known to you as Raymond Queneau, of course.'

Gabriel registered his stomach-churn and then a form of lucid panic in his mind – that he subdued with a gulp of whisky, trying to look as if he was having difficulty in recalling just who this Raymond Queneau was. He felt a biliousness course through him. He would never forget Raymond Queneau. He had shot the man and thrown him off a ferry in the North Sea. Gone for ever, he thought. Apparently not.

'My God,' Gabriel said. 'I last saw Queneau in the Café Matisse on the King's Road. He threatened to have me killed. I think I told you.'

'A bit of a loose cannon, John Hillcrest.'

'Maybe it's not him,' Gabriel said.

'The dental records suggest it is. Though these bodies do get a bit churned up by ships' propellers.'

'Ugh.'

'The interesting thing about this mangled corpse is that there was a bullet lodged low in his pelvis. A .25 bullet.' She gave another of her expressive shrugs. 'Looks like this fellow was shot before he ended up in the water.'

'So?' Gabriel tried to maintain maximum impassivity.

'When you went off to Poland you had a .25 pistol with you. That we supplied.'

'That I dumped in a ditch before crossing into East Germany on my journey home. Good procedure.'

'Right. Absolutely.'

They looked at each other, both smiling faintly, duplicitously, Gabriel thought. This was the sour undercurrent in their lives, he saw, a fundamental absence of trust that corroded all the purer, nicer, warmer feelings they might have had for each other. Now he was wondering if she had deliberately removed her engagement ring to give him faint hope. How could one live like this? he asked himself. Always questioning, always doubting . . .

'Anyway, I never saw Queneau again,' he said, as breezily as possible. 'I didn't like him particularly – a braggart, a bully. Apologies. I know he was a CIA colleague of yours, back in the Congo.'

'Very briefly. Still, as the investigation into this corpse continues – and the CIA are very interested in its outcome, naturally – I want to put a proposition to you.'

'I'm finishing my book, sorry.'

She ignored him.

'We would like you to go to Guatemala – under the cover of the *New Interzonal Review*, as before.'

'Alas, I—'

'I think, Gabriel, it would be in your best interests. A joint MI6/ CIA operation. The CIA would be grateful . . . You might benefit from their gratitude.'

'I don't understand.'

'I think you do.'

'I had nothing to do with the death of Raymond Queneau.'

'I wasn't referring to Queneau. Odd that you should bring him up.'

Gabriel looked at her. Always these games, this fencing with each other.

'Let's just say that I have no interest in appeasing the CIA,' he said.

'It would be a very good signal, if you know what I mean. You would be . . .' She thought about the right word. 'Appreciated.'

'All right. I'll think about it.'

'Come to the Institute. Wednesday? Noon? We'll brief you. Your usual wages.'

She stood up. Gabriel rose to his feet, thinking: how can she do this to me so easily? He felt like some sort of indentured servant – wash the dishes in the scullery and then mop the floors upstairs.

'It's important work, Gabriel.'

'Isn't it always?'

'Cynicism doesn't suit you, as I've pointed out many times.'

'I'm a cynic. Can you blame me? I can't help it.'

She walked to the door, folding her luxuriant coat closer around her. She turned and faced him.

'Can I kiss you goodbye?' he said.

'You can kiss me there.'

Her forefinger touched the middle of her right cheek.

Gabriel leant forward, kissed her cheek and then, swiftly, before she could react, her soft lips. For a second or two she yielded, and for that moment Gabriel felt himself transported. He put his arms around her and held her to him.

She pushed him away, forcefully.

'And that's the very last time you'll ever kiss me, Mr Dax.'

'I doubt it, somehow.'

'It's not in your gift.'

'Stay the night. You want to, I know.'

'I have a very important meeting in London.'

'Liar.'

They stared at each other. Tick-tock, tick-tock. He opened the front door.

'See you at noon on Wednesday,' he said. And she left.

He stood there, held fast in the usual turmoil of emotions that this woman provoked in him, listening to her powerful car start and then motor off up the lane.

He sat down and poured himself another dram of whisky. Guatemala, here I come, he thought.

4.

Transference

Dr Katerina Haas leant back in her chair, thinking, tapping her chin with her forefinger and looking at him, closely. Sometimes she did this in a session, Gabriel recalled, paused and reflected as if she had suddenly had some kind of revelation about him. Today she was wearing an iridescent silk scarf – magenta and a cerulean blue – loosely tied, that shimmered against the starched white collar of her lab coat.

'I'm going to make a suggestion,' she said. 'One that you're perfectly free to decline. I only ask it of some of my analysands – but I find it helps me. Significantly.'

'By all means,' Gabriel said.

'I would like to see you naked.'

'May I ask why?' Gabriel tried not to sound astonished.

'If I see how you deal with your nakedness in front of me it'll give me information that simple discussions cannot provide. I'll know you in ways I don't know you now. For example, how comfortable are you with your nakedness? Or, perhaps I'll sense if you're embarrassed, or recoil in some way. All useful information about you as a person.'

Gabriel thought for a moment. Maybe there was some psychoanalytical sense in this notion.

'All right.'

Katerina Haas pulled the cream curtains across the French windows that overlooked her back lawn. Gabriel moved to the wall opposite and began to undress, hanging his clothes on the large weighing scale that stood there. As he loosened his tie he wondered if this was actually a little unhinged, not to say perverse. What the hell, he thought, he wasn't ashamed of his body.

He stood there facing her.

'Completely naked, please.'

He slipped off his underpants. And put his hands on his hips, legs slightly apart.

'You're very thin,' she said, taking a step towards him.

'I'm an ectomorph. I don't seem able to put on weight.'

She reached out a hand and smiled.

'May I touch your penis?'

Gabriel woke with a jolt and managed to stop himself from ejaculating. Thank God, he thought, feeling the mortification course through him, his blush heating his cheeks. What the fuck was going on in his unconscious? He swung himself out of bed and sat for a minute, trying to calm down, then stood and took a few steps around his bedroom, massaging his hot face. He switched on the light and glugged some water from the glass on the bedside table. Some measure of repose duly returned. It wasn't surprising that he'd had a sexual dream, he reasoned, given what had occurred between him and Faith Green a few hours before and the intense feelings swirling in him, the desire he'd felt for her, the brief kiss . . .

What was alarming him was that, in the inevitable sex dream afterwards, the woman wasn't Faith but his psychoanalyst. What was that all about? 'Transference' was the term he believed was used. Why had he transferred from Faith to Dr Haas? Who knew? Life was full of mysteries, large and small. He had a callus in the middle of his right palm. He had no idea what friction had brought this about – some sort of mindless nail-scratching in the small of the night, a little fretting agitation that he was unaware of but had the evidence on his palm to prove that it had taken place. There are more things in heaven and earth, Horatio, than are dreamt of in your philosophy. *Hamlet*. His favourite quote from Shakespeare.

He opened the drawer of the bedside table and took out the notebook and biro that he kept there. Katerina Haas had asked him to record his dreams – to write his dream-diary, as she termed it. 'Dreams are worse than memories,' she had said. 'If you don't write them down they're gone for ever. Like melting snow, bubbles bursting.'

He wrote down: 'Strangely erotic dream. Stripped naked in front of Katerina, at her request. Potential cock-touching.' It was a sign – he should go and see her, he thought, it had been a while since his last visit. She was expensive and her rates had gone up. Still, now he had more money from the Russians he could spend it on sessions with her – the KGB bonus.

Gabriel paused as he emerged from Covent Garden Tube station and looked around, bracing himself. He felt an odd sense of foreboding, walking down Long Acre towards the Institute, wondering what this Guatemala trip might involve. Trouble, no doubt.

It was a bright blustery day, fresh and cool, the blue sky full of lumbering clouds, cloud-shadows hurrying up the street, eye-dazzling sunbursts firing from the windscreens of passing cars. Perhaps he should have worn a hat, he thought idly, glad of his scarf and duffel coat. He rang the bell at the side of the Institute's scuffed and dusty nameplate and heard the lock system whirr and click before the door opened.

Not Faith – to his vague surprise – but a young woman, about his age. She was wearing a grass-green herringbone tweed suit and was on the plump side, he thought. A pink flush to her full cheeks, brown hair in a bun, rimless oval spectacles that flashed briefly – silver coins in the angled sunshine as the door opened wide.

'Mr Dax,' she said, extending her hand. 'How do you do? I'm Mrs Dunbar.'

Polite Scottish accent, Gabriel noted, as she led him upstairs, commenting chattily on the hint of approaching spring in today's intermittent sunshine. She showed him into the first-floor conference room and Gabriel stepped inside. There was Faith at the head of the long table, and her team – the familiar faces of Harrison Lee, Anatoly Sirin and Mr Fuller, the note-taker. Gabriel was welcomed enthusiastically, shaking hands with the men like a colleague returned from a long leave, he reflected. Mrs Dunbar sat down. Gabriel's place was at the end of the table, opposite Faith. There was a carafe of water on the table and six glasses. No biscuits, Gabriel noticed. Belts being tightened at the Institute, perhaps.

Faith gestured at Mrs Dunbar.

'You've met Ishbel. She's our South American expert.'

Ishbel Dunbar, Gabriel registered, some sort of Scottish variant of Isabel, he assumed.

'Are you familiar with the current situation in Guatemala?' Ishbel asked.

'I've done a bit of homework,' Gabriel said. 'It's a military government, currently led by General Ydígoras Fuentes.' He shrugged. 'The place seems a bit of a mess. Guerrilla armies in the hills and all that. Disappearances, arrests. Sort of tinpot dictatorland.'

'Might be an interesting appendix for your book,' Lee said, smiling. He turned to Ishbel. 'Gabriel wrote a book called *Dictatorland*.'

'I know,' Ishbel said. 'I too have done my homework on Mr Dax.'

Chuckles from the men. Faith was looking at him, expressionless, as usual.

'Do please call me Gabriel.'

'Ydígoras is walking on thin ice, unfortunately. Democratic elections are promised. He may not last long.'

'At least he hasn't been assassinated,' Gabriel said. 'Like President Armas in 1957.'

'Now you're showing off,' Faith said, drily. More chuckles.

'Why exactly do you want me to go to Guatemala?' Gabriel asked. 'I can't quite see that I'd be any use.'

'We want you to meet and interview a man who may be the next elected President of the country,' Ishbel said. 'If and when democracy returns.'

'May I ask why?'

Ishbel looked at Faith.

'We want to get the measure of him. He's elusive, very much an unknown quantity,' Faith said.

'Who is "we"?'

'MI6 and the CIA.'

Gabriel took a beat to think. The CIA, again. The CIA dividend that would benefit him – somehow.

'Guatemala is in the USA's back yard,' Gabriel said. 'Why would we – the British – be involved?'

'Precisely because we're *not* involved,' Faith said. 'This man will speak to you – he's already agreed, by the way. He would never speak to an American or anyone he suspected was working for them.'

'Who is this man?'

'His name is Santiago Angel Lopez,' Ishbel said. 'He's an ex-priest who started a trade union – the Frente de Justicia Patriótica that has now become a political party. The FJP. The Patriotic Justice Front. There is a national groundswell. He's a charismatic man: still "Padre Tiago" to the common people – even if he's a *laic*, as they say. It gives him massive credibility.'

Gabriel noticed that Ishbel pronounced the Spanish words in what seemed perfect Spanish.

'What do you mean: he's agreed?' he asked Faith.

'We approached him through the *New Interzonal Review* – your familiar journalistic milieu,' she said. 'Its credentials are impeccable, as you know, in this kind of situation. Ideally, stringently left-wing. Which is why we use it and why you write for it, Gabriel, in case you'd forgotten.'

He hadn't. And he hadn't forgotten that *Interzonal* was covertly funded by MI6 – one of the reasons it paid so well.

'What does Bennet Strum say?' Strum was the editor, an old but somewhat dubious friend.

'He knows exactly what's at stake,' Faith said. 'And is very happy. Your interview with Padre Tiago will be a huge coup for the magazine. Can we move on? Harry?'

Harrison Lee pushed a large envelope down the table towards Gabriel.

'The usual stuff,' Harry Lee said. 'Visa, return plane tickets, hotel booking vouchers, your fee.' He paused. 'There's also a bit of background information on Padre Tiago, and a list of potential questions to ask, if you're so inclined.'

Gabriel picked up the envelope and put it in his briefcase. He was thinking.

'What exactly is the object of this . . . this "mission"?' he asked. 'What am I supposed to achieve? Any journalist could interview this man. Why me?'

Everyone around the table looked at Faith.

'Not any journalist, actually,' she said. 'I told you – he's very secretive. Nobody knows much about him. We want to try to get an idea of what might be his future relationship with the USA. That's the key objective.'

'You mean the CIA want to know,' Gabriel interjected.

'Yes, I admit. Hence your being recruited. That's why we were asked to find someone who wouldn't provoke suspicion. Suppose a Lopez presidency arrives sometime in the near future. What will be the Guatemala–USA axis? Friendly or hostile?'

'Or the Guatemala–United Fruit Company axis,' Gabriel said.

'You *have* done your homework,' Ishbel said.

'United Fruit had President Armas assassinated,' Gabriel said. 'The CIA obliged.'

'Wild. Wrong. Totally unproven,' Faith said, a little snappily, he thought. 'That was then. The 1950s. This is 1963,' she continued. 'Things have changed. Hence this – what would you call it? – "softer" approach. You meet the man. You talk to him, ask him certain questions, and then report back to us. It will be valuable information. Rare information. Simple as that. And information is better than brute force. Always has been.'

'Right,' Gabriel said. Now he knew. 'I hope I can, all being well, "get the measure of him" as you say.'

'You're the perfect interlocutor,' Faith said. 'Nobody else would ever be able to be this close to him. Yet you'll be there – Gabriel Dax and Santiago Angel Lopez – face to face.'

'You call the tune,' he said.

'And before you fly off we'd like you to go back to Leyton – for some basic training.'

'I do know how to interview people,' Gabriel said.

'Just for your personal protection,' Faith said. 'Some self-defence instruction. A formality. But now you're officially part of the team it's something we require. You'll be glad of it, I guarantee.'

'I'm off to Guatemala,' Gabriel told his uncle, Aldous Dax.

'Another river?'

'No. One of my dodgy little "jobs" for MI6.'

'At least you can't blame Sefton this time.'

'Poor bloody Sefton.'

Gabriel thought sadly of his older brother, his late older brother, for a moment; a man wilfully caught up in the dark world of betrayal and duplicity, and paying the ultimate price. A suicide – or was it?

'I know one shouldn't speak ill of the dead, but I never really liked Sefton,' Aldous said, reaching for the whisky bottle and topping up their drinks. 'A bit arrogant. Permanently overweight. And always very pleased with himself. Annoyingly self-assured.'

'I think that was his undoing. Got in too deep. Thought he could outsmart everyone.'

'It's a very dangerous trait, arrogance.' Aldous made a histrionic arrogant face, sneering knowingly. 'Hubris, you know.'

'Yes. Indeed . . .'

They were sitting in the large drawing room of Aldous's capacious, shabby apartment in a mansion block near the Albert Hall. Watercolours and drawings hung closely, frame to frame, from skirting board to cornice but at least the great stacks of un-hung paintings and drawings that had been ranged on the carpet had disappeared.

'I see you've tidied up a bit,' Gabriel said, keen to change the subject.

'I'm selling almost everything,' Aldous said, 'since I closed the gallery.' He made a sad face, gesturing at the ranked pictures on the walls. 'Market's very low for my stuff, however. I won't leave you much when I die, my darling boy.'

'You'll live to a hundred, Aldous. You'll outlive me.'

'It's not dangerous, this Guatemala trip of yours, is it?'

'No, no. Just journalism, sort of.'

'Where the hell is Guatemala, anyway?'

'South of Mexico. Big country, full of mountain ranges and volcanoes.' Gabriel thought. 'Actually, I must check up if there's a river there that I could use for my book. Good point.' He paused. 'Talking of books, I need to pick your brain.'

'Good luck. Let me know if you find it.'

'I'm being sued for plagiarism.'

'What? Fucking hell!'

'I know. It's pure extortion. An old, greedy, impoverished writer trying to make a buck. Picked on me.' Gabriel sipped at his whisky, feeling the slow burn as it slid down his throat. He always relaxed when he was with Aldous; there was something about his carefree, insouciant nature that was contagious. He was wearing, this evening, an embroidered caftan and, on his head, a black felt *songkok* with a tassel down the back. More disconcertingly, on his feet he had a pair of old, grubby gym shoes, sockless.

'I need a lawyer,' Gabriel said. 'A right bastard.'

'I know exactly the man. An old chum. Jump down your throat and eat your liver.'

Gabriel decided to stay up in London for a night or two as he had much to do before he left for Guatemala, not to mention his self-defence course in Leyton. He found a small hotel in Pimlico and, rather than seek out somewhere to eat in the neighbourhood, he decided to walk to Chelsea, to the Goat and Crow, his local pub as was, and have a pie and a pint in memory of old times.

He had finished what the barman had described as a 'Cornish pastry' and was contemplating another pint of pale ale when he saw Ishbel Dunbar walk into the pub. He did a momentary double-take as he thought he was mistaken – her thick brown hair was loose down to her shoulders and she was wearing a sheepskin jacket and jeans. My God, he thought: Ishbel Dunbar in jeans . . .?

She looked around and spotted him. Raised her hand and came over.

'Gabriel,' she said. 'What a coincidence!'

She sat down at his table.

'I thought you lived in darkest Sussex,' she said.

'I do. But I used to have a flat around the corner. This was always my local.'

His brain was very active, trying both to dispute and dispel her claim of this encounter being a coincidence. He offered to buy her a drink – gin and tonic, please – and went to the bar, returning with her gin and his fresh pint.

She told him she'd been visiting a friend in St Leonard's Terrace – a very ill friend, lung cancer, and had searched out the nearest pub to have a restorative drink and compose herself.

'And there you were,' she said. 'A perfect distraction from my woes.'

'Yes,' Gabriel replied lamely. 'Sorry to hear about your friend.' Maybe it was indeed a coincidence, he thought, then heard Faith's voice in his head repeating her mantra: there are no coincidences in our business. So, if that were true, what was Ishbel Dunbar up to? Engineering this encounter?

'Ready for Guatemala?' she said, pronouncing the name in proper Spanish: *Guatemala*.

'Pretty much,' he said. 'I've a few things to sort out before I leave.'

Then, for some reason, he told her about the ludicrous plagiarism claim and how he was going to fight it – how he needed to find a good lawyer.

'You don't need a lawyer,' she said, bluntly. 'Who is this person?'

Gabriel explained about Lucian Applegate – an elderly writer out of funds, a has-been, trying to extort money: any travel writer who'd written about Greece would have done as a potential target – it was just bad luck that he chose me, he said.

Ishbel Dunbar leant back in her seat and sipped at her gin.

'We can make it all go away, you know,' she said. 'Easily.'

'What do you mean?'

'Find out where he lives, let me know and I'll send some people round to have a quiet word with him. End of lawsuit.'

Gabriel felt an almost innocent sense of shock. Some people? He looked again at Ishbel – Ishbel with her polite Scottish accent, her plump cheeks, her thick hair – as she searched her bag for cigarettes.

She lit her cigarette and briskly plumed smoke from the corner of her mouth.

'It's usually the simplest way. An unmistakable, not to say brutal, word of warning. Stop what you're doing, or else. Have a think. It can be set in motion very quickly.'

'I will, thank you,' Gabriel said, still somewhat unsettled. 'But I reckon a lawyer's letter will have the same effect. He's just an old fool trying it on.'

Ishbel shrugged.

'Just let me know,' she said. 'Easy as pie.'

Gabriel took a sip from his pint, trying to compute what he'd just been offered. What actual power did Ishbel Dunbar wield? he asked himself. How did she fit into the Institute's hierarchy?

'How long have you worked with Faith?' Ishbel said, casually, reaching for an ashtray on the next table.

'Couple of years,' Gabriel said, vaguely. 'Courier work, in the main.'

'I'd hardly describe the Caldwell defection as courier work,' she said, smiling knowingly.

'Well, that's how it started out. It got more complicated.'

'As things tend to do in our business.'

'Yes. As I've discovered.'

'Guatemala should be more straightforward.' She stubbed out her half-smoked cigarette. 'You'll be liaising with me, by the way. I'll be running you.'

'Great.'

'How do you find working with Faith?'

'Entirely professional,' Gabriel said. He cleared his throat. 'Exemplary.'

'She's an amazing woman,' Ishbel said. 'Had an extraordinary war. Very . . .' She paused, searching for the right word. 'Demanding. Harrowing.'

'Really?' Gabriel said, disingenuously. He knew about Faith Green's war and her terrible ordeal. He now wondered if this was what the encounter was about. A fishing expedition. Casting a baited line towards Faith Green.

Ishbel finished her gin and stood up.

'Thank you for the medicinal gin. Better get back to Primrose Hill,' she said. 'Lovely to bump into you, Gabriel. I look forward to our Guatemala adventure.' She offered her hand and Gabriel stood and shook it.

Gabriel watched her leave – she gave him a final brisk wave at the door. What was going on? he asked himself. He sat down, mysteriously disturbed by the so-called coincidence. She must have been following him, or had him followed, he supposed. He was confident that this wasn't some kind of Faith-ruse; no, he felt sure this meeting was an instigation of Ishbel's making – an out-of-office encounter; an informal chat between two new colleagues. Sure. But what was she looking for? He felt both weary and hungry. It was wearisome – this constant need to second-guess, to analyse, to deduce, to suspect. He returned to the bar and ordered another pint and a couple of pickled eggs with toast. Funnily enough, he was looking forward to leaving for Central America on his travels – wanderlust had returned.

5.

Self-defence

It was odd being back at the chicken farm in Leyton, Gabriel thought, as he stepped out of the taxi. The smell of chicken shit had not dissipated in his absence, he noticed. Then he corrected himself: it wasn't 'odd', it was annoying. Places, people, situations that he assumed would never re-enter his life seemed to have a habit of doing the opposite. Look at Raymond Queneau, for example. And here he was, back at the chicken farm.

He recognized the unsmiling man in a boiler suit who approached him from the front door of the farmhouse. He was the man who had trained him to shoot and had supplied the gun that had killed Queneau. What was his name? Ernest? Eddie? No, Eric.

'Hello, Eric,' Gabriel said. 'We meet again.'

They shook hands.

'How are you, sir?' Eric said, unusually curious. 'How was your trip to Poland?'

'Eventful.'

'I assume you're returning the weapon.'

'What?'

'The FN-VP "Baby Browning" that we lent to you.'

'Lent?'

'It's government property, sir.'

'Well, I'm afraid I lost it in Poland. Had to dump it.'

'That's a shame.'

'What do you mean?'

'We'll have to invoice you for it, sir.'

'Fine, fine. Couldn't matter less. Send me the bill.'

Gabriel kept his anger in check at this footling piece of

bureaucracy. He'd pay for the missing gun with his Russian money, he thought. Nice irony.

Eric led him deep into the chicken farm, through the narrow lanes between the squat barrack-like buildings of creosoted timber, towards a low concrete structure, like a blockhouse, with a tall, blackened tin chimney rising above it.

'What is this place?' Gabriel asked.

'This was the abattoir,' Eric said. 'This is where the chickens were killed, cleaned, refrigerated, packed.'

'Right.'

'But now it's a gymnasium. Sort of.'

He rang the doorbell and the door was opened by a small, bald, muscled man in his fifties wearing a blue vest and matching track-suit bottoms.

Eric saluted him.

'This is Sergeant Major Begg,' Eric said. 'This is Mr Dax, what is going to South America.'

'So-ho, you're the main man,' Begg said in a strong Ulster accent. 'I'll take over, Eric, lad. See you later.'

Begg ushered Gabriel into the bare hallway and then down a corridor to a large concrete-walled room, painted white and brightly lit with neon tubes hanging from the ceiling. Judo mats were strewn on the floor and Gabriel quickly spotted that there was a table laid out with various implements – wooden clubs, iron bars, hand axes.

Begg positioned Gabriel in the middle of the room and faced him. Begg was constantly moving, Gabriel noticed. His hands, his shoulders, his feet seemed in a kind of non-stop twitching agitation, as if he was about to spring into attack mode at any moment. Gabriel felt himself stiffen, his armpits sweaty though the room was noticeably chill.

'So-ho, are you a fighting man, Mr Dax?'

'What do you mean?'

'Have you done much fighting in your life?' He threw a fake punch that made Gabriel flinch. 'Fisticuffs – a bit of a walloping on the randan. Given someone a good kicking at a football match?'

'Ah, no, actually,' Gabriel said.

'Have you ever hit a man in the face?'

'Never.'

Begg seemed to sag at this disappointing information and stopped his St Vitus dance for a moment or two.

'Even when you were a boy? Never slugged a fella who was bothering you?'

'Never.'

'You're what I call a "man of peace", would that be correct?'

'I suppose so. I'm a writer.'

Begg looked at him with new, overt suspicion.

'Why are you going to South America, then?'

'I'm going to interview someone. For a magazine.'

Begg now closed his eyes.

'Why have they sent you to me?'

'It wasn't my idea. Some basic self-defence training, I was told.'

'Right.' Begg seemed disappointed. 'This won't take long.'

He led Gabriel over to the table with the array of crude weapons. Gabriel noticed that there was a half-brick and some large stones included as well as various types of knives along with the axes and the clubs.

'Would you empty your pockets, please, Mr Dax.'

Gabriel searched his pockets and placed his wallet, his notebook and his house keys on the table.

'So-ho, you say you're a man of peace,' Begg confronted him with some aggression.

'I suppose I am.'

'Well, why are you carrying three weapons on you?' Begg pointed to the notebook, the wallet and the keys.

'I've never thought of them as—'

Begg picked up his house keys and made a fist with the sharp ends of the keys projecting through his clenched fingers. Again he mimed a hit to Gabriel's face that made Gabriel recoil.

'You punch someone with these keys – thus arrayed – and you'll tear half his face off.'

40

'My God.'

Begg picked up the notebook. He placed the edge under Gabriel's nose.

'Smash the little notebook under some fella's nose and you drive a bone deep into his brain. Good as dead. The writer's notebook – a deadly weapon.' Begg flourished it.

He picked up the wallet.

'Stick the corner of this into a fella's eye. Hard!' He swiftly brought the wallet's corner up to Gabriel's eye. Begg smiled. 'He won't be seeing out of that eye for a long time.'

Begg stepped back and spread his hands.

'Do you catch my drift, Mr Dax?'

'I'm not sure I—'

'Anything can be a weapon. Rule one.'

'Right.'

'Rule two. Don't use your hands if you can avoid it. Anything else is better. Keys, a pencil, a stone. You punch someone hard in the face and likely you'll break a finger or two. Use your notebook, a shoe, a lamp.'

'I see . . .'

'Rule three. Retaliate first. You think someone's going to aggress you. Aggress him first. You can always apologize afterwards, if you're wrong.'

'Isn't that a bit—'

'And rule four. Watch out for pretenders. Your man goes down – he seems out of it – kick him hard in the ribs. Several times. Break a few ribs.' He paused, reflectively. 'I remember my old colour sergeant. Italy 1944. He said to us: you see a dead body – a dead enemy – put a round in it. Every time. Routine. If he's dead – no matter. If he's pretending – then you've got him.' Begg rubbed his face. 'It was very good advice.' He smiled suddenly, beaming. 'So-ho, are youse getting the message, Mr Dax?'

'Absolutely.'

'Recite me Patrick Begg's four rules of self-defence.'

'Ah. Let's see. One: everything is a potential weapon. Two:

don't use your hands. Three: retaliate first. And four: watch out for pretenders.'

'Ready for action, Mr Dax. Quick learner.'

Gabriel stood on the gravelled sweep in front of the house waiting for his taxi. He felt exhausted after his brief period of instruction with Begg. There had been a few more moves and blows illustrated and explained regarding the near-lethal use of house keys, note-book and wallet, then Begg had made him a cup of tea in a little kitchen off the gym area and told him more adventures of his torrid time in Italy in '44.

'I've killed a lot of people, Mr Dax. I'm not proud of it and I'm not ashamed of it. It was war. But I learnt a lot – and I try to pass on the fruits of my experience to young fellas like you who may be going into harm's way.'

'I'm very grateful,' Gabriel had said, sincerely. 'I won't forget what you've told me. I just hope I won't have to – you know – put my learning into practice.'

He heard the crunch of footsteps on gravel and turned around to find Eric approaching him.

'Taxi'll be here in five, Mr Dax,' he said, handing him an envelope.

'What's this?'

'An invoice for the Baby Browning you lost. We'd appreciate an early settlement of the bill.'

6.

Dovehouse Gardens

Varvara Suvorina was standing outside the Café Matisse, smoking a cigarette, when Gabriel arrived for their meeting. She was wearing a long black fur coat and a Tyrolean-style olive-green hat – with a small *gamsbart* plume in the corded band.

'I would like to have our conversation outside, if you agree, Mr Dax.'

'Of course – may I ask why?'

'The tables are very close in café,' she said. 'We must be discreet.'

'Procedure.'

'This is the word.'

They wandered up the road to the garden at the end of Dovehouse Street, a small, shabby green space with mature plane trees. It had been a former graveyard off the King's Road, now open to the public. They found a bench with ancient headstones behind it, stacked against the wall like paving slabs. They sat for a moment, smoking, as the stirring, trembling leaf-shadows shifted gently around and over them. It was calming, Gabriel thought, a perfect site for quiet reflection. A pigeon cooed softly somewhere above their heads.

'What is this place, exactly?' Varvara asked.

'It used to be a burial ground, then it was the garden to a workhouse.' He looked around at the headstones. 'A place for poor people. It was badly bombed in the war.'

'Strange atmosphere.'

'But very discreet, as you wished. No one to hear us talk.'

'Yes – we should meet here in future, I think.'

'Of course.'

Then she asked him if he had any information about Faith

Green. Gabriel dutifully relayed the essential details, following Faith's instructions – namely that she ran an annexe of MI6 called the Institute of Developmental Studies with a small staff. He gave its address in Long Acre.

'Their job is to look for traitors in the British security services – MI6, MI5, the Foreign Office, the army, the navy, et cetera – looking for double agents,' he said. 'They call them "termites".'

'Termites?'

'Just a slang word. A word they use amongst themselves.'

'Termites. I must remember this.'

Gabriel suddenly realized that, in fact, Varvara Suvorina, and indeed the KGB, probably knew everything about the Institute. 'Termites' was the only piece of information that intrigued her. So why, he asked himself, had he been set this redundant task? Was it indeed some kind of test, as Faith had suggested? If he had lied or claimed not to know much about the Institute would they begin to suspect him?

Certainly, Varvara now seemed to relax. She took off her hat and ran her fingers through her short grey hair. Gabriel offered her one of his French cigarettes and she declined – preferring American tobacco, she said.

'I love American cigarettes,' she confessed. 'I prefer to Russian.' She smiled. 'I don't think they will arrest me.'

Gabriel gave a knowing laugh. Two operatives with their own share of stresses.

'We have a new message from Mr Caldwell,' she said.

'Oh, yes?' Gabriel tried to look unconcerned. 'How is he?'

'He's very well – but he would like for you to come to Moscow.'

'Why?'

'To discuss future "procedure", I believe.' She shrugged. 'Maybe next week, the week after. We can arrange it.'

'I can't go to Moscow at the moment.'

'Oh, yes? Why is that?'

'Because I'm going to Guatemala. On a trip.' He could see she looked perplexed.

'It's a book I'm writing,' he explained. 'A book about rivers.'

'Then when you come back, maybe.'

'Well, yes. If it's easy to arrange. I don't want Faith Green to think I'm a "termite".'

Varvara smiled warily, nodding at the logic of his remark, and looked at him intently.

'You're right, Mr Dax. We will find a way. Innocuous – is this the word?'

'Yes. Please do call me Gabriel.'

'And I am Varvara.'

She offered her hand and Gabriel shook it. What new bond was this? Gabriel felt a familiar enervation overwhelm him. All this pretence, all this duplicity – it was exhausting. He wondered if Varvara felt the same, looking at her as she lit yet another cigarette. He suspected so.

'Do you like music, Gabriel?'

'Yes. I listen to music all the time. All sorts of music.'

'Perhaps you will accompany me to a concert, here in London. I must say, every week in London there are musical temptations. So many concerts. Many free.'

'I'd like that,' he said, thinking: no, don't go down that road. Keep everything at a distance.

She stood up; Gabriel did also. The meeting had achieved whatever it was meant to achieve. They shook hands again and Varvara stood on her cigarette end and pulled on a pair of brown leather gloves. She flexed her fingers.

'When is your trip to Guatemala?'

'I leave the day after tomorrow.'

'How long for?'

'I don't know. Two weeks, three weeks.'

'Please to contact me when you return. Then we can plan your trip to Moscow to meet Mr Caldwell.'

'Of course,' Gabriel said, feeling that he wanted to fall to the ground and go to sleep.

'I will leave first. I will take a bus. Then you can leave.'

Gabriel watched her wander out of the garden and sat down on the bench again. The unforeseen consequences of his double life were beginning to overwhelm him. Guatemala would be the last job he would do for the Institute, whatever Faith Green said, he told himself. He felt his own private existence was being marginalized by these repeated unasked-for responsibilities and tasks. And how to get out of this damn projected trip to Moscow? he wondered, as he walked back down the King's Road, heading for his hotel in Pimlico. He would have to ask Faith, he supposed. Faith would have a solution, a smart idea.

'Why are you going to Guatemala?' Dr Katerina Haas asked him. He told her the truth – a job for MI6. The interview with the trade union leader, the former priest. There were to be no secrets, Gabriel had decided, between him and his psychoanalyst – otherwise what would be the point of these expensive hourly sessions? And besides, he liked her and she had cured him of his insomnia, almost.

'Is it dangerous? You told me your Poland trip would be easy – but in fact it was dangerous, you said.'

'I don't think this trip will be like that one,' Gabriel said, carefully. 'It's more a kind of fact-finding mission, as I suppose you could describe it. And it's Central America – not a communist state.'

They were sitting in armchairs facing each other in her cream-and-white consulting room. She was wearing her usual outfit of crisp white lab coat with a silk scarf at the neck – vermilion, today. Unusually, she had what looked like a medal pinned to her lapel – a gold star beneath a red-and-white ribbon.

'Is that an award, a decoration you've been given?' Gabriel asked, pointing.

'No, it's a medal that was given to my father. Just a week before he was killed at the battle in the town of Zborov in 1917. Part of the 1917 Kerensky Offensive. I always wear it on the anniversary of his death.'

'I don't think I've heard of the Kerensky Offensive.'

'I'm not surprised. The details of the First World War as applied to Austria-Hungary and Russia are virtually unknown – outside of Austria and Hungary and Russia.'

Gabriel nodded, as if sagely, though he couldn't think of anything to say. He acknowledged the vagaries of an individual's history. A soldier be-medalled, then being killed days after, and now his daughter sat opposite her English analysand in London forty-odd years later wearing his actual medal. We are helpless, he thought, powerless against these random forces – and then he considered his own predicament, en route for Guatemala, and felt impotent tears sting his eyes.

'Are you all right, Gabriel?'

'Sorry. Your story about your father made me feel sad. Silly of me.'

'But your own father died – brutally. And your mother. It must be that connection. You understand that loss.'

'True, perhaps it is. But I never knew my father – I was too young.'

'And there lies the sadness. There's no shame. We all have the right to feel sad at life's harsh contingencies.'

'I suppose so.' Gabriel managed a grim smile. 'How old were you when your father died?'

'I was a teenage girl. I knew my Pappi very well.'

'Lucky you.'

'Shall we begin?' Dr Haas stood up and switched on the tape recorder.

EXTRACTS FROM THE TRANSCRIPTION OF SESSION 12

GABRIEL DAX: I should start by telling you about a dream I had. A dream about you.

DR HAAS: It's quite normal to dream about your analyst.

GABRIEL DAX: But this dream was – what shall I say? – erotic.

DR HAAS: Please tell me the details.

GABRIEL DAX: You asked me to undress. You said it would be helpful if I stood naked before you.

DR HAAS: Interesting. Did I explain why?

GABRIEL DAX: You said that it would help you to know me better if you saw me naked – if you saw how I reacted to being naked before you.

DR HAAS: And did you undress?

GABRIEL DAX: Yes. And I should say I had no hesitation. There seemed a kind of logic in your request. It made sense, oddly. So I took all my clothes off. I was standing there, just there, by the weighing machine.

DR HAAS: And then what happened?

GABRIEL DAX: Well, ah . . . [clears his throat repeatedly] You asked if you could touch my penis.

DR HAAS: I see. And did I?

GABRIEL DAX: That was when I woke up.

DR HAAS: Did you have an erection?

GABRIEL DAX: Yes.

DR HAAS: Any emission?

GABRIEL DAX: No.

DR HAAS: Have you any explanation for this dream?

GABRIEL DAX: I think . . . [Pause] I think it was because I had become sexually aroused – earlier that evening. But I can't explain why the protagonist of this dream should have been you.

DR HAAS: Why were you sexually aroused?

GABRIEL DAX: Because I had kissed this woman – this woman I've told you about before, Faith Green.

DR HAAS: Your MI6 'handler', I believe you call her.

GABRIEL DAX: Yes. As you know, we were briefly lovers. And I have to say that my obsession with her hasn't really diminished.

DR HAAS: Did she respond to your kiss?

GABRIEL DAX: Yes, I think so. But then she recoiled. I think – I believe – she's attracted to me but, at the same time, she knows my feelings for her are far more powerful and she uses that as a lever against me. A way of controlling me.

DR HAAS: Do you have any sexual feelings about me?

GABRIEL DAX: What? No. No, I like you, Katerina, of course, as a friend, and I respect you deeply as my physician, if you like. I can't explain this 'transference' – if that's the right term.

48

DR HAAS: I suppose it applies. [Pause] Have you had a sexual relationship recently?

GABRIEL DAX: No. Not since the last time with Faith Green – some months ago. Some many months ago, in fact, in Southwold, in Suffolk, last year. I told you about that night I spent with her. [Pause] I've found I'm not interested in other women, I have to say. She dominates my thinking, sexually.

DR HAAS: You're obviously very frustrated. You can't have Faith Green so you choose, unconsciously, another woman – in this case it was me. I think it's significant that you so easily submitted to my demands – you did what I told you to do. Maybe this is the nature of the sexual power relationship between you and this Faith Green. She's controlling everything.

GABRIEL DAX: I feel very embarrassed but you've always demanded total honesty from me.

DR HAAS: I'm not embarrassed. You should hear some of the dreams that my patients have had about me. Sodom and Gomorrah seem like a holiday resort. [Pause] Are you attracted to other women? I believe you had a girlfriend, when we first met.

GABRIEL DAX: Yes, Lorraine. That's over. She left me for another man. It was doomed, anyway. But now I find I'm not attracted to other women – I can only think of Faith Green. It's an obsession, I realize. I admit. What can one do in these circumstances?

DR HAAS: Do you masturbate?

GABRIEL DAX: What? Ah. Well . . . Yes, from time to time. Purely for release – like every man.

DR HAAS: *Every* man? How do you know this?

GABRIEL DAX: I don't. I suppose I'm extrapolating from my own experience.

DR HAAS: But you may not be typical. You don't know.

GABRIEL DAX: That's true. I'm just making an assumption.

DR HAAS: Maybe you should start seeing other women. You

do know other women, I presume. You have had other relationships in your life.

GABRIEL DAX: Yes, several.

DR HAAS: You don't need to have sexual relationships. Just go out for a meal. Go to the cinema. I think you need to be able to make comparisons with your Faith Green. See her in the context of other women you know. It may allow you to regard her differently.

GABRIEL DAX: I'm sure you're right. Unfortunately, I feel that logic and rationality aren't going to help me in this matter.

DR HAAS: Well, at least you're going to Guatemala. Maybe there will be distractions.

GABRIEL DAX: I know there will be. Yes . . .

Gabriel knocked on Royston's door. Royston invited him in for a drink but Gabriel said he was going to the airport, off on a trip for two or three weeks.

'If I left you a set of keys do you think you could put out some food for my cat – every couple of days? There are a lot of tins of catfood in the kitchen cupboard.'

'Do you mean Edgar?' Royston said. 'Big black cat, white paws.'

'Edgar?'

'That's what I call him. He's in and out of my house all the time. Especially when you're away.'

'Right. It's not going to be a problem then.'

'No. I'll feed him well. Safe journey.'

Gabriel walked back to Rose Cottage feeling foolish and oddly hurt at the Cat's disloyalty. 'Edgar'. How ridiculous, he said to himself. The Cat lived as he pleased, entirely pragmatically. Perhaps he should learn a lesson or two from him, Gabriel thought. His bags were packed. He telephoned for a taxi to take him to the station.

7.

Welcome to Guatemala

Gabriel flew BOAC from London airport, at Heathrow, to Idlewild airport, New York, then transferred to Pan American Airways for the next leg to Miami. He spent a night in Miami before catching an Aviateca flight to Guatemala City. He felt oddly pleased and relaxed to be travelling again, wondering if constant movement was the ideal state of being for him. Staying put always seemed to provoke problems and consternations of one sort or another. When you were on the road, on the move, it was harder for life's inevitable demands to catch up with you. Or so you fondly thought. Still, he was aware he wasn't 'on the move' at his own behest – a little cloud of apprehension travelled with him on this journey to Central America, increasing steadily as the DC-6 touched down at Guatemala City's La Aurora airport one sunny afternoon.

He stepped out of the customs hall with his luggage – a small suitcase, a grip and his portable typewriter – and looked around him. There was a large banner on the wall of the arrivals hall: 'BIENVENIDOS A GUATEMALA'. To his surprise he saw a young man – in his twenties – holding up a placard that read: 'Señor Dax'. He wandered over.

'*Hola. Soy el Señor Dax.*'

The young man smiled widely but there was something twisted about his smile. Gabriel spotted a repaired hare lip.

'I am Javier,' the young man said and took Gabriel's suitcase from him. 'Señor Sartorius has organize everything.' His English was fairly good, Gabriel registered, as Javier, chatting away, led him out of the arrivals hall to the taxi rank. And he knew who Sartorius was, thanks to his briefing at the Institute: Frank Sartorius, CIA Head of Station in Guatemala. His parallel life had reclaimed him, already.

Javier's taxi was a 1950s four-door Chrysler New Yorker – gunmetal blue with added rust. Javier placed the luggage in the trunk and Gabriel settled back in the substantial rear seat. Big, confident, swaggering cars, he thought: we have nothing to match this scale back home. Again, he registered the familiar travel frisson. Almost everything he was about to experience would be new and different – and, in a way, that was the essential requirement of travel, he considered. It made the world fresh and stirring once again, curiosity stimulated, eyes wide open.

Javier pulled out of the taxi rank and they headed off through the airport's precincts towards Guatemala City. At one moment the highway from the airport breasted a small bluff and Gabriel was able to see a grand panorama of the city below him, set on its high, narrow plateau, a mile above sea level, ringed with cloud-capped mountains and mighty volcanoes. The city was built low, he saw, most houses no more than a standard two storeys, and above them loomed the grand public buildings – the cathedral, the national palace, the ministry of culture, the government offices – like great ornate ships stuck in a frozen sea of stuccoed brick and terracotta tiles. His guidebook had rather pompously said that Guatemala City was 'neither ancient nor beautiful'. He didn't agree. He had never seen a city quite like it, he realized – almost a lost world.

Reality returned in the shape of a police checkpoint as they descended into the suburbs. Javier presented his ID card; Gabriel his passport. The policemen were armed and unsmiling. They were waved on brusquely.

'What's happening?' Gabriel asked Javier.

'Students fighting, workers fighting, rebels fighting. Everybody fighting. Nobody is liking this government.' He gave a grim smile. 'It will change in November, you wait and see, *señor*.'

'What's happening in November?'

'We have elections. Democracy is coming back to Guatemala.'

The car moved slowly through crowded streets. He saw the Mercado Central as they drove by. Big American cars parked beside a fritter of brightly coloured pavement market stalls selling heaped foodstuffs. People in European-style clothing mingled with Indians in their straw hats with up-tilted brims, wearing woollen jackets with strange appliquéd motifs, vivid ponchos and shawls. Gabriel peered out of the window as the throng parted to let the Chrysler through. He felt oddly exhilarated by the marked close contrast of cultures. He was abroad – everything was vivid, new, exciting. There were compensations to be had working for the Institute, he grudgingly recognized, even if he was a temporary, lowly 'agent in the field'.

The Alcázar-Plaza was an old nineteenth-century building, near the Central Park, with a sooty, ludicrously over-decorated facade with finials, obelisks, friezes, columns, sculpted figures in niches and elaborately detailed architraves over the tall, garlanded windows. 'Encrusted' was the word that came to mind. Javier pulled up in front of the pillared portico and carried his luggage into the dark, marbled lobby, panelled with chocolate-brown wood and lit by a vast, heavy, bronze chandelier, and made his farewells. He gave Gabriel his card. 'Javier Dagoberto García', Gabriel saw, with a telephone number beneath it.

'If ever you need transport, Señor Dax, you call this telephone. They call me by radio. Day and night.'

Gabriel thanked him and assured him he'd be in touch. He checked in at reception and then followed a bellhop to an open-grilled lift that creaked up three floors to find his room.

No need for his usual upgrade, he said to himself, as he assessed the accommodation. The Institute had done him proud, for once. There was a sizeable bedroom with a bathroom en suite and, in an alcove overlooking the large inner gardens, like a modest park, was a small study with a writing desk and an armchair. The bed was wide with a crisp white lace coverlet and there was a ceiling fan set above it. The floor was polished wood with silk rugs. No complaints, Gabriel decided, looking out over the walled garden below him with its pathways and water features and clumps of carefully pruned and maintained exotic trees. Benches were scattered here and there. He saw a man in a white suit standing on the corner of a small terrace smoking a long cigar. A civilized oasis in the city, Gabriel thought. And then there was a muffled boom and the glass in the windows rattled. It sounded like a bomb going off. And then he heard the firecracker retorts of guns being fired and police sirens beginning to whoop and wail. 'Everybody fighting,' Javier had said. Gabriel turned away and began to unpack his bag. The telephone rang. It was reception.

'Mr Sartorius is here to see you, sir. He is waiting in the bar.'

'Tell him I'll be down in five minutes.'

Gabriel felt his good mood dissipate. It had begun.

PART TWO

Guatemala City
New York

March–April 1963

Frank Sartorius

Gabriel found the Alcázar-Plaza's bar. Dark-panelled like the lobby, it was lit with dim-bulbed sconces. The bar gave on to the terrace that had been visible from his room. The man in the white suit was still standing there, still smoking his cigar. Gabriel looked around. A plump figure was waving at him from a booth in the far corner. He stood up as Gabriel approached. He was a portly, short man in his fifties, Gabriel reckoned, wearing a beige seersucker suit, white buttoned-down shirt and banded tie. He had a greying, quite severe crew cut and a neat moustache. Gabriel thought he might as well have had a sign around his neck saying: 'I am an American.'

They shook hands.

'Gabriel Dax, a pleasure to meet you. I'm Frank Sartorius.'

They sat down and ordered drinks from the white-jacketed waiter. A couple of beers.

'We are immensely grateful to you, Gabriel – may I call you Gabriel?' Frank Sartorius said and offered his beer glass for Gabriel to clink his against.

'One of the unforeseen advantages of being a writer,' Gabriel said. 'I suppose it can get you access.'

'Have you made contact?' Sartorius asked, glancing about him. There was nobody sitting nearby.

'No. I thought I'd wait until tomorrow morning.'

'Good idea. Get your bearings. Be a little wary if you go out late at night. Did you hear the bomb?'

'Was it a bomb?'

'Oh, yes. A government bomb. The military explode them here and there – it's a pretext for rounding up the dissidents. Kind of crazy to set off bombs in your own capital but, hey, this is Guatemala.'

He shrugged and smiled broadly. Geniality, Gabriel noted, was clearly a Sartorius character trait.

They talked on for a while about the protocol for approaching Padre Tiago and the FJP; they ordered another couple of beers. Sartorius advised against any kind of CIA identification.

'The more anti-American you are, the better,' he said, cheerfully. 'Go for it.'

At that moment the man in the white suit came back into the bar, and walked by, glancing briefly at them both. He seemed about to raise his hand in greeting but instead thrust it in a pocket, before pausing at the bar to settle his bill.

The man in the white suit was tall and ruggedly handsome, though the skin on his cheeks seemed pitted – ravaging teenage acne, Gabriel supposed, or some kind of pox. He had wiry black hair combed back from his wide forehead. As he passed their booth the lingering smell of his cigar smoke left an invisible sour spoor behind him. Gabriel sneezed. A dedicated smoker himself, he had never been tempted by cigars. They finished their beers and Sartorius checked that Gabriel had all the contact telephone numbers he needed, then they parted.

'Let us know when the Tiago meeting is,' Sartorius said, as Gabriel walked with him through the dark lobby to the front door.

'I worked briefly, last year, with one of your colleagues,' Gabriel said, as they stood outside in the evening sunshine, waiting for Sartorius's car. 'A man called John Hillcrest. Did you know him?'

'Have you any idea how many people work for the Company?' Sartorius said. 'Thousands. Never heard of him. Why do you ask?'

'Just curiosity. Seemed a nice guy.'

A black Lincoln Continental Town Car pulled up and Sartorius opened the back door. They shook hands once again.

'We truly appreciate what you're doing, Gabriel,' Sartorius said. 'Believe me. *Hasta luego, amigo.*'

He slid into the back seat; Gabriel closed the door on him and watched the limousine pull away. We, he thought. Who in fact was We? He sensed a strange feeling settle on him, like an invisible shawl around his shoulders. He knew what he was experiencing. Unease.

He shivered and went back inside to the bar. He needed something stronger than beer.

The next morning Gabriel telephoned the offices of the FJP. In his halting Spanish he asked to speak to a certain Alvaro Guzman, head of 'Communications and Liaison'. He was put through.

'Welcome to Guatemala,' Guzman said. 'We are looking forward to meeting you, Señor Dax. However, we do not yet have a time for your appointment. May I ask how we can contact you?'

Gabriel gave him his room number and the name of the Alcázar-Plaza. There was silence on the end of the line.

'You are staying at this hotel?'

'Yes. My magazine booked it for me. Why?'

'There is no problem. We will call you.'

'Have you any idea when the interview will take place?'

'No. We will contact you.'

Gabriel hung up after saying he was at the FJP's disposition – whenever was convenient. He sighed. Obviously, he would have some time on his side – the tone of the conversation had been polite but cagey, in his estimation. The FJP seemed in no hurry to set up his interview with Padre Tiago. Perhaps it was a good time to look for a river for his book.

2.

Rio Motagua

Gabriel stood in the lobby of the Alcázar waiting for Javier to arrive with his taxi. They were going on a trip to the Motagua river, about a three-hour drive from the city. He lit a cigarette. The Motagua was the largest river in Guatemala, running west to east towards the Gulf of Honduras and the Atlantic. The interesting fact about the river, as far as he was concerned, was that its long valley marked the boundary of the North American and Caribbean tectonic plates. The Motagua fault had generated some of Guatemala's most severe and destructive earthquakes. He rather liked the idea of including a dangerous river in his book. All he needed to do was to find a suitable village somewhere on its banks and the rest would fall neatly into—

'Morning.'

Gabriel turned. It was the man in the white suit, except he was wearing an olive-green suit today. A tall man, tall as he was, Gabriel noted, limber, broad-shouldered.

'Do you have a light?'

Gabriel offered him his lighter and the man lit a small cigarillo.

'Thanks. Are you a friend of Frank Sartorius? I saw you in the bar yesterday with him.' The man had an American accent, seasoned with some foreign note. Spanish? Italian?

'He's a friend of a friend. That's the first time we've met,' Gabriel said, trying not to sound wary, and immediately wondered if that had been wise. But the man seemed amiable enough, unperturbed at the information. His pocked face was more evident in the morning light, Gabriel saw. A handsome man, marred.

'I'm Dean Furlan,' the man said, offering his hand. Gabriel shook it; the grip was strong.

'Gabriel Dax. How do you know Frank?' Gabriel asked.

'I don't. I just happen to know who he is,' Furlan said, looking at Gabriel intently. Blue eyes, olivey skin, Gabriel noted. 'There are very few secrets in Guatemala City.'

'I see.'

'I'm in the restaurant trade,' Furlan said. 'Looking to buy Guatemalan coffee – in bulk. Cut out the middleman. The American ambassador has been very helpful.'

Gabriel picked up the subtext, but decided not to pursue it. He told Furlan he was a travel writer, here to complete a new book that featured Guatemala, amongst other countries. 'I was introduced to Frank Sartorius,' he said. 'Frank will introduce me to important others, I hope. Saves a hell of a lot of time.'

'Interesting,' Furlan said, nodding, suddenly seeming oddly relieved. 'I know what you mean. Everyone needs a facilitator.'

Furlan looked round. A small thickset man in a cheap shiny blue suit and two-tone shoes had come into the lobby. He looked more Indian than Spanish, Gabriel thought. Furlan gave him a brusque wave.

'Here comes mine,' Furlan said. 'Mr Coffee Bean.' He turned back to Gabriel.

'Enjoy your day,' Furlan said. 'See you around.'

He and the man exchanged a few words and wandered out to the hotel's forecourt. Gabriel was thinking: was there anything significant about that conversation? Or were they just two hotel guests passing the time?

The drive to the river was smooth and uneventful. They motored steadily along a near-traffic-free two-lane blacktop with wide verges and, beyond the verges, thick vegetation – scrub and forest, undulating still distances of dense greenery.

Javier was chatting as they drove. He told Gabriel that he could buy jade if he wanted – the Motagua river valley was the only place you could find jade in Guatemala.

'Well, I don't really need any jade,' Gabriel said.

'You buy a present for your wife – your girlfriend,' Javier said. 'She will be very happy.'

'I don't have a wife or a girlfriend,' Gabriel said, thinking of Faith.
'I don't believe you, *señor*. No, no!'

They had a laugh – but Gabriel was pondering. Yes, a present for Faith from Guatemala: that would shake her up.

At midday, they stopped in a small town on the river called Dos Vados. There was a Mayan site there – not particularly significant: a ruined temple and a weed-badged, crumbling pyramid in front of a wide paved square – also good material for the chapter, Gabriel thought. Earthquakes and an ancient civilization – ideally rich, easily expanded on.

It was the dry season and the Motagua river was low and shallow, meandering between large banks of white sand, looking like a river in Africa in time of drought, Gabriel thought, except that the forested hills on either side were lush and verdant. He found a set of stone steps that led down to the riverbank. He stood on the white sand and looked around. Over the forest there were high parapets of white clouds and the air was noisy with a gibbering chatter of parakeets in the riverine palm trees. He looked down at the turbid pool by his feet and, beneath the wobbling glare of the sun on the water, saw a gloomy tangle of weeds amongst which small shoals of silver fish cruised. He turned and looked upstream at the lazy swerve of the Motagua. A long-legged bird hauled itself into the air and, its wide wings spread, it coasted low across the water to another sandbar. The unfolding moment seemed unending, he thought, timeless. He could have been back in the era of the Mayas.

He shook himself out of his reverie and took some photographs – and then he climbed back up the steps to rejoin Javier. They went to a *cantina* and ordered some food. Gabriel had *huevos rancheros* with sliced avocado pears. He bought Javier some *tamales* and invited him to join him but he insisted on eating in the car, leaving Gabriel alone to enjoy his lunch.

Gabriel jotted down a few notes about the Motagua and Dos Vados – the chapter was writing itself, he thought. Whatever else was involved with this trip at least he had profited by it in a literary sense. The book, *Rivers*, was almost done, he realized with quiet satisfaction – and completed under unprecedented extraneous pressures during its composition. If only his future readers knew. He felt oddly proud at his doggedness; his refusal to abandon his own, real life.

When Gabriel had finished his meal he met up with Javier who led him to a small native shop in a dusty square off the main road, selling straw hats and leather-worked goods – sandals, aprons, wallets – and brightly woven ponchos and scarves. The shopkeeper – a shrunken, ancient woman – opened a drawer and showed him some small pieces of green jade. He bought, for twenty quetzals, an inch-long stone, curved, like a tusk from some fabled beast. He would have it mounted and hung on a gold chain, he thought, and would present it to Faith Green as a love token, whether she welcomed it or not.

They drove back to Guatemala City later that afternoon, Gabriel wondering if there would be a message waiting from the FJP, but there was nothing when he checked with reception. He decided to put a call in to the Institute, following the simple code they had agreed on. In the telephone cabin at the rear of the lobby he had the hotel switchboard operator connect him with the number in London that he'd been given. The time difference meant that it would be early afternoon there.

'Hello,' said a male voice.

'Hello. It's Mr Simpson here, I wonder if I could speak to my wife.' He felt a bit of a fool but this was how he'd been told to make contact and he was to speak in plain-code, as they termed it. Low-rent skullduggery, he thought. Procedure. There was a pause.

'Hello?' He was expecting Ishbel Dunbar but he instantly recognized Faith's voice.

'Hello, darling,' he said, deliberately, feeling his lungs inflate with pleasure at hearing her. 'I've met Uncle Frank, but no news from our friends, yet.'

'Fine. Stay in touch. Hope the visit goes well.'

Click. She hung up, probably irritated by his endearment. Good, he thought.

He stepped out of the booth, suddenly feeling hungry, but not wanting to eat alone in the gloom of the Alcázar's vast dining room.

He asked at reception for the name of a decent restaurant and directions to its location, and was given a card with a map on the back. Don Pepito on Calle 1, Zona 1. A five-minute walk away, he was told.

He headed off into the night.

Don Pepito had pretensions. Printed silk on the walls, small red candles with crystal glass shades on every table and a guitarist playing quietly in the corner. Gabriel ordered *carpaccio de lomito*, an *ensalada tropical* and *tacos de camarón*, washed down with a pungent red Malbec from Argentina. He ate and drank, notebook on the table, jotting down more memories and impressions of his trip to the Motagua, thinking that this was his old life, gifted back to him for an hour or two – a stranger in a strange city, everyone talking Spanish around him, the guitarist playing some rhythmic *bossa nova* number. The travel thrill was present, still functioning – he hoped it would never leave him.

It died as he paid his bill and headed out of the restaurant. As he approached the door on to the street Dean Furlan entered with his friend, Mr Coffee Bean. Furlan, Gabriel saw at once, was not delighted by this encounter even though he managed a smile.

'I guess the concierge at the hotel must be on some kickback, here,' Furlan said.

'Still, the food is good. Try the *tacos de camarón*, delicious.'

Mr Coffee Bean lit a cigarette, stepping back a pace. Gabriel was very aware that Furlan didn't want to introduce him. He wasn't sure why but the idea came to him and he held out his hand and said, '*Hola. Buenas noches. Soy* Gabriel Dax.'

Surprised, the man shook his hand and gave his name in a half-mumble, unreflectingly, spontaneously. But Gabriel registered it: Denilson Canul. Gabriel sensed Furlan's immediate annoyance at the ruse but they parted with false cheer and false smiles. Walking back to the hotel, Gabriel had a feeling that this chance encounter was important in some way. Denilson Canul, he repeated to himself, Denilson Canul. Canul, an Indian name. Then he heard the distant, flat thump of a bomb going off somewhere in the north of the city. A police car sped by, lights flashing, red luminescence bouncing off the plate-glass shop windows. His new life – and its jeopardy, its uncertainty – was back again, emphatically, it seemed to him.

As if to underline the observation there was a message waiting for him from the FJP when he returned to the hotel and picked up the keys to his room.

'Please call us tomorrow morning at your convenience,' was all it said. Unsigned.

3.

El Frente de Justicia Patriótica

'*Puedo hablar con el Señor Guzman*,' Gabriel said quietly, holding the telephone receiver close to his mouth. He felt oddly edgy, his armpits sweaty. Guzman answered after a longish pause.

'Please to come to the FJP headquarters at midday tomorrow,' he said. He gave the address. Gabriel scribbled it down on a notepad.

'Midday tomorrow. I'll be there, thank you.'

'It's very important, *señor*, that you tell no one of this rendezvous.'

'Of course. I guarantee. Many thanks.'

Gabriel immediately thought of calling the Institute to convey the information that the meeting was on – but he resisted the impulse. If he told Faith, Faith would tell Frank Sartorius. He decided to hold back and respect the instructions of the FJP; he could inform everyone after the event, claim that the meeting arrangement was very spontaneous.

And now, he thought, he had twenty-four hours or so to kill. He became a tourist: he visited the cathedral, he strolled around the Parque Central and had a bite of lunch at a small café. In the Central Market he marvelled at the heaped profusion of lurid fruits and vegetables, some that he'd never seen before, as if dreamt up by a mad cartoonist. He diligently visited a few churches that were recommended in his guidebook – particularly relishing the stark white beauty of the church of Santo Domingo. He photographed it from several angles. He thought about going to the zoo. A city's zoo, he had found, told you almost as much about the place, or indeed a country, as famous public buildings, museums and art galleries did. But all the time he was playing the tourist he sensed his nervousness slowly mounting. Not to any alarming degree, but like a kind of building tinnitus in his inner ear – impossible to ignore.

Consequently, he decided to have a drink, or a series of drinks, and try to forget what was inevitably approaching. A taxi took him to a club called Bar Coco. It was suitably dark, nearly empty, and he found a seat in a corner and ordered a cocktail called a Diablo Rojo. A small *marimba* band was playing and, as the time passed, it became annoyingly louder as saxophonists and trumpet players joined the original ensemble and eventually the squawking, blaring din succeeded in driving him out. He returned to the Alcázar-Plaza and took a Seconal.

The next morning, he again called the number of the taxi firm that Javier had given him and booked him in for an 11.30 pick-up. He felt calmer – the sleeping pill had helped. He went through his notes and the list of questions for Padre Tiago that he had compiled with the Institute's help. There was to be no recording of the interview – a condition – his rudimentary, personal shorthand would have to suffice.

Javier was on time – spruce, smiling his uneven smile, eager. They drove south to a small, shabby square at the edge of the city. The two huge volcanoes visible from the city – Acatenango and Fuego – loomed larger. A pillar of smoke drifted from Fuego, the more distant one. Under the volcano, Gabriel said to himself, remembering Malcolm Lowry's novel that had also featured two volcanoes – and he hoped it wasn't a grim presentiment. He had no desire to repeat the hapless protagonist's end. However, the random literary association energized him – at least his brain was functioning – and he told Javier to drive by and park at the furthest end of the square. He didn't want to be dropped off at the FJP's front door.

The FJP's headquarters were in a large three-storey 1930s building – it looked like a barracks with its plain, stained, stucco facade and rows of identical windows. There was a huge banner hung above the main entrance, green letters on a white background – '*REFORMA AGRARIA!*' – and half a dozen men in paramilitary uniforms stood outside on guard. They were wearing unmatching olive-green military fatigues, trousers tucked into heavy boots, and peaked forage caps with 'FJP' stencilled on the front. Some had long truncheons hanging from their belts. No doubt they were further armed, Gabriel supposed. Javier parked the taxi on the other side of the plaza.

'Are you going there?' Javier asked, surprise heightening his voice. 'Do you know who these people are?'

'Yes,' Gabriel said, guardedly. 'I'm meeting a man who will help me with my book – Señor Guzman.'

'Do you know the name of Padre Tiago?'

'No. Who's he?'

'He is the FJP. He begin this movement of workers. They say he will be the next President of Guatemala when the elections come.'

'Oh. Right.' Gabriel opened the door. 'Good to know. *Gracias*, Javier. You can go now.'

'Are you sure? I can wait for you.'

'No, no. I'll be fine. I'll call if I need you.' He gave what he hoped was a reassuring smile, waved his hand and wandered off across the plaza towards the FJP building. He felt a small sword of acid indigestion burn in his oesophagus. Relax, he told himself, relax. I'm just a journalist on assignment. This will all be over in an hour or two.

Gabriel's passport was taken away by one of the stern paramilitary men guarding the building. After five minutes, he was admitted, his passport was returned, and he was asked to wait in a lobby that smelt strangely of cheese – he assumed it was mould – it made him feel slightly bilious. He asked for a glass of water but was told that was not possible. After another five minutes a young woman came and wordlessly led him upstairs to an office where Alvaro Guzman was waiting for him.

Guzman was in his thirties, lean and balding with a Leon Trotsky goatee beard and heavy, black-framed spectacles. He was sitting behind a desk and did not offer Gabriel a seat. He looked like a cross between a university professor and a state prosecutor in some ruthless autocracy, Gabriel thought. He was polite and reserved, reminding Gabriel that this was an unprecedented opportunity he was being given but there would be security measures put in place that he might find uncomfortable. He was free to pull out, if he wished.

'No, no need,' Gabriel said, a little alarmed, nonetheless. Security measures? 'I'm looking forward to meeting Padre Tiago.'

'Please do not refer to him as "Padre",' Guzman said. 'To you he is Señor Lopez.'

'Of course.'

Guzman stood up from behind his desk and managed a thin smile.

'Please, come with me.'

Guzman led him down the stairs and further down into a basement garage. They walked over to a mud-splattered Chevrolet Corvair Greenbrier van. Two men were waiting outside it. Gabriel noticed that the rear windows were curtained. He climbed into the back and one of the men joined him.

'Forgive me,' Guzman said, peering in. 'But these are the security measures I told you about.'

The man then placed a cloth sack over Gabriel's head.

'Is this really necessary?' Gabriel said. 'I'm on your side.'

'We can take no risks, Mr Dax,' Guzman said. '*Mis disculpas.*'

Gabriel heard the door slam and then the engine start. They jolted forward. Under his sack, Gabriel was aware of the light changing as they emerged from the basement garage but apart from that he had no idea of any direction they took as they drove through the noisy city streets. From time to time he covertly lifted the edge of his head-covering and checked his watch. The city noise soon disappeared and then all he heard was the grind of the engine, driving on steadily. He sat back and closed his eyes. After about half an hour the van stopped and the cloth sack was removed from his head. They were on a dirt track somewhere far beyond the city, dense vegetation on either side. The driver gestured for Gabriel to step out of the van and he did so, blinking in the oblique rays of the afternoon sun as he looked around him.

The driver led him over to a Ford Fairlane station wagon with fake wooden trim on the side. Another man sat at the wheel. Gabriel climbed into the rear seat and they pulled off. They drove to a metalled road and, judging from the position of the sun in the sky, headed northwards, as far as Gabriel could determine.

An hour later they turned off the road and motored up another dirt track toward a cluster of farm buildings. There were picket fences and livestock – horses, cows, sheep – all corralled. The main farm building was solid-looking with small windows, painted white. Gabriel noticed a tall wireless mast. He stepped out of the car and another paramilitary led him inside to a sitting room with a tiled terracotta floor and some rudimentary pieces of furniture: a dresser, a dining table with chairs, a divan and a fireplace stacked with logs and with a wooden bench set in front of it. There was a black crucifix on a wall but otherwise the decor was robustly ascetic. At one end some glazed doors led on to a low-walled terrace. Gabriel sat down at the table and waited. He was feeling very strange, he realized, almost as if he had been kidnapped and was being held hostage. He asked the paramilitary for some *agua* and a glass was brought to him. A good sign, he thought.

Presently, the doors on to the terrace opened and a silhouetted figure appeared, framed in the doorway.

'Señor Dax, please will you join me.'

Padre Tiago himself, Gabriel thought, rising to his feet, and putting down his glass. Maybe this will be all right, after all.

Padre Tiago was a tall man, with wiry grey hair and a neatly trimmed, pointed grey beard; he was in his late forties, Gabriel knew. He spoke good, accented English and his slightly rheumy eyes seemed both kind and watchful. He was wearing a black shirt buttoned to the throat and black trousers with sandals on his feet. The effect was both ecclesiastical and revolutionary, as it was no doubt intended to be. They shook hands and sat down at a wrought-iron table. Coffee was on offer and Gabriel gladly accepted. The paramilitary poured cups for them both. No milk, no sugar.

From the terrace Gabriel could see a split-rail fenced meadow containing a horse and a pony in the far distance. Beyond that, forested hills unfolded. There were glimpses of blue sky between dense, slowly migrating clouds. It all seemed very timeless and remote, Gabriel thought – Padre Tiago in his own private Shangri-La.

There was absolutely nothing, no single detail, that would allow Gabriel to identify this location. A farm in the countryside would be his best description. All very thorough and pre-planned.

Padre Tiago said he was enjoying the opportunity to speak English. He had spent many months in London, he said, in 1948. How was London today? he asked. It's becoming more lively, Gabriel said. The city had seemed stuck in its post-war gloom for years, he added. Now, things are changing. They chatted some more about Padre Tiago's London memories. He had stayed in a place called Earl's Court – it sounded very grand but was the opposite. They laughed. Yes, I know Earl's Court, Gabriel said. No earl has ever been anywhere near there, let alone held court.

'And you are English?' Padre Tiago asked.

'I am.'

'Do you live in London?'

'I used to. Now I live in the countryside. I'm a writer,' Gabriel said. 'Peace and quiet is important.'

Padre Tiago smiled.

'Like here. For the moment.' He gestured at the sunlit meadow, then his face hardened. 'We need peace and quiet in Guatemala. No soldiers. No American CIA. No United Fruit.'

Gabriel thought this was the ideal opportunity to set the interview under way and took out his notebook and biro from his jacket pocket.

'May I take notes?' he asked.

'Of course. But before we start the interview, please pass on the message you bring.'

'The message?'

'From Fidel.'

'Fidel who?'

'Fidel Castro.'

Gabriel felt his throat contract.

'I think there must be some mistake.'

Padre Tiago looked perplexed for a moment.

'I was told you had been in Cuba and had met Castro recently and that he had given you a personal message for me.'

'May I ask who gave you this information?'

Padre Tiago rose to his feet and went back inside. Gabriel heard some terse conversation ensue. What the hell is going on here? he said to himself, suddenly feeling sick. He took a gulp of his cold coffee.

Padre Tiago returned with a sheet of paper and spread it in front of Gabriel. Gabriel noted the familiar letterhead. It was from the editor of the *New Interzonal Review* requesting an interview with Padre Santiago Lopez. It was signed by Bennet Strum. In the second paragraph he read that:

Mr Dax was recently in Cuba where he met Fidel Castro. On learning that Mr Dax was travelling to Guatemala in the hope of interviewing yourself Señor Castro passed on a personal message of respect. Mr Dax will be more than happy to deliver this personal message to you if and when you meet.

Gabriel took another slug of coffee. He saw the hand of Faith Green everywhere. He closed his eyes.

'It's true,' he said. 'I was once offered the opportunity of meeting Fidel Castro but it did not take place. The editor was . . .' he paused. 'Presumptuous.'

'Presumptuous?'

Miraculously, the Spanish word for 'presumptuous' sprang into his head.

'*Presuntuoso.*'

'So. You have no message for me from Fidel Castro,' Padre Tiago stated, coldly.

'No. I'm sorry.'

'I only granted you and your magazine this interview because of this message you were bringing from *El Commandante.*'

'I'm very sorry, sir, I repeat. I had no idea that this . . . this promise had been made. It has nothing to do with me.'

'But this changes our agreement,' Padre Tiago said, looking around him. He shouted a name: 'Raul!'

'We can still do the interview,' Gabriel said, insistently. 'My magazine is very pro-Cuba, pro-Castro, very anti-American. We want to know everything about your thoughts, your ambitions, your policies. How you will fight the election in November. How you will—'

Raul, the paramilitary who had provided the coffee, appeared. He and Padre Tiago went into a huddle. For a second, Gabriel wondered if he would be imprisoned or even killed. No, he thought: it's an innocent mistake, surely that was obvious – just an absurd promise to gain access—

Padre Tiago returned to him.

'You must go,' he said, flatly. 'Go back to Guatemala City. I cannot speak with you.'

'This had nothing to do with me, Señor Lopez. I came here in good faith—'

'In bad faith. This is your magazine.'

'I could have lied to you – given you any invented message from Castro.'

Padre Tiago smiled, sadly.

'Of course, I know this. You seem to be an honest man. And this is the only reason I am allowing you to return. *Ve con Dios.*'

He made a brusque sign of the cross and strode back into the house.

Gabriel sat in the back of the Ford Fairlane, hot with shame and feeling his anger build. It was almost as if there had been a deliberate attempt to subvert and abort the interview, as if whoever – Faith Green, Frank Sartorius and other unknown parties – wanted it to fall at the first hurdle. But why? Why the Castro promise, so easily exposed as a stupid ploy? He experienced the familiar sense of being used again, recognizing that his old role as the 'useful idiot' had been imposed on him. But this time, he considered, he was wiser than in the old days – he would plot some retribution.

The Fairlane duly took him back to the Greenbrier van. He was bundled into the rear seats and the sack placed over his head once more. His sour mood made him feel scratchy and irritated as he sweated under his blindfold, his mind a riot of thoughts and suppositions, curses and imprecations. No, he would never write for

Interzonal again, he told himself. He would personally beat the shit out of Bennet Strum. More importantly, he would find some way of getting his own back on Faith Green. But, but – the question nagged at him persistently – what was the motive behind this carefully constructed fiasco? It certainly wasn't about embarrassing Gabriel Dax.

It was evening when Gabriel's hood was pulled from his head and he was ushered out of the Greenbrier in Guatemala City. He found himself in a narrow side street by the Parque Central. He could see the ornate towers of the cathedral high above the rooftops of the alleyway. The Greenbrier drove off abruptly and left him there, dazed and uncomprehending, as if coming around from some surreal dream. He had not the faintest idea of where he had been these past few hours of his life.

He wandered back to the hotel, distracted and fretful – still wondering what the larger, secret narrative was, the story within the story. But, after all, this was the constant nature of his engagement with the Institute of Developmental Studies, he told himself, trying to calm down. He only ever descried a corner of the big picture – full revelation only occurred, if he was lucky, much further down the line. Still, he thought, he had met Padre Tiago and they seemed to have connected. It had all been genial and warm – laughing about Earl's Court – until the revelation of the stupid Castro ruse. Bastards, he thought – and then thought again. Maybe there was still an article to write: the non-interview with Padre Tiago. A bizarre adventure that he could publish where he liked – perhaps when Padre Santiago Lopez eventually became President of Guatemala. That might irritate some people – stir things up. Good. He began to feel better: there was maybe something to be gained, after all.

Back at the hotel he was handed a message by the desk clerk, along with his keys. He stepped away and opened it. 'Please call at your earliest convenience. FS.' He had no desire to speak to Frank Sartorius this evening, he decided – it could wait until tomorrow. He went up to his room, ordered a cheese omelette and a bottle of red wine and, when he'd finished, took a Seconal and fell into an untroubled, dreamless sleep.

4.

United Fruit

Gabriel arranged to meet Frank Sartorius in the hotel bar at noon. While he waited he investigated the airline timetables, planning his return to London. His job was done – or aborted, through no fault of his own.

Sartorius was in his usual corner booth, his seersucker suit a pale blue, today. There was another man with him, in his forties, Gabriel assumed. Navy blazer, beige chinos, tall, very fair-haired with a flushed face. Hypertension level five, Gabriel thought. They were both drinking coffee.

They were introduced.

'This is Don Van Hoff from United Fruit,' Sartorius said. They sat down and Gabriel ordered a beer, a Gallo. He was developing a taste for the Guatemalan lager. All three lit cigarettes.

'So, how did the meeting go with Padre Tiago?' Sartorius said.

Gabriel stiffened.

'How did you know I'd met him?' he asked.

'We know about these things, Gabriel. It's our business.'

Gabriel thought: yes, of course, Javier, the taxi driver. He managed a thin smile. Javier – not to be trusted henceforth. Fool.

'It didn't go well,' he said. 'He terminated the meeting after about ten minutes.'

Intriguingly, Gabriel thought, this information didn't seem to perturb either Sartorius or Van Hoff.

'We met, we chatted, it all seemed to be going well, and then he suddenly changed his mind,' Gabriel said. 'Called it off. And I came back to the city.'

'How did he seem to you?' Van Hoff asked.

'Personable, calm, a kind of inner strength.' Gabriel paused. 'An impressive man.'

Sartorius and Van Hoff looked at each other.

'Did he say anything about United Fruit?' Van Hoff asked.

'He did say one thing, very forcefully,' Gabriel said, trying not to let his pleasure show at the revelation. 'He said that what Guatemala needed was: "No soldiers. No American CIA. No United Fruit." I quote. He was very emphatic.'

'Fuck,' Van Hoff said.

'That's very interesting,' Sartorius said.

Van Hoff pointed a finger at Gabriel.

'He didn't say anything about nationalization, did he?'

'No,' Gabriel said.

'He has threatened to nationalize the United Fruit plantations and return them to the workers. Do you know how many acres we're talking about?'

'No. I assume it's a lot.'

'Well over a million, give or take. We are the largest landholders in this country.'

Gabriel gave a fake whistle of astonishment.

'Maybe that's the problem – from their point of view.'

'We – United Fruit – made this country,' Van Hoff said, with hoarse passion. 'We built the ports. We built the railway, the roads – and now this Lopez bastard wants to take it all back.'

'Take it easy, Don,' Sartorius said. 'He hasn't won the election yet.'

'He will win,' Van Hoff said, lowering his voice. 'Because he's a fucking priest *and* a trade unionist. He's got the religious vote and the workers' vote. Ydígoras doesn't stand a chance. You know that as well as I do, Frank.'

'Well, there's many a slip betwixt the cup and the lip,' Sartorius said enigmatically. Of the two men, Gabriel noted, Van Hoff was clearly in a state, his flushed face flusher. Sartorius radiated unconcern, almost indifference. Van Hoff turned to Gabriel.

'Did you know that bananas are the fourth-most consumed foodstuff on planet earth?'

'No, I didn't know that,' Gabriel said. 'Fascinating. What are the other three?'

Van Hoff ignored him.

'We're just meant to stand aside and let decades of, of, of . . .' He waved his hands about. 'Decades of investment, agriculture, infrastructure fall into the hands of a few thousand peasant small-holders? Not to mention the money in bananas. We're talking millions of dollars. Millions of United Fruit dollars. Come on, get real, fellas.'

'The election isn't until November, Don,' Sartorius said, almost soothingly, signalling a waiter. 'A lot can happen. Padre Tiago doesn't want to bankrupt Guatemala. He'll see sense. He needs United Fruit.'

'I wish I had your confidence,' Van Hoff said. 'But I know a Commie when I smell one.'

Sartorius paid the bill. They all stood up and shook hands. As they were leaving, Sartorius drew back and spoke quietly to Gabriel.

'You did a great job, Gabriel. You're the only "outsider" to have seen Tiago face to face in over four months. We're very grateful. I'll let Faith Green know how pleased we are.' He clapped Gabriel on the shoulder, grinned and went to join Van Hoff. Gabriel sat down and ordered another beer, thinking: what exactly had he achieved in his short meeting with Padre Tiago? What seemed to be an overt, maladroit failure was now being presented as some kind of personal coup. He lit a cigarette and sipped his beer.

Dean Furlan stepped into the bar, looked around, saw Gabriel, gave him a wave and left. Gabriel stood up and walked to the door. Keeping out of sight as best he could, he peered into the hotel lobby. Frank Sartorius and Dean Furlan stood by the main door, talking quietly to each other. Then Sartorius's car arrived. He and Furlan parted. Van Hoff had gone already, Gabriel assumed – there was no sign of him.

He returned to his seat and took his notebook and pen out of his pocket. He jotted down a list of names. It was a habit of his – seeing names in black and white sometimes encouraged clarity, exposed links where none had been discerned.

Padre Tiago
Frank Sartorius
Dean Furlan
Gabriel Dax
Faith Green

He stared at the names – nothing was forthcoming. He added another. Denilson Canul. And another: Ishbel Dunbar. What was the connection? Or was he the connection? Maybe it was as simple as that.

In the afternoon, he went to a travel agent and booked a flight to New York via Miami for the 30th. He would spend another forty-eight hours in Guatemala, he decided, and maybe dig up some more information on the Motagua river and its Mayan ruins.

Contemplating his imminent book always improved his mood. He had reception reserve him a table in one of Guatemala City's more upscale restaurants, called La Alhambra. He would leave Guatemala City in style – thank you, Institute of Developmental Studies. He showered and shaved and sent two shirts to the laundry. As he stood in the window of his small study-alcove, smoking a cigarette, he saw Denilson Canul wander out of the bar and take a seat on a bench under a mango tree. Canul, he thought: where does he fit in? He pulled on his jacket and headed downstairs.

Canul looked up as he approached. It was clear he recognized and remembered Gabriel. He gave a nod and a weak smile.

'*Hola*,' Gabriel said, and offered him a cigarette. He handed over his lighter and Canul lit up. Gabriel noticed that Canul's fingernails were grimy and the laces of his two-tone shoes didn't match. There was a stain on the arm of his jacket. He looked surly, Gabriel thought, fairly fed up.

'*¿Está bien?*' he asked, in his rudimentary Spanish.

Canul assured him he was all right, returned Gabriel's lighter and drew heavily on his cigarette.

'*Soy amigo de Señor Furlan,*' Gabriel said. '*Lo conoces bien?*'

'*Si,*' Canul said, not meeting Gabriel's eye, and rose to his feet. '*Discúlpeme.*' He walked back into the hotel – the conversation was over. Another mystery, Gabriel considered: what was someone like Dean Furlan doing with someone like Canul? He was pretty sure it had nothing to do with coffee beans.

State of Siege

The next morning, when he went down to the lobby, Gabriel was instantly aware that something was wrong. He could hear somebody sobbing down a corridor and he saw small groups of the hotel staff conferring urgently, some visibly upset. Two policemen stood at the main door. Outside in the city, sirens wailed and howled.

'What's happening?' Gabriel asked the desk clerk. 'Is there something going on?'

'Is a big tragedy for our country,' the man said, lowering his voice. 'Everyone is very frightened. Very.'

'An earthquake? A volcano?'

'No, sir. An important person has been killed. Has been murdered.'

Gabriel felt a slipping and a sliding inside him, as if his guts were rearranging themselves.

'Who?'

'You do not know him, sir.'

'What's his name?'

'Padre Tiago Lopez. *Un gran hombre.*'

Back in his room, Gabriel tried to calm himself and called Frank Sartorius. After a short wait, Sartorius came to the phone.

'Have you heard?' Sartorius asked.

'Yes, just now.'

'Kind of uncanny, huh?'

'Do you know what happened?'

'Some guy with a grudge, apparently,' Sartorius said, his usual geniality unaffected. 'Shot him dead.'

'Where was he killed?'

'I don't know.'

'Did they get the killer?' Gabriel asked.

'Not yet.'

'United Fruit will be opening the champagne.'

'No.' Sartorius was emphatic. 'It gets worse. There's been a military coup. President Ydígoras has been removed.'

'What? What the fuck!'

'Yeah. Real Banana Republic stuff. Couldn't make it up.'

Sartorius explained. It looked like the new President was going to be one Colonel Azurdia, Minister of Defence. A 'State of Siege' had been installed. There was a city-wide curfew from six p.m. to six a.m. The airport's going to be closed, he added.

'I was meant to be leaving tomorrow.'

'That ain't gonna happen,' Sartorius said. 'Just stay in the hotel. They'll look after you. They'll be taking to the streets – the students, the workers – heads will be broken, or worse. Lie low. Stay safe. It'll pass over.'

Gabriel thought.

'Had you any inkling this might happen?'

'Of course not. Just some lunatic with a gun. Everybody loved Padre Tiago. We're all in shock.'

Yeah, sure, Gabriel thought as he hung up.

He went down to the lobby to the telephone cabin and asked the hotel switchboard to connect him with his London number.

'Hello, it's Mr Simpson here. Can I speak to my wife?'

He hoped it would be Faith but Ishbel Dunbar replied.

'You may not have heard yet,' Gabriel said, slowly. 'But there's been a bit of a family tragedy. Dramatic. Cousin Tommy died suddenly of a heart attack.'

There was a pause as the information was ingested.

'Cousin Tommy?'

'Yes, I'd just been to visit him.'

'Ah. Right. We actually didn't know you'd visited him. We haven't heard any news here. That's a great shame.'

'Everything's turned upside down, consequently. In a major way. I won't be coming home for a while.'

'Keep in touch. Be careful.'

Gabriel hung up. He felt sick, nauseous. He had a horrible, growing conviction that somehow he had been a key component – a vital
catalyst – in the murder of Padre Tiago. And now the military coup
in Guatemala was a direct consequence of that murder, also, he felt
sure. But how? What? Why? He couldn't join the dots. There were
too many pieces missing from the jigsaw puzzle that was his life,
currently. He went back up to his room and wrote down everything
he could remember about his fateful, clandestine visit to the farm,
every little detail of the meeting and the truncated conversation
with Padre Tiago that had taken place. He covered pages, searching
his memory ruthlessly.

Outside in the city he heard noises build: shouting, chanting
crowds, baleful police sirens, gunshots.

That evening he went down to the hotel dining room. It was
almost empty. Then he saw Dean Furlan sitting alone at the rear.
Furlan beckoned him over.

'Why don't you join me?' Furlan said. 'Two refugees waiting for
the war to end.'

For a moment, Gabriel wondered if this invitation was one he
should accept. But – how could he duck out of it? He smiled and said
he'd be delighted and took a seat opposite Furlan at the table. They
ate well – Furlan had a steak, Gabriel ordered a pork dish, hot with
chillies, called *manchamanteles de cerdo*. Furlan seemed in a good mood
and talked freely. He told Gabriel that he owned 'a couple of restaurants and a diner' in Buffalo, New York State. He said he had found a
reliable supplier of Guatemalan coffee and was about to 'clean up'.

'I mean, everybody drinks coffee, don't they? And now I've got
the best.'

'Are you from Buffalo?' Gabriel asked.

'My family are from Italy,' Furlan said. 'The Veneto. Do you
know it?'

Gabriel said he did. He was a travel writer, he reminded Furlan,
author of three books. He had been to almost every country in
Europe. Furlan noted down the titles on a paper napkin. He would
buy them, he promised, though he had to confess he was not much
of a reader.

'Movies, that's my thing,' he said.

At one stage, just before they ordered their desert, there was a loud rip close by of what sounded like machine-gun fire. Everyone in the restaurant paused. There was a silence. And then people resumed eating and talking – the clink of silverware on china an undercurrent to discreet conversations.

'What do you know about this *coup d'état*?' Furlan asked. 'Nobody saw it coming.'

'Not much,' Gabriel said carefully. 'One colonel replacing a general, as far as I can tell. I can't remember the new one's name.'

'What does Frank Sartorius think?'

'I haven't spoken to him,' Gabriel said, deciding on discretion. 'I'm sure he's got a lot on his plate.'

Gabriel finished his ice cream.

'Have you heard about this man who was killed, murdered? Padre Tiago Lopez?' he asked.

'No,' Furlan said. 'A priest? What's he got to do with anything?'

Gabriel explained, briefly. Charismatic priest turned populist trade union leader, turned potential presidential candidate.

'That's why everyone is out on the streets,' Gabriel said. 'It's not the army changing guard, so to speak. It's about the death of this man.'

'Maybe this new colonel has some questions to answer,' Furlan said. 'I bet you. You want to get a brandy?'

They wandered through to the bar and ordered their drinks. Furlan lit one of his long cigars. Beyond the high garden wall of the Alcázar they could see a shifting yellow light in the night sky – some building burning, Gabriel supposed.

'I was meant to be heading home tomorrow,' Gabriel said.

'They're closing the airport,' Furlan said. 'I'm staying on, got to sign the contracts with the coffee exporters.' He paused, thinking. 'The airport may be closed but you could always get a train to Mexico. Easy.'

'Maybe I will,' Gabriel said. He felt ambivalent about Furlan, watching him relight his cigar with due concentration and blow on the glowing ash at its end. He seemed open and friendly, but some questions remained. Was Furlan really just a Buffalo restaurateur who was trying to buy coffee wholesale? What was the connection with grubby, edgy Denilson Canul? No coffee-broker, that was for sure.

They chatted on, and ordered another round of brandy. Gabriel told him about his book *Rivers*. Furlan gave him his business card and invited him to Buffalo, telling him to check out the Buffalo river. 'Full of history,' he said. 'You got the Seneca nation, you got the British, the War of Independence. There's a real story there.'

'Maybe I will,' Gabriel said. 'I'm going to New York to catch my plane to England. Might take a detour.'

'Let me do you a favour,' Furlan said. 'If you're staying in Manhattan – go to this hotel. My cousin's the manager. You'll get a great discount.' He retrieved his business card from Gabriel and wrote on the back of it, returning it to him.

Gabriel read: 'Blakelock Hotel. Giancarlo Ruffini'.

'Great, thanks,' he said. 'I'll take you up on that.'

'It's near Grand Central Station. Very nice – you know: not too big, classy, civilized. And when I say discount I mean discount. Just mention my name to Giancarlo. In fact I'll call him. Tell him you might be checking in.'

Gabriel was duly grateful. Then Furlan stood up and wished him goodnight, saying he had to go to his room and make a few calls. Gabriel sat on in the bar and smoked a final cigarette. All seemed quiet in the city, for the moment, the wailing police sirens finally silent in the curfew. The Alcázar-Plaza seemed a strange oasis in the sudden turmoil of the audible but largely invisible political convulsions gripping the country. He was trapped, but his prison had all mod-cons. Could have been worse, he thought. He signed for the drinks and went upstairs to his room. Perhaps he could factor this bizarre adventure into his chapter on the Motagua. Nothing is wasted, after all: it was one of his personal mottos.

Gabriel lay in bed, his mind active, running through everything that had happened. He knew he'd have to take a sleeping pill again tonight. He thought back to his meeting with Padre Tiago. The tall man in black with his knowing, rheumy eyes, shot dead . . . But by whom? And why? Actually, the 'why' was pretty obvious, he reflected. But who was the killer? He looked up at the ceiling fan spinning above his bed. Stop thinking, he told himself – imagine you're back in Rose Cottage, in your bedroom, very tired, wanting to go to sleep. Sometimes the thought-experiment worked.

Boom! The glass in the windows rattled as the bomb went off some streets away. The vision of Rose Cottage abruptly disappeared. Gabriel reached for his bottle of Seconal.

The next day the newspapers were full of images of the marching protestors, the burnt-out cars, police with batons charging makeshift barricades. The hotel guests were still not permitted to leave the hotel precincts so Gabriel remained in his room. He packed; he asked at reception about trains to Mexico; he even began to write up his chapter on the Motagua river. He saw no sign of Furlan all day – perhaps he was in his room buying more coffee beans. The coffee king of Buffalo.

In the evening, as he headed down the main stairway towards the bar, keen to have a drink before dinner, Gabriel paused on the final turning, noticing Denilson Canul, in his creased and shabby blue suit, crossing the lobby. Interesting. Gabriel ran quickly down the final flight in time to see Canul enter the bar, and spotted Furlan waiting for him on the terrace. Gabriel found a corner table from where he could safely observe the two of them as they talked. Canul seemed agitated, waving his arms around, and Furlan was clearly attempting to calm him down. It was dusk and the light was fading fast, bats beginning to dip and dart about in the gloaming. Furlan pointed to the far wall of the Alcázar and almost physically pushed Canul in that direction. He then strode briskly back through the bar, not looking left or right, and not spotting Gabriel in his corner. Where was Canul going? Gabriel wondered, stepping out on to the terrace.

Then he saw the man hurrying down a path beside a terraced water-feature at the garden's end – gentle two-foot waterfalls planted with rushes and other aquatic flora that disappeared into a subterranean tank by an area reserved for the gardeners where there were heaps of compost, wooden stakes, coils of chicken wire, stacked sacks of fallen leaves. There was a wooden door there that gave on to an alley beyond the Alcázar wall. Unlocked, Gabriel saw, as Canul opened it. Canul slipped through and, seconds later, Gabriel followed.

The streets in this quarter of the city were narrow and badly lit, dank lanes with parked, clapped-out cars and a fair amount of rubbish clogging the gutters. Canul turned a corner and Gabriel broke into a run, keen not to lose him, asking himself, at the same time, what the hell he thought he was doing, following the man. He had always sensed an oddness in the Furlan–Canul relationship and he had a sudden suspicion that this might be the moment when he found out its source. That was his rationale, for what it was worth, he told himself, as he ran on. Would he be vindicated?

Canul turned another corner but by the time Gabriel arrived at the junction there was no sign of the man. Fuck. Gabriel ran to the next intersection – no sign. He looked about him and wandered around for a minute or two, trying to get his bearings. The buildings in these narrow alleys were not houses – they appeared to be workshops or storage facilities with metal grilles and shuttered windows, all closed tight at the end of the working day. There was no sign of human or family life. He turned and headed back to the hotel. So much for his sleuthing. He had—

He heard the gunshot. A single flat detonation – like a backfire – a couple of streets away, he reckoned. A dog began barking somewhere. He ran back to the last junction where he had seen Canul. He walked slowly along the alley, dim street lights casting a faint glow on cracked and potholed tarmac. Dirty cars all parked on one side. He paused.

Canul was sitting behind the wheel of a dusty dark green Dodge Coronet. He seemed to be asleep, his head resting against the wheel. Gabriel knocked on the window – Canul didn't move. He walked round to the other side of the car and peered in.

Above Canul's ear was a bloody, weeping, rose-sized exit wound. There was a splatter of blood on the window. Gabriel stood there in rigid, breathless shock. He looked around. No one. It must have been only two or three minutes since he heard the gunshot. Gabriel shaded his eyes and peered in. Canul had a gun – a snub-nosed revolver – half-held in his right hand, limply extended along the Coronet's front bench seat. There was a folded sheet of notepaper on the seat beside the gun. Suicide?

Gabriel took some steps away from the car. Canul had certainly seemed agitated when he was talking to Furlan. But what crisis would have provoked such a severe and fatal outcome? What made Canul go to his car, sit there for a few short minutes – that was why Gabriel had lost him, he realized – and then put a gun to his head and pull the trigger? What had Furlan said to him . . .?

Gabriel walked away, mouth dry, a small, persistent tremor of worry running through his body, and headed back to the hotel, his mind typically full of clamouring questions and unsatisfactory answers. What were the facts as he knew them? Furlan and Canul had had some sort of dispute, or at least an intense conversation, on the terrace outside the bar, that was clear. Furlan had urged him to exit the hotel grounds clandestinely through a door reserved for the gardening staff. Canul had duly done so and had gone to his parked car and then taken a gun from – where? – the glove compartment or his pocket, placed the barrel on his temple and pulled the trigger. Somehow Gabriel knew this was not caused by a disagreement about the price of coffee beans. It was time for him to leave Guatemala City.

6.

New York, New York

It had been a long, tedious, two-day journey from Guatemala City to New York. A train to La Mesilla, on the border, another train to Mexico City, a night in a hotel near the airport in Mexico City, then Aeroméxico to Miami, then United Airlines to New York. But it had given him plenty of time to think. Everything was wrong. Everything he thought he knew was, in fact, simply evidence of his ignorance.

Ignorance that was dissipated to a certain extent when he bought a copy of the *New York Times* at the airport. There was an article about the coup in Guatemala and the change in the military government, and, more vitally, a paragraph within it about the assassination of Padre Tiago. There was a blurry photograph of a young Padre Tiago and beneath it the account of how a lone gunman by the name of Denilson Canul had taken his own life, leaving a confessional note as to his responsibility for the murder. He was the man who had killed the much-loved priest and populist leader who had possibly been in line to become President at the elections scheduled for November. Elections, not surprisingly, that had now been cancelled.

Not for the first time, Gabriel noted how honest, diligent reportage could be so far from reality, so distant from the truth. Whatever that was.

He checked in to the modest midtown hotel that Furlan had recommended, the Blakelock, not far from Grand Central Station, and settled in. He had been given a very good discount on the room just as Furlan had promised. His cousin, Giancarlo, the manager, had been warmly welcoming. He had wanted to say goodbye to Furlan before he left the Alcázar-Plaza but to his vague surprise had been told Señor Furlan was no longer staying in the hotel. Maybe the death of Canul had put paid to his wholesale coffee-purchasing plans.

Gabriel felt oddly insecure, all the same, still troubled by his discovery of Canul's body and its numerous worrying implications, whatever they might be. He went to a post office and sent a telegram to the Institute: 'IN NEW YORK FOR SEVERAL DAYS. STOP. WILL MAKE CONTACT SOON. SIMPSON.' That should buy him some time, he thought, and maybe cause some mild consternation now that Faith would realize he was out of Guatemala.

That evening in a bar, searching his wallet for some dollars, he came across Dean Furlan's business card and recalled his invitation to visit Buffalo and explore the Buffalo river. It wasn't a bad idea, he recognized, though he didn't fancy meeting Furlan again so soon. And, anyway, thinking further, inspired, he didn't need the Buffalo river as he had another river on his doorstep – the Hudson. What with the Motagua and now the Hudson, *Rivers* would effectively be finished. The prospect gave him real pleasure. *Il faut profiter*, he said to himself in French, for some reason. Whatever the fallout from the Padre Tiago disaster he would have a completed book.

He left the bar and went in search of a shop he knew on Lexington Avenue that appeared to sell every known newspaper and magazine in the world. He bought two Guatemalan newspapers – *Prensa Libre* and the *Diario de Centro América* – and a Mexican newspaper, *El Universal*. He assumed the coup in a neighbouring country would be covered. He went back to the Blakemore and began to read as methodically as he could, wishing his Spanish was better.

The death of Padre Tiago was covered but not in much detail. 'A grudge killing', was one interpretation, but there were no details about the grudge. 'A solitary man, a psychopath', was another theory. There was no information about the weapon used or the location of the murder. Padre Tiago was no more and Guatemala had a new military government, helmed by one Colonel Enrique Peralta Azurdia. *Cui bono?* Gabriel asked himself. Who was happy? The soldiers in charge? – yes. United Fruit? – yes. The USA? – yes. Regime change but no regime change, seemed to be the outcome of the coup, as far as he could see. One authoritarian soldier replaced by another. But no democratic elections in November, significantly. Civil unrest quashed and the status quo in Guatemala preserved. Maybe that was the simple object of the exercise.

He ordered up a hamburger and a Scotch and soda from room service. Where did Gabriel Dax fit in, however? he asked himself. What was his role in the affair? Why had this interview been set up and then so easily undermined? He knew that the only person who could answer was Faith Green. He would bide his time, he thought, there was no hurry and he had a book to finish.

Gabriel caught a train from Penn station to Poughkeepsie in the Hudson river valley. He had decided to choose the town of Hyde Park as his locus on the river. Home of President Franklin D. Roosevelt, and his wife, Eleanor, of course. Hyde Park offered many opportunities. Washington Irving territory wasn't far away, either – Sleepy Hollow and Tarrytown – there was rich Gilded Age material to hand as well, vast nineteenth-century mansions set in their landscaped estates.

The station at Hyde Park was defunct so Gabriel taxied the few miles there from Poughkeepsie. He had good views of the river from the back of the car. The day was bright, with a spring shimmer in the air, and a breezy coolness that invigorated. The Hudson was impressive, he had to admit; 'America's Rhine' it was called, broad and still, thickly wooded on either bank and, even though the trees were bare, there was a kind of romantic majesty about the Hudson valley that was stirring and inspiring.

In a Hyde Park bookstore he bought a guidebook to the town and its environs – a small, thick volume, filled with illustrations and maps. He realized he could easily spend a week here, and the book would help flesh out his chapter. He went to a diner for a late break-fast, enjoying his fried eggs and hash browns as he flicked through the pages of the guide. Maybe he should have another taxi drive him to the Roosevelt house, he wondered, and take some photographs.

He paid the bill, pulled on his duffel coat and sauntered outside. It was still bright and still chilly – the kind of day that made you walk briskly and he did so, setting off through the town, guidebook in hand, to the river's edge.

As he walked he became aware of somebody following him, footsteps steadily becoming closer. He turned. It was a young man, in his twenties, Gabriel thought – thin, with a lick of dark hair falling over his brow. He was wearing a short red jacket with a large white 'A' embroidered on it.

'You Gabriel Dax, by any chance?'

Could it be another fan? Gabriel thought, puzzled. An American, also. It was uncanny how his readers spotted him. Who'd have thought, here in Hyde Park, of all places?

'Yes,' he said, 'I am,' thinking it odd that the man didn't smile at the acknowledgement being made as he stepped forward. 'Gabriel Dax, at your service.'

Then he saw the glint of a blade in the man's right hand.

Unthinkingly, instinctively, Gabriel smashed the hard spine of the guidebook into the young man's face, pulverizing his nose. He screamed, and flailed out with his knife. Gabriel felt the tear in his coat. But the man then wheeled away, doubled over, blood streaming from his ruined nose, spitting, making an agonized grinding, moaning noise. He ran off, turned a corner and was gone.

Thank you, Patrick Begg, Gabriel thought, breathing deeply. Anything can be a weapon. Then he looked down to see that he was standing in a widening puddle of his own blood, feeling a warm wetness on his right side, his trousers quickly sopping with the flow of blood from his wound. He dropped his book and fell to his knees. Some passer-by was shouting for help, he heard. Gabriel blinked. Now he felt the spearing pain in his side. He passed out and keeled over.

7.

The Wound

Gabriel's wound required some fifteen stitches to close the wild slash above his right hip. The thin blade had gone in about an inch deep, its point emerging about six inches later, and was then whipped out causing a neat, linear incision. No vital organs were damaged, no severance of any part of his intestinal system. A butcherly precise flesh wound – but some infection had followed so he was put on antibiotics and the sutured lesion was probed and drained daily. Very painfully.

He had now been six days in a substantial hospital, not far from Hyde Park, set in a former country estate. He had his own room on the second floor and through the window, when he was allowed out of bed, he had a view of a wide, terraced parterre and a carefully planted avenue of shagbark hickories leading down to a manufactured oxbow lake surrounded with huge rhododendrons. Newer buildings, other facilities – administration, nurses' quarters, paediatrics, a tuberculosis unit – had been built here and there, tastefully echoing the architecture of the original 'big house', now fully adapted as a large modern American hospital.

None of this was free, of course, and he was grateful to his travel insurers, Barrow & Plumstead – a firm he'd been using since his first book – for so quickly picking up the tab. After lunch, when the sun was out, he was steered down to the parterre in a wheelchair and, leaning on the elbow of a nurse, was then walked around the gravelled pathways. Mobility was key, he was told. He began to feel better, stronger, though the infection of his wound was persistent. Tiny fibres from his coat that had been missed when the cut was first cleaned and abraded were the cause, apparently, hence the daily probing and sanitizing.

Gabriel closed his eyes, enjoying the early April sunshine. He was sitting on a bench – no need for a wheelchair, even though he still limped, somewhat – warm in his neatly repaired duffel coat, a blanket over his knees. He had been told he would be able to leave the next day – news that had destabilized him somewhat. It was funny, he thought, but the total, twenty-four-hour security of these places, where all your needs – medical, gastronomical, hygienical – were catered for by smiling, helpful nurses and other staff, always made the idea of your own normal diurnal autonomy a little alarming. What would he do? he thought. Go back to England, he supposed. Finish his book. Try to forget Guatemala—

'Sorry to interrupt your reverie,' came a familiar voice.

Gabriel opened his eyes.

Faith Green stood there, wearing her shaved-rabbit coat, no hat – her usual Alice band (scarlet) securing her tousled hair.

She leant forward and kissed his cheek and sat down on the bench beside him. She took his hand.

'How are you?'

'I'm better, apparently. They're kicking me out tomorrow.'

'I'm so sorry this happened, Gabriel.' She seemed sincere, then she released his hand. 'Was the man who stabbed you a thief, do you think?'

'Thieves don't usually confirm your name before they rob you,' he said and gave her a brief description of the encounter. 'No. I think he was trying to kill me.' He paused. 'For a reason I still can't fathom.'

Faith sat back and crossed her arms.

'Fair point.'

'Thank you for coming,' Gabriel said.

'I'm on my way to Langley – big MI6–CIA brainstorming session.' She smiled. 'I thought I'd detour and see how you were.'

Oh, right, Gabriel reflected. He had managed to have a telegram sent to the Institute, shortly after he'd been hospitalized, detailing the bare facts of his current crisis and giving his address. There had been no reply, but here was Faith sitting beside him, looking down at the oxbow lake, thinking. Her strong pale face inert, expressionless.

'How many people knew you were coming to New York?' she asked.

'A lot,' he said. 'Everyone at the Institute, the hotel staff, Frank Sartorius, and a man I met in Guatemala City called Dean Furlan.'

'Who was he? This Furlan?'

'He said he was a restaurateur looking to buy wholesale coffee. We were staying in the same hotel and got to know each other, especially once the coup erupted. We spent some time together. But there was something suspicious about him. He also knew the man accused of killing Padre Tiago, for example.'

'Really?' Faith said. 'My God . . .'

She opened her handbag and took out a small diary, She wrote Furlan's name down, asking Gabriel how to spell it.

'Maybe the people at Langley will have some intelligence about him.'

'Maybe. I can't imagine why he'd want to kill me, however.' He threw the blanket off his knees. 'Shall we go for a stroll?' he said.

They walked together down the gravelled pathways towards the neatly sculpted oxbow lake. Gabriel was enjoying being with her in this visitor–convalescent mode – it was different, almost caring, not like the usual fractious to-and-fro tensions of their normal encounters. And she had kissed his cheek, spontaneously. Ex-lovers, he reminded himself. Still, he had some pertinent questions for her.

'Why was I sent to interview Padre Tiago?' he asked, as casually as he could manage.

'You know why. The CIA couldn't get to him – so they asked us. We set it all up.'

'But it all went haywire very quickly,' he said, telling her about the fake Castro message and Padre Tiago's instant angry reaction.

'Yes, that was a mistake,' she said. 'In hindsight. But the personal message from Castro was the only reason Padre Tiago would have met you, you see. We rather thought you could finesse it, once you were face to face.'

'He was furious.'

'We weren't to know that.'

'If you'd warned me I might have been able to "finesse" it.'

'It was better you didn't know.'

They walked on. He knew the answer to that: if he'd been aware of the Castro message, given that he'd never met Fidel Castro, he'd have realized that the interview was a set-up. The unsuspecting go-between would have been very conscious that he was simply a means to an end. He had been here before, of course, working for Faith and the Institute – and, as ever, sometimes a useful idiot was more useful than he knew.

'How was Padre Tiago killed, by the way?' Gabriel asked. 'Do you have any information? There's nothing in the newspapers.'

'A sniper, I believe. One shot.'

'A sniper?'

'Yes.'

'Where was he killed?'

'Some remote farm in the countryside where he was in hiding.'

Gabriel almost laughed.

'Well, that's it, don't you see?'

'Lost me, Gabriel, sorry.'

'The only reason this "interview" was set up was to find out where Padre Tiago was hiding.'

'No, that's—'

'I must have been followed to that farm from the city. The fucking taxi driver who took me to the FJP headquarters was working for the CIA. That's how they were able to kill him.' Gabriel closed his eyes, feeling suddenly weak. 'I led the killer to Padre Tiago.'

'That's ridiculous.'

He turned and looked at her.

'You know exactly what happened, Faith. Frank Sartorius set this all up. I was the lure, the bait. I flushed Padre Tiago out. They didn't know where he was.'

'Nonsense.'

'Ask Sartorius when you see him at Langley.' He paused. 'Padre Tiago Lopez is dead. Assassinated. There's been a military coup in Guatemala and a new bunch of soldiers is in power. Nothing will change. Elections conveniently cancelled. A neat piece of geo-political manipulation. Everybody happy, particularly the United

Fruit Company. And the CIA, of course. No chance of a charismatic, popular "Commie" union leader as President, mobilizing the workforce, nationalizing the agricultural industry, kicking out the multinational companies making their fortunes. And thank you, MI6, by the way, for facilitating things – by sending that numbskull to interview the target.'

She looked at him, levelly, unperturbed.

'This is paranoia. You couldn't be more wrong,' she said.

'Well, leave me to stew in my paranoia. Thanks for coming by, Faith. I appreciate it.'

He turned away, his chest tight, but seeing things clearly through his anger – he felt unhappy, that old bitterness – as he walked away back to the hospital and his room.

'Gabriel!' she shouted after him. 'Don't be stupid! Nothing is what it seems!'

PART THREE

East Sussex
London
The Cotswolds

April 1963

I.

Home Sweet Home

Gabriel unlocked the front door of Rose Cottage and felt his sphincter loosen momentarily with the sudden, intense relief he was experiencing at being back. Home. He shivered, lugging in his suitcase, grip and typewriter and setting them down before closing the door behind him. The Cat stalked out of the living room into the hall, looked briefly at him, and headed down the corridor to the kitchen. Food – now – was the clear message. How had the Cat known when he was returning? Gabriel wondered, following it to the kitchen where he emptied a tin of catfood into a saucer and left the beast to its lunch.

He unpacked and had a bath, contemplating, as he dried himself off, the row of neat black stitches – fifteen in all – that were knitting together the two sides of his wound. It seemed to have properly healed though it was still a gleaming pink stripe. The hospital had advised him to have the stitches removed as soon as possible on his return to Britain. He would ask his doctor, Muir Kinross, to do the deed. Another trip to London beckoned.

As he shaved, he began to think that, in fact, he needed to rent a *pied-à-terre* in London. He was spending too much on bed-and-breakfasts and hotels, however modest. He had enough money – thanks to the Russian subventions – and it would make life easier for him. Faith would approve, also: another more ostentatious use of the Russian windfall. Somewhere in Chelsea, he thought, his old stamping ground. The idea cheered him up and made him forget his recent trauma – and the perplexing mysteries of his Guatemala trip. Think positively, he told himself. He could have been stabbed to death – and he had managed to find two new rivers for his book. Not everything was going against him.

His phone rang. It was Ishbel Dunbar.

'Welcome home,' she said. 'Would it be possible for you to drop by the Institute the next time you're in London?'

'Yes, of course. I have to come up to see my doctor.'

'I heard about the incident,' she said. 'Glad you're fit and well.'

'I'll let you know,' he said. 'Sometime later this week.'

They exchanged banalities and he hung up. Yes, he thought, he definitely needed his own place in London. The city seemed to be claiming him again.

Muir Kinross was wearing an emerald-green silk tie that offset his white shirt and charcoal-grey pinstriped suit to perfection. Gabriel was concentrating on the tie's shimmering iridescence as Muir snipped away at the sutures and then pulled the threads out with a small pincer, each tug causing a mini-spasm of pain.

'Going to make a very nice scar,' he said. 'Obviously an ideally sharp knife. Like a wire through cheese, as they say.'

'We must count our blessings, I suppose,' Gabriel said.

'Was it a robbery?'

'Or a madman. Maybe a disappointed reader.' Gabriel tried not to think back. 'I smashed his nose in – some compensation. Then he ran off. Nobody was arrested.'

Muir wiped some disinfectant over the now stitch-free wound.

'Are you still going to that psychoanalyst?' Muir asked. Katerina Haas had been his suggestion.

'I'm heading there now,' Gabriel said. 'You'll have noticed I'm not asking for more supplies of sleeping pills.' Gabriel thought for a moment. 'It was an excellent idea of yours, Muir, I must say. I find her very . . .' He paused. 'Still very helpful – even though the initial cause seems to have been resolved. The insomnia is minor, intermittent, tolerable.'

'Well, whatever gets you through the night, as they say.'

'She was psychoanalysed by Freud, you know,' Gabriel said, adjusting his trousers and tightening his belt.

'That old fraud. Is that a recommendation?'

'She claims to be a follower of Adler, now.'

Muir's thin smile was eloquent.

'I like her,' Gabriel said. 'I'm at ease with her. I tell her everything.'

'Well, if it works, it works,' he said. 'Very good to see you again, Gabriel. Looking forward to the new book.'

EXTRACTS FROM THE TRANSCRIPTION
OF SESSION 13

DR HAAS: But this attack, this stabbing, hasn't – what can I say? – hasn't destabilized you?

GABRIEL DAX: Well, it has. But not in a consequential way. I relive the moment – but I can banish it. It doesn't stop me sleeping at night, that's the main thing.

DR HAAS: What was the cause, the provocation?

GABRIEL DAX: I can only think this person was trying to kill me.

DR HAAS: My God. Why?

GABRIEL DAX: Because of what happened in Guatemala. But I can't analyse it further. It's connected to Guatemala but I'm not sure who had the motive. It could be one of several people. [Pause] But I do feel safer now I'm back in England. For some reason.

DR HAAS: And you said that when you were in hospital in America you were visited by this woman, Faith Green.

GABRIEL DAX: Yes, I was very touched, actually. I think it was a sign of some concern. Very unusual for her.

DR HAAS: Do you think she felt some responsibility for the injury?

GABRIEL DAX: I don't know. She sent me to Guatemala, so maybe she did feel a bit responsible.

DR HAAS: How are your feelings for this woman, now?

GABRIEL DAX: Exactly the same. I can't really get her out of my mind. But, also, I just can't figure her out. We have been lovers, as you're aware. And she knows what I feel about her – but I've no concrete idea what she feels about me. It's not normal, our relationship – such as it is.

DR HAAS: Are you familiar with the concepts of the 'true self' and the 'false self'?

GABRIEL DAX: No. I mean, of course, I understand the division, the opposition, but not in a clinical sense.

DR HAAS: Some people call it a division between the 'original self' and a 'pseudo self'. A person exhibiting a 'false self' occurs when other people's expectations override the spontaneous expression of the 'true self'. The 'false self' is a kind of masquerade – a self that is presented to the world. A 'social self'. Not the true, private self, inside.

GABRIEL DAX: I don't see what this has to do with me and Faith Green.

DR HAAS: I've never met this woman but, from what you say, I believe that maybe the root of the problem is that you are showing your true self to her – and she is responding with her false self. In a case like that there can be no – what's the word? – *Vereinigung* . . . [Pause]. Yes, fusion. Is that a good English word?

GABRIEL DAX: It makes a kind of sense. But, if that's indeed the case, what am I meant to do about it?

DR HAAS: Well, first of all I think you have to try to make this Faith Green show you her true self. Then fusion has a chance of taking place.

GABRIEL DAX: I think that might be quite difficult.

DR HAAS: But worth the effort, no? And until that happens I suggest that you try to have an ordinary sexual life. You're a young man, attractive, clever, successful. You should be in the full flush of your sexual being. Not obsessing about this woman with her false self.

GABRIEL DAX: Easier said than done. But I promise I'll give it some thought.

2.

The Studio

The estate agent handed Gabriel the keys, wished him a happy tenancy of Studio 3 and left him to contemplate his new London home.

Ruskin Studios was a late nineteenth-century development of purpose-built studio apartments constructed around a courtyard that was accessed through an archway from Flood Street. It was a red-brick building with a conspicuous decorative frieze high up on the outer wall. There was a caretaker's cottage next to the main door which gave on to a wide, tiled corridor lined by the various-sized studios on offer – some single units like Gabriel's; others grander duplexes with two bedrooms as well as the sizeable workspace. The studios were about two hundred yards away from his old flat in Redburn Street and their very proximity to his former existence seemed serendipitously apt. He had his country life in Claverleigh and now here was a new toehold in his former Chelsea world. Trips to London were to be welcomed. He could spend a night or two in town and enjoy the city. Thank you, KGB, for your largesse, thank you, Varvara Suvorina.

The studio was unfurnished. Wooden-floored, white-walled, it consisted of a substantial, high-ceilinged room (previously occupied by a photographer, he had been told) with a very large multi-paned window giving maximum luminosity. A gas fire provided heat. There was a small, open kitchenette with a stove, a fridge and a sink and – through a door – a lavatory. Sleeping quarters were in a mezzanine overlooking the main studio space, reached by a narrow twisting stair. £10 a week. No bathroom or shower but he could easily wash and shave at the kitchen sink – very nineteenth century, he thought – and, anyway, his stays would be short: a night, two nights at the most. All he needed was a bed for the mezzanine sleeping area, a desk, a chair, a rug, a couple of table lamps, sheets, blankets, some pots and pans, dishes and glasses, essential cutlery and it was ready for occupancy. One trip to Peter Jones at Sloane Square would see the place furnished. He felt his mood surge – a fizz of elation – things were looking up. The key objective, he realized, was to keep it a secret. This was his safe house, his bolthole, should his life ever become precarious or threatened in some way. The courtyard entrance and the communal corridor made it especially discreet. Nobody need know who was occupying number 3 Ruskin Studios. Certainly not Faith Green.

He locked the door of the studio behind him and set off towards Sloane Square and the department store that would answer his every domestic need. His buoyant mood sustained him: the Motagua river chapter was finished and he was near the end of his Hudson river chapter. Once that was done his book was effectively completed. Time to hand it in to Inigo. Maybe his old life would return, wholesale . . . But then he remembered he had an appointment at the Institute. What did they want him for, now?

It was strange being in the Institute with no Faith Green present. Ishbel Dunbar had greeted him at the door and had invited him into her office, a small, cramped space, just fitting her desk and two chairs and a bookshelf full of Spanish and South American books – dictionaries, almanacs, manuals and histories, as far as he could tell. A window looked on to a yard with bins and several parked bicycles.

Ishbel's hair was back up in its sensible bun and her checked-saffron tweed jacket had a large thistle-shaped amber-and-silver brooch on the lapel. She offered him a glass of sherry that he gladly accepted, experiencing a sudden sensation of being back at university having a tutorial with a don, one of the few memories that remained of his truncated sojourn as an undergraduate at Cambridge – that feeling of being slightly tense, conscious of not being fully prepared. How would things have been different, he momentarily wondered, if he had stayed on at Cambridge and become the doctor he had so fervently wished to be? He wouldn't be sitting in the Institute of Developmental Studies drinking sherry with Ishbel Dunbar, that was for sure.

'Are you all right, Gabriel?' Ishbel asked. 'Thought I'd lost you there.'

'Some distant memory triggered, that's all. Apologies. Is Faith joining us?'

'She's away – in Italy, I believe.'

'Holiday?'

'No. I'm pretty sure not.'

'Right.'

So – no Faith, Gabriel thought, sensing something unorthodox approaching.

'How are you?' Ishbel asked. 'I mean, after the attack in New York. Shocking.'

'I'm very lucky,' Gabriel said. 'The wound's well healed. My doctor thinks it'll make rather a fetching scar.'

'Doctors,' Ishbel said, rolling her eyes.

'I still have no real idea of a motive. Something to do with Guatemala, that's for sure. But what? Who? Why?'

'Mistaken identity?'

'The man used my name. He wanted to check it was me.'

Ishbel frowned and fiddled with her brooch, thinking.

'Faith came to see you at the hospital – in New York.'

'Yes. Very good of her.'

'Did she tell you what she was doing in America?'

'She said she had to go to a big meeting at Langley. CIA, MI6, brainstorming sort of thing.'

'There was no such meeting scheduled.'

Gabriel said nothing for a moment, aware that this discussion had a subtext he couldn't discern. Some internal issue in the Institute, no doubt – little power shifts under way, Ishbel taking advantage of Faith's absence. He didn't want to know.

'Perhaps I got it wrong,' he said. 'I was pretty woozy most of the time. Pumped full of painkillers.' He smiled. 'Maybe it was a personal matter. Maybe she was visiting friends.'

'Yes, probably something like that,' Ishbel said. 'Did she mention any names?'

'Not that I recall,' Gabriel said, sipping at his sherry. Sherry from Jerez, he thought, remembering his brief visit there.

'Ever been to Jerez?' he said, keen to change the subject.

'Yes, I have, actually, several times,' Ishbel said. 'Frank Sartorius was your CIA contact in Guatemala City.'

'Yes.'

'Did you come across a CIA agent called Austin Belhaven?'

'Never heard of him.'

'Faith didn't mention his name?'

'No.'

'Hmmm . . .' Ishbel murmured to herself and fiddled with her brooch again. Annoying habit, Gabriel thought.

'Might I smoke a cigarette?' he asked, the sherry stimulating his need for nicotine.

'I'd prefer if you didn't,' she said. 'Apologies. I don't smoke in the office.'

'Right. Of course.'

She stood up, seeming slightly irritated, Gabriel thought; as if she hadn't received any of the answers she was expecting, clearly signalling that the meeting was now over.

'Very good to see you looking so well, Gabriel, after your ordeal. Thank you for everything.'

She saw him to the door and out into the street.

'Off back to Sussex?'

'Going to see a lawyer,' he said. 'Bit of legal trouble in my other life.'

'Oh, yes. You told me about it.' She smiled. 'My offer still stands, if you want to take it up. The way of least resistance.'

'Thanks, but I think we'll scare him off. He's just an old fool trying to extort money.'

'How is Aldous?' John Saxonbridge asked.

'Very well,' Gabriel said. 'Struggling to cope with being a retired art dealer but making a go of it.'

'Send him my best. Tell him I'll invite him to lunch at the Garrick. He always liked that.'

John Saxonbridge was the rapacious lawyer Aldous had recommended. He was immensely tall – six foot six – with a skewed broken nose. His suit and his shirt were clearly bespoke, his tie was discreetly banded with a little undiscernible motif on it. He had a deep, plummy voice and pronounced the word 'off' as 'awf'. What had Aldous said? 'He'll jump down your throat and eat your liver.' He didn't look or sound like that kind of person to Gabriel but maybe, he reflected, it was a very clever disguise. The patrician smiler with the sharp, concealed, deadly knife.

They were sitting in his dark, dusty office on Chancery Lane. Dying spider plants lined the windowsill. On the walls were framed portrait photographs of the Queen, Winston Churchill and a much-decorated senior officer – a colonel or a general – whom Gabriel didn't recognize. Aldous had said John Saxonbridge had had a 'good war', whatever that meant.

A butler figure in a morning suit brought tea and biscuits on a silver tray. Once the tea was served, Gabriel told Saxonbridge all about the Applegate plagiarism claim.

'Applegate? I know that name,' Saxonbridge said. 'I think I've even read some of his books. I thought he was dead.'

'Very much alive, alas.'

'Have you read any of his books?'

'Yes. All of them. I'm a huge admirer – he was a massive influence on me.' Gabriel shrugged. 'I've even written articles about him – but I didn't steal from his book.'

'Yes,' Saxonbridge said, pulling strongly at his nose as if he was trying to force it back into its original shape. 'Interesting. I think the first step is a truly ferocious "Cease and Desist" letter. If that doesn't work we can counter-sue, for ridiculous damages. Have you a compliant doctor who could testify to the mental wear and tear this absurd and harmful claim is having on you?'

'Yes, and I've a psychoanalyst, as well.'

'Even better.' He paused. 'Do we know where Applegate is living?'

'I can find out,' Gabriel said. He'd ask Inigo.

'I'll have the letter served by a bailiff – that adds to the general terrifying heft of our response.'

Saxonbridge made some notes and they chatted about Aldous and the old friendship between the men. After precisely an hour Saxonbridge ended the meeting and showed him out.

'Very glad to be of help, Gabriel, but did Aldous happen to tell you I'm extremely expensive?'

'Yes. "Eye-watering" was his assessment. But don't worry – I'm in funds. Just delivering my new book.' They shook hands.

'We'll well and truly fuck up Applegate for you, don't worry.'

Gabriel felt reassured by the casual expletive. Saxonbridge was going to dine on Applegate's liver. Serve him right.

3.

The Mistake

Gabriel placed the small Swiss cheese plant on the corner of his new desk and stepped back. Plants added to the feel of domesticity, he reckoned – he'd been inspired by John Saxonbridge's office – even though number 3 Ruskin Studios was still a bit under-furnished and minimalist. Perhaps he needed an armchair. Some paintings for the walls. Maybe a bookcase and some books. Yes. He could bring up a couple of dozen from Rose Cottage . . .

He had bought all the furniture and the bits and pieces he'd need in half an hour at Peter Jones. They were delivered the next day and installed. Getting the bed up the stairs to the mezzanine had been a problem and he'd had to call on the aid of a new neighbour in the studio across from number 3, a man of about his age called Roland Reed, an artist. Once the bed was in place, Gabriel had offered Reed a drink and they had a whisky together. Reed was a short, broad-shouldered, stocky man, prematurely balding with a West Country accent. Gabriel asked him what he painted and he said, somewhat bafflingly, portraits of portraits and offered to show him his work one day. He said he was pleased to learn that Gabriel was a writer as there were too many bloody fashion photographers and dress designers in Ruskin Studios, adding that they weren't proper artists.

'That ponce who used to be in here. A "photographer". Don't make me laugh. Music playing day and night. Comings and goings at all hours. They should be kicked out,' he said, fiercely. 'All of them. Only artists allowed.'

Gabriel detected a flicker of mania in the vehemence with which Reed spoke.

'Well, each to his own,' he said, vaguely.

Maybe it was good that he knew at least one of the other studio occupants, Gabriel thought, might be useful even though there was a full-time caretaker. It made the move seem more real, somehow valid – he wasn't totally anonymous, he had a neighbour that he knew. Anyway, he thought, now he had his bed he could spend his first night in the place, a true and proper initiation. He was back in Chelsea – and he felt all the better for it.

He thought, by way of celebration, that he would go to the Goat and Crow for a few drinks, a local pub once more, and return to being a regular. He sauntered along St Leonard's Terrace and turned left into Smith Street. There was the Goat – he felt a surge of happiness. He would enjoy getting slightly drunk tonight, he thought: the Guatemala chapter of his life over and done with, the wound well healed.

His surge of happiness quickly disappeared when he saw Lorraine and Tyrone Rogan sitting at a corner table. Sister and brother – each with a complicated shared history in his recent existence. They beckoned him over and greeted him warmly. He duly bought them drinks.

Tyrone didn't stay long – he had 'a job to do', he said. Gabriel wondered if he was back burgling again or whether it was some emergency that his locksmith's profession required him to attend. As he left he bent down and whispered in Gabriel's ear.

'Cheer her up, Gabe. She's down in the dumps.'

Gabriel turned to Lorraine.

'So. How's life in the sandwich bar?' he asked.

Tears flowed as Lorraine told the story of manipulation, bad faith, duplicity.

Ken Lubbock, the owner of the sandwich bar – and her lover – had turned out to be a rat, a 'perve' and a liar. She had put some of her own money into the place – money she had received when made redundant from the Wimpy Bar where she and Lubbock had both worked, money that he had promised to repay but never had. She had finally ended their relationship and quit, still being owed two months' wages.

'I should never have left you, Gabe. You were a good man – a true man. I don't know what I saw in that . . .' She searched for a suitable epithet. 'That piece of scum. That stinking turd. I was blind, Gabe, blind.'

Gabriel looked at her as she dabbed at her eyes with a tissue, thinking of their long affair, one that had lasted many sexually charged months. Her hair was different, he noted: blonder, with a short fringe that enhanced her strong, sharp features. She was wearing a white T-shirt with a single blue anchor printed on it between her breasts and he could tell from their soft unsupported sling and the subtle, shadowed protrusion of her nipples that she was wearing no bra. He felt his throat dry. She reached for his hand and he let her take it, feeling the old Lorraine effect – a singular, pure form of atavistic lust – begin to creep over him.

'Have another Bacardi and Coke,' he said, standing, and headed for the bar.

They stayed in the Goat for another hour or so, drinking, smoking and reminiscing, and Lorraine steadily regained her usual demeanour of feisty self-reliance. She kept reaching for his hand and kissing his knuckles. Just so happy to see you, darling, she said. Everything seems better now you're here.

'What're you doing in Chelsea, anyway?' she asked, as they pulled on their jackets and prepared to leave. It was near closing time. 'Tyrone said you were living in the country. Sussex somewhere. Yeah?'

'I'm renting a little flat around the corner,' Gabriel said without thinking. 'An artist's studio.'

'Not Ruskin Studios?' she said.

'Yes, actually.'

'Amazing! Can I have a look? Always wanted to see one of them.'

Gabriel sat on the end of the bed and looked at Lorraine's pale naked back as she slept, snoring slightly. He had a mild hangover, he noted. The early-morning light shone evenly, filtered through the parchment blind over the big window, no shadows cast. He closed his eyes and exhaled, savouring the healing stillness of the moment. Fool, he said to himself. Why? Why? They had both been drunk, he realized, that was why. Reason, ratiocination, simple prudence were out of the question, under the conspiring circumstances. And he had been aroused, he had to admit. Lorraine did this to him – a near-instant erection. The minute he closed the door behind them as they stepped into number 3 they both knew what would ensue. And it had been very satisfying, Gabriel had to admit. They were old and seasoned lovers and fell back into their routines as if no time had passed. They made energetic love. Then Lorraine brewed them both a mug of tea. Then they made more deliberate, measured love once again before falling asleep in each other's arms in the narrow bed on the mezzanine.

The narrow bed on the mezzanine, Gabriel said to himself, pulling on his underpants and picking his way quietly downstairs. Wasn't that the title of a Chekhov short story? He lit the gas hob on the stove and placed the kettle over the blue flames. He recalled Katerina Haas's advice – to resume his normal sex life. Well, yes, now he had – with his ex-girlfriend, if that was wise. He tried not to think of Faith Green – and then rebuked himself. What had Faith Green to do with his private life any more? She herself seemed happy to forget that they had been lovers – deliberately – as if the night they had spent together and the love they'd made had never happened. What was he feeling? he asked himself. Guilt? How could sexual guilt intrude in his complicated relationship with Faith? Absurd. Sad? No, he was a free man – exactly as she wished him to be. But was he free? He thought back to the kiss he had cleverly stolen from her. No, he wasn't. Damn it. Fuck.

'Morning, Gabe,' Lorraine called from the top of the stair.

He looked around. She stood there, entirely naked, entirely unselfconscious.

'You got anything to eat? I'm starving.'

They went to the Café Matisse and ate eggs and bacon and drank several black coffees. They each smoked their first cigarette of the day, Gabriel thinking that it was as if their months of separation – a break-up caused and initiated by Lorraine's new love for the bastard Ken Lubbock – had never occurred. She seemed very happy as she sat there, smoking and chatting – all her self-assured Lorraine-style *joie de vivre* back – and this troubled him. Now she knew where his Chelsea safe house was – suddenly not so safe.

'I love your studio,' she said, as if reading his mind. 'It could be just, you know, a bit more cosy. A sofa – oh, and a bigger fridge. And you need a mirror. What about a telly?' She went on to enumerate all the other furnishings and extras he required in order to make it even more ideal, almost as if, Gabriel thought with some alarm, she was thinking of moving in.

'It's not my home,' he said, a little impatiently. 'It's a convenient base – somewhere to stay if I'm up in London instead of a hotel. I'm not sure how long I'll keep it.'

'It could be lovely, Gabe,' she said. 'Could be special.'

They said their goodbyes on the King's Road – a kiss, a hug, a deeply meaningful look and thanks from Lorraine – and went their separate ways. Gabriel bought a pint of milk and the *Manchester Guardian* and wandered, head full of thoughts, back to Ruskin Studios. He was about to unlock the door of number 3 when he was approached down the passageway by the caretaker, one Mr Corless, a man in his fifties with thin, oiled hair and the insincere smile of a long-term manager and go-between of other people's annoying demands on his time.

'Mr Dax,' he said. 'Message for you.'

Corless had a telephone in his cottage and was obliged to take messages for those tenants who were without telephones. He handed Gabriel a slip of paper and turned away.

Gabriel opened the folded slip.

'Please call me. We should meet soon. Varvara.'

4.

The Kit Caldwell Situation

Two days later, as mutually agreed, Gabriel met Varvara Suvorina in Dovehouse Gardens. They sat on their usual bench and lit their cigarettes. She was wearing more make-up, Gabriel noticed, a blue eyeshadow and orange lipstick, and her greying hair was longer, tucked back neatly behind her small ears.

'May I ask how you knew how to reach me at Ruskin Studios?'

'We know these things, Mr Dax. We like to know where you are and what you're doing. This way we can help you, if it is necessary. For your security.'

'Of course. I understand. I was a bit surprised, though – I'd only just moved in.' He had to do something about this, he thought, he had to be more aware of when there was surveillance, when he was being followed, logged and scrutinized.

'How are you, Mr Dax?'

'Please call me Gabriel. I'm fine. I've just delivered my new book. Thinking of the next one.'

'*Pozdravlyayu!* Congratulations! And you must call me Varvara. As you English say, we are all in this together.'

'Indeed, Varvara.'

She looked at him, closely, as if preserving the image of his face in her mind, he thought.

'You are a most interesting man, Gabriel. Most interesting to me.'

'Right. Good. I'm not sure I'm all that interesting, to tell the truth.' What were these compliments all about? he wondered.

'Oh, yes. I have bought your books. Our contact is very important to me.'

He smiled and nodded, not knowing what to say. Important in a covert, espionage sense? he asked himself. Or was she hinting at something else, something more personal? No, he told himself. Keep it resolutely professional – if only for Kit Caldwell's ongoing protection.

It was a mild spring day, with gauzy beams of sunshine angling through the young leaves on the plane trees in the garden. Varvara put on a pair of sunglasses. Gabriel unwound his scarf and laid it across his knee.

'What did you want to see me about?' he asked.

'We have a message for you from Mr Caldwell. He wishes for you to bring another drawing to Moscow.'

'A Blanco drawing?'

'That would be preferable.'

'I can't go back to Blanco – I'm compromised there.'

Varvara thought for a while.

'I suppose, in that case, any other drawing would be acceptable. Of course, it needs to have a message inscribed.'

Yes, Gabriel thought, a handwritten message on a drawing that contained a microdot. This was how Caldwell communicated with – and duped – the KGB. But now he'd 'defected', why did he want a drawing? There must be another motive. It must be some sort of cry for help, Gabriel thought, feeling slightly queasy. Caldwell wanted Gabriel in Moscow. Maybe Faith Green could explain the reasoning.

'It's difficult for me to go to Moscow at the moment,' Gabriel said. 'I have to be here for my book's publication.'

'There is no hurry, Gabriel,' Varvara said. 'Acquire the drawing and we can make arrangements. We can invite you to Moscow very easily.'

'No, I can't do that,' Gabriel said. 'I mustn't be invited. I have to go under my own auspices, if you see what I mean. If you invite me, MI6 will be suspicious.'

Gabriel felt a small fire of fury build within him. He resented being Caldwell's MI6 contact, with all that was implied by the role. He resented having to play the small-fry double agent to keep Caldwell safe, out of harm's way, and to placate Varvara Suvorina and her KGB colleagues. All a result of Faith Green's clever manipulations, he realized – but she never gave any thought to the consequences for the person being manipulated, how it might affect their life . . .

'Are you all right, Gabriel?'

'Yes. Sorry. Just thinking things through.' He paused. 'I believe I can find a way to get to Moscow that won't arouse suspicions. Though it may take a little longer,' he added, keen to buy himself some time.

'We will let you find the proper moment,' she said. 'And I will have message sent to Mr Caldwell. He will be pleased to know you will come, for sure.' She reached into her handbag and produced the brown paper parcel that was another book, cheaply bound, the pages interleaved with his KGB stipend, no doubt.

'I think you will enjoy this book.'

Gabriel tore open the paper wrapping and held the volume in his hand. *The Death of Ivan Ilyich* by Leo Tolstoy.

'A truly remarkable work of art,' Varvara said, standing. 'Please wait here the usual ten minutes.' She shook his hand, firmly, smiled and walked away towards the King's Road.

Faith asked for an orange juice as she said she had to go back to the office for an important meeting. They were in the pub, the Prince Regent, that Inigo Marcher had taken him to, though not in the fetid basement. Through the windows of the ground-floor saloon they had a good view of Kingsway and the steady flow of traffic and pedestrians. It was lunchtime and the place was busy with suited office workers surviving their daily shift with a few midday pints. Gabriel was drinking a large gin and tonic. He felt a bit agitated, as he usually did in Faith's presence. She was wearing a navy-blue jersey coat and matching skirt, with cream piping, and looked, he thought, both rich and alluring, as if she were going to some grand garden party, nothing like an MI6 spy-catcher having a lunchtime meeting in a Kingsway pub. He glanced at her shoes – also cream, patent and sharply pointed. She was wearing a tangerine-coloured lipstick. He liked to note the details of her appearance when they met – seeing them as indicative of the false self she was presenting to the world, and to him, he thought, thinking of Katerina Haas's categories. He asked permission to smoke; it was granted and he lit a Gitanes.

'What I don't understand,' Gabriel said, 'is this request for a drawing. It doesn't make sense. He's defected – he has no access to secrets.'

'Maybe they think you have access?' she said. 'You are his contact in London, with MI6, after all.'

'A minute's investigation would establish that is wholly impossible,' Gabriel said, conscious that he was beginning to sound neurotic. 'It must be something else.'

'I think he simply wants you in Moscow. That's his way of signalling the need.'

'But why?'

'I don't know, Gabriel. Caldwell is acting alone. We have absolutely zero contact with him. It would be fatal. You're the only link. He knows he can communicate with you through this Varvara Suvorina woman – so he's sending a covert message. Let me have a think about it.'

She sipped at her orange juice.

'Actually, could I have a shot of vodka in this?'

Gabriel went to the bar and returned with her reinforced juice.

'How much do I owe you?' she said.

'It's on me. My pleasure. I've just had another five hundred pounds from the KGB.'

'Rather nice to realize they're paying for our drinks, isn't it?'

They sat there for a moment, both thinking.

'You'll have to go to Moscow,' she said. 'There's no other option – and we owe it to Caldwell. We'll find a way.'

'I don't want to go to Moscow.'

'Caldwell needs you. Don't let him down.'

'All right, all right – but at a time of my choosing.'

'Goes without saying.'

Gabriel looked at her, sensing the usual mingling cross-currents of feelings and emotions that she provoked: irritation, resentment, frustration, admiration, respect, sexual desire.

'Another thing,' he said. 'The Russians are following me. Constantly. Must be. They seem to know my every move.'

'Not surprising. They're probably still checking that you're bona fide – that you are who they think you are.'

'I was also followed in Guatemala – unmistakably. I was obviously tailed to Padre Tiago's hideout. I've no idea how. What I'd like is some training – how to spot people who are following me, and I'd like to know how to get rid of them, to lose them, of course.'

Faith pursed her lips, sipped at her drink.

'Well, there are tried and tested techniques. Specialists who can advise you. I can arrange that, if you like.'

'I do like.'

'I'll set it up.' She smiled. 'You're becoming quite the professional.'

'Needs must, Faith. You landed me in this position.'

'I don't think that's entirely fair. I've never put a gun to your head, in a manner of speaking. I've simply asked you to do things and you've said yes.'

'Without knowing the full consequences.'

'That's life, Gabriel. None of us knows the full consequences of our decisions. History is the history of unintended consequences. Life is random, unpredictable.'

'Yes, yes. Thank you for the philosophy lesson.'

'You seem in a very bad mood today.'

'I think I need another drink.'

'I'll join you. Same again, please.'

At the bar he told himself to be calmer, to adopt a more insouciant, indifferent mood. He should try not to let her see how he was reacting to these pressures, how she affected him. He carried their drinks back to the table. Faith looked at her watch.

'One thing before I go,' she said. 'You had a meeting with Ishbel Dunbar at the Institute while I was away.'

'Yes, she called me in. I was surprised you weren't there.'

'What did she want?' She took her compact out of her handbag, and her lipstick, and carefully reapplied the tangerine gloss. She checked her lips and, satisfied, closed the compact with a snap, and sipped at her vodka and orange.

'You suit that colour of lipstick.'

'Thank you. What did she want to talk to you about?'

'A debrief about Guatemala. What had happened.'

'How's the stab wound?'

'Seems fully settled. Oh, yes. Ishbel knew you'd been to see me in hospital.'

'Really?' Faith stiffened. Gabriel urged himself to be very circumspect. He was beginning to sense when she was a little rattled, now. 'How did she know that?'

'I don't know. But she did. I said I was very touched by your concern.'

'Ha ha. Anything else?'

'Well, she asked me if – in Guatemala – I'd come across a CIA agent called Austin Belhaven. I said I hadn't.'

Gabriel could practically hear Faith's brain working at this news. 'Did she, indeed . . .'

'Who is Austin Belhaven?' he asked.

'A senior CIA agent.'

'And?'

'That's all you need to know.' She looked at her watch again. 'I'd better run. I'll set up a training session for you.' She stood up. Gabriel rose to his feet, also.

'Can I kiss you goodbye?' he asked. 'Just *les bises*, I promise.'

'No. We'll be in touch.'

Gabriel watched her stride out of the pub and dart across the Kingsway traffic, heading towards the Institute, her demesne. He took a long gulp of his gin and tonic. Something was going on between her and Ishbel Dunbar, he was almost sure about that, and it wasn't just office politics. Anyway, he thought, it was none of his business. Life was random and unpredictable, after all.

5.

Artifice

As ever, he was glad to be back in Rose Cottage. He felt more and more that the place was coming to represent his old life – agreeably – of writing and reading and familiar routine. London was now the focus of his other, unsought-for parallel life: fraught, annoying, perplexing, duplicitous. He had sent off the completed typescript of *Rivers* to Inigo and, as always when a book left the house, so to speak, he felt a bit aimless. It was a useful spur to start him working on the next one.

He had been back half an hour, had unpacked the groceries he'd bought, lit a small fire, had a swift lunch at his desk of bread and cheese and a glass of cider, when he heard the cat-flap in the kitchen door click open and close and the Cat appeared.

'Yes, I'm back,' Gabriel said. 'Did you miss me?'

The Cat sprang up on to the armchair, made itself comfortable and proceeded to lick portions of itself clean. Gabriel turned back to his papers, oddly pleased that the Cat had deigned to return, relinquishing its 'Edgar' persona next door.

The phone rang. The Cat leapt off the armchair and headed immediately upstairs, clearly irritated. Gabriel answered. It was John Saxonbridge.

'Well, we had a very swift reply from your Lucian Applegate,' he said.

Inigo Marcher had found Applegate's address from his former publishers and Gabriel had duly passed it on to Saxonbridge.

'Good news?'

'No. Our "Cease and Desist" letter had the opposite effect.' Saxonbridge paused. 'He simply returned the letter but with – what shall I say? – noxious additions.'

'I don't understand.'

'Well, look, there's no euphemistic way to express this, but he'd clearly used my letter to wipe his arse, after a good shit, I presume, and then sent it back.'

'My God!'

'Yes, that's a first for me, I must say.' Saxonbridge's tone was dry. 'I think it's time for a merciless counter-suit. Don't you?'

'Actually, I've had an idea,' Gabriel said. 'Now we know Applegate's address I think I should go and see him myself. Beard him, you know, face to face.' Gabriel thought on, quite pleased with the idea. Writer to writer, eyeball to eyeball. 'At least I'll know how serious he is – or how vulnerable.'

'Fair enough,' Saxonbridge said. 'Just don't beat him up. Leave it to me to scare the life out of him.'

'I'll let you know how I get on,' Gabriel said. He hung up, feeling oddly excited by his spontaneous decision. For once he was taking matters into his own hands, not waiting for unforeseen circumstances – or Faith Green – to dictate a course of action. And anyway, he thought further, he'd never met Applegate. Perhaps it was time for the fan to meet the idol and see if he had feet of clay.

The next day he had another phone call from a man who identified himself as Tom Brown. He had a languid, nasal London accent and Gabriel couldn't resist the question.

'Like Tom Brown of "Schooldays" fame?'

'Sorry?'

'*Tom Brown's Schooldays*. It's a well-known book.'

'You've lost me, I'm afraid, Mr Dax.'

'Never mind.'

It turned out that this Tom Brown was to be his instructor in the art of discerning followers and of how to throw them off the scent. Faith Green had asked him to make an appointment, Brown said. He suggested they meet in any modest or middle-sized town with a significant main street.

'How about Lewes?' Gabriel said. 'East Sussex. Tomorrow? Will that be possible for you?'

They arranged to meet in front of the town hall at midday.

'How will I know you?' Gabriel asked.

'Don't worry, I'll know you.'

Gabriel biked to Lewes, parked the Navigator and waited in front of the town hall for this Tom Brown to appear. He smoked a cigarette, scanning the passers-by, wondering what Brown might look like. Somebody cleared his throat behind him and he turned to see a man in his forties, wearing a black snap-brim trilby and a creased beige raincoat. He had round tortoiseshell spectacles perched on a beaky nose and a somewhat weak chin.

'Mr Dax? Tom Brown.'

They shook hands. Brown said he would kill for a cup of tea so they found a café on the high street and a pot of tea was duly ordered. Brown didn't remove his trilby.

'Wouldn't mind a bun of some sort.'

The waitress offered him a choice of a Bath bun or a currant bun.

'How about a slice of cake?' Brown enquired.

'We've a cherry cake and a Battenberg.'

'I'll go with the cherry,' Brown said.

Brown demolished his cherry cake in a few swift bites and had two cups of tea. He seemed more content, though Gabriel's confidence was beginning to wane. Who was this person Faith Green had sent him? There was something of the prep-school master about him, Gabriel thought – an amateur, in other words.

'So,' Brown said. 'You want to know when you're being followed and how to get rid of the "tail", as our American friends describe it.'

'Yes. Are you attached to the Institute?'

'I do work for them, from time to time. I'm MI5, really.' He inclined his head, modestly. 'They usually ask for me when it's anything to do with "artifice".'

'Artifice?'

'That's what we call it. Anything to do with the nuts and bolts of our curious trade. Phone tapping, letter drops, surveillance, bugging and debugging, breaking and entering. That sort of thing.'

Gabriel told him about the conviction he had that he was being constantly under surveillance by the Russians and how he'd been followed in Central America – keeping the details vague – still followed, somehow, even when they had changed vehicles halfway through the journey.

'It's all pretty straightforward,' Brown said, picking at the remaining crumbs of his cherry cake. 'You just have to keep checking. Look back all the time. The reflections in shop windows are the most useful. Take a few turnings, change course. Then doubleback. Look for the same person. Though, in fact,' he shrugged, 'you could be being followed by a team. Two, three, four people. Somebody ahead of you could be following you. It's a paradox, I know, but it does work, if the team's communicating well.'

He went on. Turn back, then turn again. Watch for people – men and women, he emphasized – who have suddenly stopped walking when you have stopped. People reading a newspaper, tying a shoelace, looking into windows.

'When you start moving, check to see if they start moving.'

'How do you get rid of a tail?' Gabriel asked.

'The best and simplest way is to go into a building with a rear entrance and exit as quickly as you can.' He signalled the waitress. 'I'll have another slice of that cherry cake, if I may,' he asked her. He turned back to Gabriel. 'It's common sense, really. Speed up, take some unexpected turns. Go up stairs, come down stairs, take a lift, come out at a random floor, go down fire stairs.'

'Right,' Gabriel said.

'If you know you're being followed then it's actually quite easy to shake them off. Even a well-drilled team. Of course, most people being followed don't realize it.'

'I suppose so. Makes sense.'

'Artifice is fundamentally about common sense,' he said, gnomically. 'Shall we have a go? You head off down the high street and I'll follow you. See if you spot me.'

Brown stayed on to finish his cherry cake, Gabriel settled the bill and stepped out on to Lewes High Street, feeling a little heart-thump of excitement. He wandered off down the pavement, crossing and re-crossing the road, heading for a large church, pausing from time to time to peer in shop windows and scan the reflections. Sure enough, there was Brown in his trilby, some thirty yards behind him. Gabriel crossed the road again and went into a Boots the Chemist that had two doors. He came out the second door a few minutes later, and abruptly turned left into a side street, ducking into a pub called the Kingfisher. He went to the bar and paid for a half-pint of bitter and then strode down a corridor to the gents' toilet. It was in a yard and there was no exit. Damn. He took a few sips of beer and walked out of the pub and back up to the high street. He scanned the ambling pedestrians. No sign of Brown. Yes, he thought, if you knew you were being followed it wasn't that difficult to become un-followed. He resumed his progress down the high street, checking windows, no sign of Brown in his trilby. He walked down to the church – St Anne's, he saw it was called. He turned around: where was Brown? Crossing the street towards him, as it happened. Gabriel felt frustrated. Brown had removed his trilby and spectacles and was carrying them in his hand.

'Elementary mistake, Mr Dax. You were looking for a man with specs wearing a trilby hat. I took them off and you never noticed me.' He replaced his trilby and spectacles. 'The pub was a good idea, however. Shall we go back there and have a drink?'

Back in the Kingfisher, Brown – having requested a pint of lager and a cheese-and-pickle sandwich – regaled him with more tips from the 'Artifice' manual. The same rules applied to the followee, he said. They are following you, a man with a red scarf and a coat. Go into a shop or a restaurant, remove hat and coat and re-emerge. When you come out of a building try to be talking to someone, as if you were a couple. They might not clock it's you as you no longer fit the first description.

'What about cars?' Gabriel asked.

'Easier to be spotted,' Brown said. 'That's why I always advocate a motorbike. But cars are confined to roads – all you can do, really, if you're in a car and another car is following you is to speed up and take rapid turns at junctions. U-turns. Sudden stops. Run red lights. It's not an arcane science, Mr Dax,' Brown continued. 'Any intelligent person, if they apply their mind to the issues of artifice, can come up with their own solutions. Maybe better ones.'

'I see what you mean.'

'In your case, if you suspect you're continually being followed – always take precautions. Change routines. Change trains. Get out at the station before your final stop. Jump on a bus.'

'Or get out and get back on in a different carriage.'

'To the manner born, Mr Dax. You're getting the hang of it.' Brown smiled. 'I could handle another cheese-and-pickle sandwich, no bother.'

'Another pint?'

'Thank you, Mr Dax. Much obliged.'

Gabriel went to the bar to put in Brown's order and added another gin and tonic for himself. Yes, he thought, 'artifice' was all that was required. Simply apply your mind to the particular problem, so Brown advised. He had a feeling that he was a natural-born artificer – Tom Brown had opened a door for him.

6.

Lucian Applegate

Gabriel didn't bother to take any artifice precautions when he travelled to the Cotswolds to confront Lucian Applegate. He didn't care if Varvara Suvorina knew where he was going. This was his business, not the Institute's. He took a train to Oxford and hired a car – a Ford Anglia – and drove to Chipping Norton. Applegate lived in a remote village a few miles away in Gloucestershire called Perton Magna. Chipping Norton would be the base for Gabriel's reconnoitre. He wanted to be prepared, ready for anything.

He found a pub with accommodation and booked in for a night. His room seemed comfortable enough – low-ceilinged, heavily beamed – with a large, soft-quilted bed. There was even a jug and ewer on the chest of drawers under the leaded window. The bathroom and WC were at the end of a corridor. He located a nearby Italian restaurant and ate a lasagne (served with chips) and drank several glasses of red wine. Back in his room, replete, he lay on the bed and planned his assault on Applegate. After a few minutes he realized that the effort was futile. Everything, he decided, would have to be a spontaneous reaction to the way Applegate received him. He had the element of surprise, he reasoned. Applegate would never expect to be challenged in his own home by the man he was accusing of plagiarism. It would be, he hoped, a real shock – advantage Dax.

It was raining the next morning – a fine but persistent drizzle coming from lumbering pewter clouds, soaking the hills and dales of springtime Gloucestershire. Perton Magna was reached by a high-hedged single-lane road that wound its way through puddled farmland like a river following primordial contours. The tiny village – more like a hamlet – was ancient and the houses looked

126

decrepit – some of them clearly empty, judging from their unkempt gardens. The soft Cotswold sepia sandstone of their walls, pocked and eroded by centuries, was the colour of dark ochre from the rain. There was a fourteenth-century ashlar church with a small battlemented Perpendicular tower with a spirelet – door padlocked – and a Jacobean manor house that was occupied; Gabriel could see smoke coming from the tall, decorated chimneys. He parked in the modest market square where there was a pillared corn exchange supported by rusty scaffolding. He knew that Applegate lived in a cottage called Foxgloves – Foxgloves, Perton Magna, Gloucestershire was the address Inigo had retrieved from his former publishers – but where was Foxgloves? There was no pub, no shop, no post office. No people either, Gabriel saw, as he wandered the few narrow streets. Perton Magna was like a Cotswoldian *Marie Celeste*. Then he heard the noise of a tractor engine and an orange Massey Ferguson duly appeared with a slopping trailer behind, full of manure judging from the acrid smell emanating from it. Gabriel hailed the tractor and the lad driving – he looked about twelve – switched off the engine. Foxgloves was not in the village, he was told, but was half a mile down a lane – straight on, turn left where the road forks to Bourton-on-the-Hill. Gabriel thanked him and headed off. The drizzle was turning to proper rain and he covered his damp hair with his duffel coat's hood. He should have brought some wellington boots, he told himself. His suede brogues were getting soaked.

Foxgloves was a large cottage – dark rotting thatch was visible through the moss on the roof. Two windows were boarded up with planks of wood. The garden was overgrown and untended but there were lights burning inside and smoke was wafting from a chimney. A Morris Minor with three flat tyres was parked next to the front door. Desuetude, Gabriel thought, the word coming suddenly into his head. Applegate was in his eighties – he wondered how on earth he could live like this, or for how much longer. Maybe this neglect explained the foolish and desperate attempt at extortion. He looked further down the lane – there seemed to be another farm there and he could hear the mournful lowing of cattle, adding to the atmosphere of decay and decrepitude. All that was required was the tolling of bells from Perton Magna's disused church tower to complete the auditory picture and fix the sombre mood.

Gabriel took shelter under a tree and thought about what to do. Applegate was at home, evidently. So, simply knock on the door and introduce himself, he reckoned, then see what happened. Then he thought: what if Applegate attacked him, or had a fierce dog? The encounter, fraught as it was, could get out of hand, he was aware. Applegate might be crazed – manic – for all he knew. He looked around him and, with the toe of his shoe, unearthed a stone the size of a large potato from the side of the lane. He remembered Patrick Begg's never-to-be-forgotten words: anything can be a weapon. He slipped the stone into his duffel-coat pocket. Good artifice, he thought.

Gabriel banged the door-knocker three times. Silence. No response. He banged again.

'Who's there?' Applegate shouted.

'Gabriel Dax!'

'Fuck off! Go away!'

'I'm not going away, Mr Applegate. We have to talk – or else all hell will break loose.'

Silence. Then he heard a key turn in the lock and the door swung open.

Applegate presented a tiny shrunken figure, stooped. His face was gaunt and his hair was wild and completely white, as was his pointed beard. He looked like some sort of mad magus or soothsayer, Gabriel thought, as he stepped past him into the dark sitting room. A small fire was burning in the fireplace but it was the smell that struck Gabriel – dirt, everything unclean, unwashed. The smell of poverty. Applegate was wearing a buttonless maroon cardigan held together by safety pins, a Viyella shirt and a greasy, dark tie. His trousers were pyjama bottoms. He had slippers on his feet.

Gabriel looked around the room. Books were everywhere, in crammed bookcases and piled on the floor. There were pictures on the walls but he couldn't make them out in the gloom. A large, fat black Labrador, snoozing by the fire, hunched itself effortfully to its feet, gave a dry cough, and wandered away. One light was burning on a side table. Gabriel felt the scene was almost medieval – as if he were an acolyte visiting some reclusive sage.

'What do you want, you bastard?' Applegate said.

'I want to talk to you about this ridiculous lawsuit you're threatening.'

'You stole from me.'

'Well, if I did, so did every writer who's written about Greece and the archipelago. You know it's a preposterous claim. I just don't want you to suffer the consequences.'

Applegate collapsed in an armchair and covered his eyes with a hand, as if shielding himself from a blazing sun.

'You don't understand, Mr Dax. I'm in desperate straits.'

'We can sort things out,' Gabriel said, pulling forward a bent-wood chair and sitting down, wary of anything upholstered.

'What made you do this insane thing?' he asked.

Applegate explained – his mind seemed still very active, Gabriel thought – and he listened carefully.

An old friend who lived in Oxford had recommended Gabriel's first book, *The Wine-Dark Sea*. Applegate had read it – 'with admiration' – and realized that it covered Greek islands that he had also written about. 'And so the clever scheme was hatched,' Applegate said, and then coughed violently for a few seconds.

'I never expected it to go to court,' Applegate continued, recovered. 'You must understand. I just thought I'd be paid some money to make the whole issue go away. Then I had that fearsome letter from your lawyer.'

'He was very put out by your unique reply.'

'Lawyers need to be shocked. A very complacent profession, I've found.'

'That's why I've come all this way to speak to you,' Gabriel said. 'We have to bring an end to this dispute, this non-dispute. I'm a huge admirer of your work. You were an inspiration to me. But I did not plagiarize you. Full stop.'

'I know that,' Applegate said, finally removing his shielding palm from his eyes and looking directly at Gabriel. 'I apologize.'

Applegate straightened himself as best he could in his chair.

'Can I offer you a drink? I only have rum.'

'Very welcome,' Gabriel said.

Applegate shuffled into the kitchen that was off the sitting room. Gabriel wondered what horrors lurked there. Through the door, he saw a teetering moraine of plates and dishes piled in a ceramic sink and quickly turned his eyes away, back to the fire. He took the liberty of throwing another couple of logs on to the glowing ashes.

Applegate returned with two thick-looking glasses with short stems – rummers, Gabriel recognized – filled to the brim.

'Rum, water and sugar,' Applegate said. 'Charles Dickens's favourite drink.'

He picked up a poker and thrust it deep into the fire.

'Give it a minute,' he said, searching around his armchair for a cloth. After a few moments he withdrew the poker, wiped its end with the cloth and plunged the point into each rummer, one after the other. There was a hiss as the liquid heated instantly. He handed Gabriel his warm glass.

'They knew a thing or two, the Victorians,' Applegate said.

Gabriel sipped at his drink, feeling the glow in his throat and stomach.

'Very nice,' he said. 'Cheers.'

'Have you ever written a novel?' Applegate asked.

'I've tried,' Gabriel said. 'But my mind isn't made that way, isn't geared to write novels. I can't make things up, for some reason. Can't invent stories and people. I realize I need to see things in front of me and then write about them. New things, unexpected things – that's why I travel to write.'

'Yes. I tried several times to write a novel,' Applegate said, rue-fully. 'Inferior stuff. I abandoned them all.'

'We have to make do with what talents we have,' Gabriel said.

'How many books have you published?' Applegate asked.

'Three. I've just delivered my fourth.'

'I've written seventeen. And do you know what income they pro-duced for me this last year?'

'Tell me.'

'Nothing,' Applegate said, jutting his chin. 'Zero. *Nihil. Rien. Nada. Niente. Nichts.*'

'It can be a harsh world, literature.'

'Hence my folly of threatening you. I'm at the end of my tether, Mr Dax. I have my state pension, that's all. Thin gruel.'

Gabriel looked at the old man – defiant, slightly mad, without doubt – and felt a creeping admiration for his spirited belligerence.

'I was born in the nineteenth century,' Applegate said, musingly. 'In 1881. Queen Victoria on the throne, the map of the world half red. My father was a veteran of the Crimean War, can you believe it? In the 1920s and 1930s newspapers paid me to travel – paid me well, anywhere I wanted – and I turned these travels into bestselling books. I had a lovely Queen Anne house in Hampstead. And look at me now.' He spread his hands. 'Pathetic. I'm ashamed.'

'It's not your fault,' Gabriel said. 'Your books are still there. I read them, avidly. They were inspirational.'

'Yes, well, they're not there any more, except for the odd volume gathering dust in antiquarian booksellers, going for a shilling or two.'

Gabriel didn't know what to say. The old Labrador padded back and settled itself carefully by the fire again, grunting, tongue lolling. Gabriel sipped his warmed rum. Powerful stuff, he thought.

'Is there anything I could do to help?' he asked. 'Talk to my publisher, my agent. Perhaps your books could be reissued with new introductions—'

'Cash,' Applegate said. 'Sorry to be so blunt. That's the beginning and end of it. I need money. Hence this absurd foolishness about you. I worry I'm losing my mind.'

'I don't think so. Would you accept a cheque?'

'I'll accept anything.'

Gabriel had his cheque book on him – he had settled his bill at the pub in Chipping Norton with a cheque. He drew it out of his pocket, unscrewed the top of his fountain pen and made out a cheque for £100 to the order of Lucian Applegate. He handed it over.

Applegate looked at it, and began to sob, quietly, hunched over, shoulders gently rocking.

'Please, Mr Applegate. It's my pleasure – as a devoted admirer.'

Gabriel walked away from Foxgloves, heading back to Perton Magna and his Ford Anglia. He reached into his pocket for his weapon-stone and flung it into the hedgerow. The rain had stopped and there was a pearly, hesitant sunlight shining somewhere behind the thinning clouds. He felt oddly shriven by the encounter, quite depressed, in fact, he noted, even though the object of the exercise had been achieved. Applegate had promised that the threat of a lawsuit was gone for ever. He was absurdly grateful, permanently in Gabriel's debt.

It wasn't the money he'd given away, Gabriel considered – it was unsought-for Russian money, anyway – it was the vision of the future that Applegate, his wheezing old dog and the dire state of Foxgloves had presented to him. Was this how he, Gabriel Dax, would end up in 1983 or 1995 or 2010 – whatever that world would be like – if he lasted that long? A forgotten, ancient writer on his uppers, bitter and full of anger at his neglect. Meeting Applegate in his home was a chilling presentiment of a possible future and it made Gabriel's mood increasingly dark. He was glad he had given Applegate that money – he had left his address, moreover, urging him to make contact in case of any further crisis. Was he a fool, himself, to have done so? He didn't think so. He felt he had done the correct, humane thing. He would call John Saxonbridge in the morning and tell him the case was closed.

7.

The Complete Surprise

Gabriel interrupted his return from the Cotswolds to spend a night at Ruskin Studios before heading back to East Sussex and the cottage. Corless handed him five messages from Lorraine. 'Please call me when you're back. Lorraine.'

He had an early supper at the Matisse and then a couple of post-prandial whiskies in the Goat and Crow – peering through the window before he entered to make sure Lorraine wasn't there. He wasn't happy about the Lorraine situation. It was all very well for Katerina Haas to tell him to resume his normal sexual activity but these things didn't happen in a vacuum. No, Lorraine was obviously keen to renew their affair. It was tempting, also, thinking about Lorraine and her particular and familiar allure, but he was aware of an annoying feeling of unease – guilt, he recognized – as if he were betraying Faith, somehow.

He wandered back to Ruskin Studios in a souring mood, irritated with himself and his inadequacies, as he saw them, swithering between an agreeable reality and an unattainable fantasy. Make up your mind, man, he told himself. He arrived at Ruskin Studios the same time as Roland Reed. Gabriel had an idea.

'Could I buy a drawing off you, Roland, a small one – if you have any for sale?'

'I've got plenty,' he said. 'Come on in.'

Reed's studio was slightly larger than Gabriel's. He had a bedroom and a bathroom off the main studio space. Reed switched on the lights and Gabriel saw stacked canvases reversed against the walls, only their backs visible, and two easels opposite each other. On one was a finished portrait of a young woman, head and shoulders, and on the other was a half-finished version of the same portrait.

'Ah-ha, now I understand what you meant,' Gabriel said. 'A portrait of a portrait.'

'It's quite amazing what happens,' Reed said. 'It's not a copy, no, no, it's another unique portrait. Differences seem to emerge of their own accord.'

He went over to a large architect's plan chest and opened some drawers while Gabriel studied the two paintings. It was true, he saw, there was something different about the expression of the eyes already.

'It's as if,' Gabriel began, forming the idea as he spoke, remembering Katerina Haas's concepts, 'the first portrait – which you do from life, I assume – is the formal public self on display and the second one is . . .' He paused. 'Somehow more guileless and honest because the sitter isn't present. The first one is the "false self" and the second one is the "true self". You are the only arbiter.'

'Interesting notion,' Reed said, though Gabriel couldn't really tell if he was sincere. 'If I haven't got a sitter I just copy another portrait. From a print.' He turned a canvas round. 'This is a Rembrandt self-portrait. But it's different from the real thing.'

He had half a dozen small drawings in his hands and showed them to Gabriel. Gabriel chose a sketch of a corner of the studio, about six inches by four, the size of the Blanco drawings.

'Yours for ten pounds,' Reed said. 'Neighbourly rates.'

Gabriel asked him to sign it and handed over two £5 notes. He looked back at the two portraits. It was not just the eyes that were different in the new portrait, he saw: the mouth also – something almost sneery about the set of the lips.

Reed handed him the signed drawing.

'What was it you said? A "false" self?'

'And a "true" self. It applies to all of us, or so my psychoanalyst claims.'

'Maybe I should try it with a self-portrait,' Reed said. 'Though it might freak me out. How about you, Gabriel – fancy sitting for me? You could show the two portraits to your psychoanalyst.'

'I might have a think about that,' Gabriel replied, diplomatically. The idea didn't appeal.

He and Reed said their goodnights and he crossed the passage-way to number 3. He propped Reed's drawing on the mantel above the gas fire. He would have something to report to Varvara – now he had a drawing for Kit Caldwell. All it needed was a dedication.

The next morning he took proper artifice care as he returned to Claverleigh. He walked to Sloane Square Tube, caught a westbound train and disembarked at the next station, South Kensington. He waited to see if anyone who had left the train at the same time was still waiting on the platform. He didn't think so and continued his journey on the Circle Line, in the other direction, to Victoria station where he spent a good few minutes wandering the passageways, climbing stairs and descending again, taking the opportunity to look back to see if there was a figure that he could recognize. There was a man with a red tie and a rolled umbrella who looked familiar. Had he seen him at Sloane Square? Noted, Gabriel thought.

On the train to Lewes, Gabriel walked through the carriages looking for Mr Red Tie but didn't spot him. Still, he left the train at Burgess Hill and caught a bus to Lewes. As he motored home to Claverleigh on the Navigator he felt quite pleased with himself. Tom Brown would have complimented him on his artifice skills, he reckoned. Then the thought came to him: was this the future for all his journeys? Stop-start, ducking and diving, changing forms of transport . . . The idea that this might be so depressed him, aware that the realities of his espionage life were beginning to infect him like a contagion. Would he ever be unwatchful and carefree again? Was this one of the many prices you paid for being Faith Green's spy?

His mood improved once he settled back in at Rose Cottage. There was no sign of the Cat, though he left some food out, just in case milord was hungry. He went to Claverleigh's only pub, the Duke of Marlborough, and had a pint of beer and two sausage rolls. He took out his notebook and jotted down some ideas for his next book, *On the Beaten Path*. Where would he go? He started to make a list:

The Eiffel Tower
The Pyramids at Giza
The Colosseum
The Rock of Gibraltar
St Mark's Square
The Empire State Building
The Grand Canyon
The Tower of London
Victoria Falls
Machu Picchu
Angkor Wat
Mount Everest

He paused – a lot of travelling, he saw, sensing a presumptive excitement. And quite a challenge, as well, he realized. How was he to make these most familiar landmarks, written about endlessly, new and interesting again? Still, the larger idea was good and original. Then he thought, and wrote down:

The Kremlin, Red Square

Yes. Perhaps that was the ideal way to finesse a trip to Russia and meet Kit Caldwell . . . But why was he bothered about this? he asked himself angrily. He had other priorities. He finished off his pint and wandered home. He would type his proposal up and send it to his agent who could pass it along to Inigo. He was glad about this new project, he concluded, it would keep him sane as he tried to cope with the madness and mayhem of his parallel life.

He went out to the woodshed in the garden and chopped and split logs for a while, stacking them neatly and filling the log basket. Good honest work, he thought, keeping his mind from straying, keeping images of Lucian Applegate and his impoverished, diminished life at bay. When he came into the sitting room, his arms full of the last load of logs, he saw that the Cat had returned: there was a dead blue tit on the hearth – a love offering – and the catfood had been devoured. Status quo re-established, normal business resumed.

He typed up his proposal for *On the Beaten Path* and then cooked himself a supper of a couple of pork chops and boiled potatoes, washed down with a few glasses of Beaujolais. He watched a documentary on the television about the Suez Crisis and felt himself nodding off. It had been a complicated few days, one way or another. Time for bed. Then the doorbell rang. He looked at his watch. Nine o'clock, full darkness outside. He hadn't heard a car in the lane. Royston? Not at this hour – and he'd have telephoned, anyway. He picked up the poker from the fireplace and quietly walked to the front door, opened it and stepped back.

Faith Green stood there, in her green Loden coat, a small suitcase in her hand.

'Hello, Gabriel,' she said, smiling. 'I wonder if I might come and stay for a few days.'

PART FOUR

Rose Cottage, Claverleigh

27 April–2 May 1963

I.

Faith takes her seat by the fire and accepts a glass of Glenfeshan while Gabriel darts upstairs to the guest bedroom and quickly makes the bed with clean sheets. He switches on an electric heater, checks there are coat hangers in the cupboard and returns downstairs to ask her if she is hungry, by any chance. To his frank and total astonishment, the Cat is curled in her lap, happily being stroked, purring.

'What a lovely cat you have, Gabriel. I never thought of you as a cat man, somehow. More of a dog lover.'

'There you go,' he says, noting his aggrievance at the Cat's rank disloyalty – and immediately feeling stupid that he is aggrieved.

'Are you hungry?' he asks. 'Sandwich? I have some tins of soup.'

'No thanks, Gabriel. I had a bite to eat before I headed off.'

'May I ask why you want to stay here? You're very welcome, however.'

She frowns and gently pushes the cat off her lap. It pads off into the kitchen, unperturbed.

'I need to – what's the expression? – disappear "off the radar" for a few days. Four, maybe five, if that's all right with you. I need to see what will happen when I disappear. It's a kind of experiment.'

'To do with the Institute?'

'Yes. If you don't mind, I won't even leave the house. I had the taxi stop in the village. I walked here. I don't think anyone's seen me arrive.'

Gabriel looks at her. What new enigmas has she brought to his doorstep?

2.

Gabriel turns in his bed, wide awake, trying to come to terms with the fact that Faith Green is sleeping a few paces away down the corridor.

The door opens and Faith stands there in a cotton nightdress.

'It's very cold in that guest room of yours,' she says. 'Do you mind if I snuggle up with you?'

3.

They lie in each other's arms, the buttery morning light squeezing in through the curtains.

Gabriel kisses her forehead, her cheeks, her lips. He feels heady, intoxicated.

'I think,' he says, 'as your host, I have to ask you what's the real reason you've come here. Otherwise I might have to show you the door.'

'Fair enough, Mr Dax. I'll tell you over breakfast. Promise.'

4.

Faith stirs her freshly poured cup of tea and adds a splash more milk. Gabriel asks her if she'd like some toast. Yes please, she says. All that exercise has made me famished. Faith is sitting at the kitchen table wearing Gabriel's dressing gown. Gabriel is fully clothed – he's been out to buy a pint of milk. The Cat is sitting nearby, eavesdropping.

'Is this about Ishbel Dunbar?' Gabriel asks.

'It is indeed. She's after my job. She wants me ousted.'

'How does coming here and hiding out frustrate that?'

'She'll interpret my "disappearance" in a way that furthers her cause. What she'll do will make her vulnerable – when I reappear.'

Gabriel takes this in, remembering his meeting with Ishbel.

'She did seem to know exactly what you were doing in the States,' he says. 'She told me that there was no meeting at Langley with the CIA.'

'There was a meeting with the CIA, but not at Langley. She doesn't know everything.'

She stands up and comes round behind him to his side of the

table. She puts her arms round his neck and kisses the top of his head. He feels her breasts flatten against his shoulders.

'It was a lovely night,' she says. 'Thank you.'

'The morning wasn't too bad either.'

5.

'When you go shopping,' Faith says, 'make sure you only buy what you would buy for yourself. Don't shop for two.'

'All right. Good procedure. Good artifice.'

'What about your neighbour? Is he nosey?'

'Royston? No. He keeps himself to himself.'

Gabriel goes shopping in the village and, in the butcher's, buys one veal escalope and half a pound of mincemeat. A pound of potatoes and some spinach in the greengrocer's. A loaf of bread and a single Danish pastry in the baker's. A bachelor, leading his solitary life.

6.

Gabriel lies at the tap end of the bath, water brimming, up to his chin. Faith is at the other end, their knees touching.

'This is a first for me,' he says. 'Bathing together.'

'It's fun, isn't it?' she says, smiling. 'We'll be all lovely and clean when we tumble into bed.'

He feels a small sob in his throat. He can't remember when he has been happier. It's very important to register these moments, Katerina Haas has told him. Hoard those times when you feel happiness, she advised – it's like money in the bank of your life. He duly deposits the bullion of being in a bath with Faith Green.

She leans forward and reaches under the water for his cock.

'What're you doing?' he says. 'It's bath time.'

'Looking for the soap. Sorry.'

7.

'What was Guatemala really all about?' Gabriel says. 'I think you can tell me now.'

They are in the sitting room, after supper, the fire blazing, finishing off their bottle of red wine. The Cat is back in Faith's lap, much to Gabriel's disgust.

'Exactly what we told you,' she says. 'They – the CIA – needed someone who could legitimately talk to this trade union leader. I thought you would be perfect. Authentic. No suspicions.'

She sounds so plausible, he thinks, but he isn't going to buy her story.

'You know it didn't end up that way,' he says.

'No. We – you – were used by elements within the CIA. And that's the problem. A major problem, as it happens.'

'Who is Austin Belhaven? The man Ishbel Dunbar asked me about.'

'He's the man I was meeting in the States when I came to see you. A good man. He's "concerned" about what's happening in the Company.'

'What does that mean?' Gabriel asks, not particularly interested.

'There's a lot of disaffection, resentment within certain factions within the CIA. After the total fiasco of the Bay of Pigs invasion some people in the CIA feel betrayed by Kennedy – the fact that he refused air support, let the Cubans die, be captured, be humiliated. And then President Kennedy sacking Allen Dulles and his team. People are unhappy. Kennedy – and his brother – are not universally popular, despite what the press may want you to believe.'

'Who's Dulles?'

'Head of the CIA, as was. Ex-director. Not a Kennedy fan.'

'Oh. Right. What about Frank Sartorius?'

'Sartorius is a complicated figure. He was – is – close to Dulles.'

'Is Sartorius still in Guatemala?' Gabriel thinks that while Faith is being forthcoming he should keep asking questions.

'No. He's been promoted – a senior executive, now, in the CIA hierarchy. I don't know what his role is, precisely.'

'What fun and games,' Gabriel says. 'The ring-a-ring o' roses in your murky world of espionage.'

'Our world, Gabriel.'

'I know.' He leaves his armchair and kneels beside her, taking her hand and kissing her cheek.

'I'm your spy, remember? More wine? Or shall we go to bed?'

8.

'Surely you can go out into the garden?' Gabriel says. 'Look, it's a lovely day. We could have a picnic.'

'After dark. I can't risk being spotted.'

'We'll have a picnic after dark. A May Day picnic under the stars.' She looks at him.

'How many times do I have to tell you? Cynicism doesn't suit you.'

'Just trying to make your stay as enjoyable as possible, that's all.'

He takes her in his arms and kisses her lips, gently. Once again he rejoices in the moment, and her lack of resistance. He deposits it in his happiness bank. He hugs her to him and she hugs him back, strongly.

'Thank you, Gabriel. I'm so grateful, you know. It means everything.'

It means everything in her war against Ishbel Dunbar? he asks himself, or it means everything to her, having him as a lover? There is no obvious answer.

'What would you like for lunch? I can do you my special spaghetti Bolognese.'

9.

'This is excellent spaghetti,' Faith says. 'And I'm an expert.'

'It's the little bit of chicken liver in the *ragù* that makes the difference, the *sine qua non*.'

They are lying in bed. He has brought them tea and toast – now a normal gustatory prelude to their morning lovemaking. A good moment to ask further questions while her guard is halfway down.

'I want to know more about Guatemala,' he says. 'You still haven't told me everything. What's the true story behind the killing of Padre Tiago?'

She sits up in bed, covers her breasts with the quilt and reaches for her mug of tea. She takes a sip. He can see she is deciding whether to tell him the truth or some sort of semi-truth that will pacify him. He can't catch her out.

'Well, Austin Belhaven told me that Tiago's murder was a classic Mafia hit – the pattern, I mean,' she begins, thoughtfully. 'A "lone gunman" kills the target but there are always other gunmen on hand – or shooting as well. Then the lone gunman is somehow killed. Case closed.' She pauses. 'Look at the assassination of President Armas. Shot by a lone gunman who then committed suicide. The Mafia pattern, as I say.'

'Conveniently. Like Denilson Canul.'

'Exactly.'

Gabriel takes this on board. Denilson Canul, ostensibly, had been the lone gunman. Then he had killed himself and left a letter, confessing. Yet Padre Tiago had been killed by a sniper's bullet on the terrace of his remote farmhouse. Was Canul the sniper? Or somebody else? No, he thinks, whoever killed Padre Tiago, Canul's suicide was a fake. Canul had been shot by a person or persons unknown and the death was made to look like a suicide – including the handy confession. He thinks back to Furlan and Canul's last agitated conversation and the way Furlan ordered Canul to leave through the garden entrance of the hotel, unobserved, to go back to his car – where the killers were waiting and Canul's 'suicide' took place, he assumes.

'Why would the Mafia kill Padre Tiago?' he asks.

'Obviously they were paid to do so,' Faith says. 'It was a conspiracy. I'm sorry you were caught up in it.'

'Who paid them?'

'*Cui bono?* The old question. Who benefited from Tiago's death?'

'United Fruit.'

Faith spreads her hands.

'Look at the recent history of Guatemala,' she says. 'The CIA organized a coup in Guatemala in 1954 to depose President Árbenz. In 1957 President Armas was assassinated by a lone gunman. And this year, 1963, the probable victor of the next general election has been assassinated by a lone gunman. And a military coup takes place with President Ydígoras ousted.' She frowns, as if she has only just analysed this sequence of events for the first time. 'Status quo re-established. This is the recent history of Guatemala and this is what's exercising Austin Belhaven. He may have good reason.'

'The CIA and the Mafia working hand in hand.'

She tells him how it came about. It all started in the Second World War, she says, after the invasion of Sicily in 1943. The Americans effectively handed over control of the island to the Mafiosi and worked with them as the Allies moved on to conquer the mainland. The links, the bonds were established then. When you want to keep your hands 'clean', then you covertly franchise the job out to professionals you know and trust. It's a pattern, she says. But that's how they do it, the Mafia. Their signature, if you like. The 'lone gunman' signature.

'So that's what I was inveigled into,' Gabriel says, thinking of his short, fraught meeting with Padre Tiago.

'We genuinely didn't know,' Faith says. 'We were all led up a garden path.'

'By whom?'

'Good question,' she says with a brief frown.

'How about Frank Sartorius and United Fruit, Guatemala's biggest landowners, who didn't want a radical new President of Guatemala committed to agrarian reform?'

'That's speculation.'

'Come on, Faith.'

'We have no proof, no evidence. Maybe it was just a lone gunman with a grievance, after all. We may never know.'

They look at each other. She doesn't flinch.

II.

After supper they play Scrabble and drink wine. Faith doesn't want to watch the television news, she says, with its round of stories about the Beatles, Fidel Castro's forthcoming visit to Moscow, the fallout from the Campaign for Nuclear Disarmament's Aldermaston march, the end of National Service and what Dr Beeching's cuts will mean for the future of British Railways. No, she'd rather beat Gabriel at Scrabble, she says. She hasn't stepped out of doors since she arrived. Occasionally she asks Gabriel if she can use the phone and she makes a few calls, ensuring that he is out of earshot. Who is she calling? he asks himself. What Machiavellian scheme is being enacted? he wonders, as he chops onions for their beef stew. She seems calm enough, he registers: maybe everything is going swimmingly as far as the Faith Green grand plan is concerned.

He doesn't really care, happy to live in this moment, this strange limbo. They enjoy each other's constant company, they have a unique shared history, they make love at night and in the morning and occasionally in the afternoon, when the mood takes them. Fondly, stupidly, he wonders if this state of affairs can possibly continue, yet he knows full well that it will come to an end whenever she decides. Take it a day at a time, he tells himself. He has never felt so content, has never felt so at ease with another person. This is as good a life as he has ever experienced.

12.

In his euphoric mood, he thinks it's time for a feast. Champagne, three courses, fine wine. Push the boat out.

Faith is still asleep when he decides to head out, leaving her a note on the kitchen table – 'Shopping in Lewes' – and drives off on the Navigator. He takes proper artifice precautions on the way: turning up side roads, retracing his route for a quarter of a mile, pausing at the outskirts of Lewes to watch the passing traffic and then weaving his way through various streets to park his bike at the train station. No one is following him, he's convinced.

As he makes his meandering way from Claverleigh to Lewes he thinks about the Faith he's come to know these past few days. Is this Faith's true self, he wonders, as opposed to the false self she presents at the Institute? He feels he has connected with her – her person, her nature – in a way that is different from the past, and not just because of the lovemaking they've been enjoying. Maybe because she needs him on a personal level for once, he thinks; therefore the power relationship has shifted significantly and the real Faith Green is finally before him, her true self. He looks forward to his discussion with Katerina Haas – no doubt she'll have something perceptive to say.

In Lewes he buys a thick slice of *pâté de campagne*, a capon, some streaky bacon, a wedge of Stilton and two small apple tarts for pudding. In a wine merchant's he chooses a bottle of champagne and a bottle of Calvados to go with the apple tarts. He has plenty of wine in his cold pantry. They will eat well tonight, he says to himself, anticipatory pleasure growing as he remounts the Navigator, its pannier loaded, ready for the journey home. His final stop is at a jeweller's in the high street where he picks up the piece of Guatemalan jade he bought in Dos Vados. The curved piece of stone is now held in a tight gold pre-notched prong setting, with a gold chain. It looks both beautiful and ancient, nestled in its bed of cotton wool in the small cardboard box. He'll give it to her after their feast, he thinks.

Artifice prevails once more on his route back to Claverleigh and Rose Cottage – doubling back, driving up narrow lanes, waiting to see if anyone is following. Nothing. All clear. Faith will approve of the good procedure, he knows. Her stay at Rose Cottage has preserved an ideal secrecy. Only the Cat could bear witness to her presence.

He lugs his provisions inside, entering the cottage through the kitchen door and dumping them on the table. The house is very quiet. No sign of the Cat. Then he sees the note propped against the toaster. He picks it up.

Darling Gabriel,

Everything has worked out as I hoped. Perfectly. I have to go back to London to resolve the crisis that my absence has generated (and destroy Ishbel Dunbar). Thank you for coming to my rescue. Thank you for an unforgettable, lovely few days. I will miss you tonight, for sure. But we will see each other very soon.

With my love, Faith

He feels an acrid taste at the back of his throat. Bile. Caused by what? Disappointment? Suspicion? Resentment? For an instant he thinks of throwing the ingredients of his feast into the dustbin – the spoilt child recourse, he tells himself. Be calm. Nothing has changed. He realizes that she has to go back to London – the object of the exercise has to be completed. But their relationship is now altogether different – since the Rose Cottage interlude it has become solid and sincere. He lets out a groan of frustration, none-theless. Perhaps he'll invite Royston round for supper – he can't eat all that food himself. But not tonight – it's too soon. Everything should keep until tomorrow, he considers. He needs to be alone tonight, to brood and to drink too much.

He goes to bed, half-drunk, but can't sleep, thinking of Faith and what they've experienced. He takes a sleeping pill but it doesn't seem to work, and so he takes another. For the first time in months he dreams about the night his family home burnt down and his mother died.

PART FIVE

London
Berlin

May–June 1963

True Self/False Self

Gabriel sold the British and Commonwealth rights to his next travel book, *On the Beaten Path*, on the basis of his detailed outline, to Mulholland & Melhuish for £1,500. He signed the contract and received a cheque in the post for £450. His agent, having taken his commission, was very confident about a US sale also, not to mention potential foreign publishers who were professing interest. Suddenly Gabriel felt almost rich. All he had to do now was write the book.

But this good fortune in his literary career couldn't cancel out his constant low-grade anguish regarding Faith. He hadn't heard from her for two weeks. It was now the middle of May. It was as if those five days, five nights and their intense emotions had never happened. Or had happened and were now in the process of being erased or eroded, or becoming merely memories – something that had occurred in the recent past. Gone.

He wrote to Faith at the Institute, professionally terse: 'Can we meet? Sincerely yours, Gabriel Dax'. There was no reply. A few days later he telephoned the Institute on the private number he'd been given and was told that Miss Green was 'on leave'. A lie, he knew. It made his mood more sombre and unstable. So much, he thought, for his encounter with Faith Green's true self. It seemed the false self was the one that predominated.

He booked an appointment with Katerina Haas.

It was a balmy, breezy afternoon in Frognal Way, Hampstead. The stirred freshness of the acid-green leaves on the lime trees made his mood better, more relaxed – the foliage seemed to be practically spreading and growing in front of his eyes, Gabriel thought. The hazy sunlight cast blurry shadows and the air seemed thronged with pollen, making his eyes sting. He was early and he walked the streets around Katerina's house smoking a Gitanes, rubbing his itchy eyes and trying to reassure himself, telling himself to be rational, logical. He was behaving, he sensed, like some sort of love-lorn teenager and felt vaguely ashamed that he had come running to Dr Haas, as if she would have the answers to his complicated affairs of the heart.

He sat for another five minutes in the waiting room, aware that, in the years he'd been coming here, he had never encountered another of Katerina's analysands. The fantasy that he was her only patient amused him for a few seconds – then she opened the door to her consulting room.

He gave a start. For the first time she wasn't wearing her habit-ual lab coat and silk scarf at the neck. She was in a cream wool suit with black lapels. Neat brown shoes with a two-inch heel. Three-string pearl necklace and pearl earrings. Dark, violet lip-stick. She looked as though she was going to a reception or a formal lunch.

'I'm a bit taken aback,' Gabriel said, sitting down in the arm-chair. 'First time with no lab coat. Have I interrupted something social?'

'No, no,' she said. 'It's just the next phase in our professional rela-tionship. Symbolized by the removal of the "doctor's garb". We meet now as two equals, if you like. Almost as friends. It changes the discourse in a subtle way.'

'Well, you look very smart. Very chic.'

'This is my style. This is me. Just as you chose your clothes for this encounter, so did I. I haven't seen that tie before.'

Gabriel looked down at his tie. Moss green with a pink polka dot. Where did he buy that? What made him choose it?

'I believe it was a present from my sister-in-law, now I come to think about it.'

'You see? We're talking about our clothes. Subtle differences, Gabriel. We're moving on to the next phase.'

She stood up and went over to the tape recorder and clicked it on. The spools began to revolve.

EXTRACTS FROM THE TRANSCRIPTION
OF SESSION 14

DR HAAS: So you have had further sexual relations with this woman, Faith Green.

GABRIEL DAX: Yes. She came to stay with me for a few days. At my cottage in East Sussex.

DR HAAS: Did you invite her?

GABRIEL DAX: No. She invited herself. She said she needed to hide away – to disappear – for a while.

DR HAAS: Why?

GABRIEL DAX: I don't really know. Something to do with a power struggle in MI6, I believe. It was part of some plan she was working out – a way of exposing a colleague, a colleague's manoeuvrings. She didn't tell me much.

DR HAAS: Was the sexual intercourse a transaction in some way?

GABRIEL DAX: What do you mean?

DR HAAS: Did you feel that she felt obliged to sleep with you because you were sheltering her, so to speak?

GABRIEL DAX: Not at all. She wouldn't do anything like that, anyway. Or at least it didn't seem so. We both wanted to make love. It seemed very natural and mutual. And I saw a different side of her. I saw her 'true self' – to use your category. Those days were, to me at least, almost magical. I was very happy.

DR HAAS: And what has happened afterwards?

GABRIEL DAX: She left suddenly. And I haven't seen or heard from her since then.

DR HAAS: And how do you feel about that?

GABRIEL DAX: Well . . . [Pause] Disappointed. Frustrated. Even a little bitter. And angry with myself for feeling so . . . so 'needy'.

DR HAAS: There's nothing wrong with that. We all have needs.

GABRIEL DAX: Yes, but we're mature adults. Yet I can't stop thinking about her and the time we spent together. I thought that there was genuine feeling, genuine emotion between the two of us. That we had become close, intimate.

DR HAAS: Did you declare this to her?

GABRIEL DAX: Not in so many words. But I'd have thought it was obvious to her what I was feeling.

DR HAAS: Did she make any declaration?

GABRIEL DAX: No. Again, not in so many words. But I felt I was reading her feelings accurately, also, if you know what I mean. I wasn't kidding myself. It was sincere, fulfilling. A kind of dream come true – for me, anyway. We made love many times. Passionate love, I would say.

DR HAAS: Physically passionate, you mean?

GABRIEL DAX: Physically and emotionally. It couldn't have been better.

DR HAAS: Have you tried to make contact with her since?

GABRIEL DAX: Yes. No response. It's as if she's returned to her 'false self', as it were.

DR HAAS: Maybe there's a logical explanation for her silence. You won't know until you see her again.

GABRIEL DAX: True. But when will that be?

DR HAAS: What about your other relationship, with your former girlfriend?

GABRIEL DAX: Lorraine? Well, I took your advice. We met. We . . . [Pause] We went to bed together. I now regret that – it was a mistake. She wants to re-establish the relationship. Her own life is something of a mess. I think she sees me as secure, someone she can trust.

DR HAAS: Maybe that's the answer. Maybe this Lorraine is the person you should be concentrating on.

GABRIEL DAX: There's no point. I can't stop thinking about Faith Green, now. After her stay with me. Those few days and nights. It's gone too far.

Gabriel pondered a return to Claverleigh but decided to spend a night at Ruskin Studios. He would go to the London Library tomorrow, he thought, and borrow some books for *On the Beaten Path*. He should concentrate on his work, that's what he should do, he told himself. Start booking some flights – focus his mind on his writing, not his so-called romantic life. He felt almost disgusted with himself. But what can you do? he remonstrated, internally, as he journeyed homeward on the Tube to Chelsea. He was a sensitive, emotional human being – that was his nature, his character, his true self. He couldn't turn himself into an unfeeling automaton, as though flicking a switch. Surely it was healthier to acknowledge these emotions and try to deal with them, not supress them. That's the whole reason why he went to Katerina Haas, for fuck's sake.

Corless hailed him as he was about to enter the front door.

'Message for you, Mr Dax.'

He handed over the folded slip of paper. A grotesque half-leer forming on his lips, Gabriel saw.

'Lady friends keep on ringing.'

He really was an objectionable little creep, Gabriel thought, noting Corless's sly man-to-man wink. Perhaps he should have a telephone installed in number 3 and avoid having Corless as prurient go-between.

'Thank you, Mr Corless.'

Gabriel hoped his contempt was evident in his dry tone of voice and he deliberately didn't look at the message until he was inside the building. Lorraine, no doubt. What was he to do with Lorraine?

He unfolded the note. Corless only wrote in capital letters.

'Please call me. Faith.' There was a number he didn't recognize. He turned and went out in search of a phone box. He was aware that he had a stupid, happy smile on his face.

2.

Austin Belhaven

Faith didn't answer the phone, much to Gabriel's disappointment. It was a man – but a man who was a functionary, Gabriel could tell, relieved. He told Gabriel that Miss Green wanted to meet him at an address in Curzon Street, Mayfair, the next day at 10 a.m. Would that be possible?

'Yes,' Gabriel said.

The house number was supplied: 47 Curzon Street, Flat 4.

'There was a reminder from Miss Green that every precaution should be taken prior to the meeting.'

'Understood,' Gabriel said. So, full artifice required. This didn't sound like a romantic assignation, he noted. He felt pleased that they would see each other again but was aware of the unwelcome tug of his parallel life. No trip to the London Library to borrow a book or two – Curzon Street took priority.

The next morning, he set off early. He changed Tube lines three times – Circle, District, Piccadilly. He emerged at Piccadilly Circus and mingled with the hurrying commuters, heading for their offices. He jumped on a bus; he jumped off the bus. He entered a shop, removed his jacket, and he exited the shop, jacketless, asking the person beside him the time. He walked to Hyde Park Corner, went down to the Tube station, stepped on to a train and stepped off at the last moment before the doors slid to. He arrived at 47 Curzon Street wholly convinced that no follower or team of followers could have any idea of his destination. Tom Brown would have been proud of him.

He rang the doorbell for Flat 4 and was buzzed in. He rode up to the top floor of the building in a small narrow lift, trying to urge saliva into his dry mouth. Faith was waiting for him, the door to the flat open. She was wearing one of her dark suits with sensible flat shoes. She smiled, but Gabriel knew this was not the moment to try to kiss her, even though he was experiencing that feeling of breathlessness and heart-hammer. The lover meeting his loved one again, after a long and trying absence.

'Very good to see you,' he whispered as she showed him in to a shabby, semi-furnished flat. The fitted carpets were worn and the armchairs and sofa had that shiny, greasy feel of overuse. No pictures on the walls; no books in the bookcases. There was a small dining table with four chairs, one of them occupied by a tall, thin, gangling man in a charcoal-grey suit and purple knitted tie. He stood up. Gabriel was tall, over six foot, but this man had two or three inches on him – almost as tall as John Saxonbridge. He had a low parting and his thin hair was carefully flattened over his cranium. In his fifties, Gabriel reckoned, pale blue, shrewd eyes, almost handsome in a gaunt, ascetic, intellectual way.

'This is Austin Belhaven. Gabriel Dax,' Faith said.

They shook hands, exchanged pleasantries and sat down at the dining table. There was no coffee, no biscuits or even water on offer, Gabriel observed. Strictly business. Belhaven took a notebook out of his pocket and flicked through some pages.

'You know a man called Dean Furlan, I believe,' Belhaven said with a vague smile, looking up from his notes.

' "Know" is a bit strong,' Gabriel said. 'We met in Guatemala City a few weeks ago. We were holed up in a hotel together when riots broke out on the streets.'

'But he would recognize you and vice versa.'

'Yes. It was a strange, alarming time. I suppose that is some kind of bond, a shared history, of sorts.' Gabriel glanced at Faith who was looking at him, intently. 'May I ask why Furlan is important?'

'You won't be aware of this,' Belhaven said, closing his notebook, 'but there have been at least two failed attempts to assassinate President John F. Kennedy in the US in the last five weeks. One in Los Angeles and one in Miami.'

'My God.'

Faith stared down at her hands.

'What's going on?' Gabriel asked them both. They looked at each other, as if trying to ascertain how much information should be given to him.

'In each instance, in each city,' Belhaven said, 'there was a long motorcade procession. And in each situation a man was arrested along the route of the motorcade in possession of a firearm, a rifle. And then released.'

'What was the point of releasing these suspects?'

'Good question, Mr Dax. Not enough evidence was the reason given.' He shrugged. 'No shot was fired. No motive was apparent. Both men had histories of mental disturbance. And in our country people have the right to bear arms.' Belhaven pursed his lips. 'To be fair, it's more complicated than that. Law enforcement in all its aspects and capacities – local police, FBI, Secret Service – was – shall we say? – less than diligent. Reluctant to draw conclusions. Complacent.'

Gabriel glanced at Faith. She gave a quick nod. He remembered what she had said about rogue elements in the CIA.

Gabriel sat back in his chair.

'What's this got to do with me? With respect.'

'It's because you know Dean Furlan. Dean Furlan was in Los Angeles and Miami at the time of these possible assassination attempts.'

'Well, that's interesting. But, I repeat, what's that got to do with—'

'President Kennedy is making an official visit to Berlin in a few weeks, in June.'

'I think I've read about that.'

'Dean Furlan has just arrived in Berlin.'

Now it was Belhaven's turn to sit back in his seat.

'We would like you to go to Berlin,' Faith said, evenly. 'And find out what Furlan is up to.'

Gabriel was about to blurt out: why me? but stopped himself. He took a deep breath.

'All right. All right, yes, I could go to Berlin and contrive to bump into Furlan. But – wouldn't he be suspicious? First Guatemala City, then Berlin?'

'There are ways of arranging these things,' Faith said, patiently, as if speaking to a not very intelligent child, Gabriel thought. 'Maybe he would bump into *you*. You have excellent cover as a journalist and renowned travel writer – you travel the world, by definition. A happy coincidence.'

'I thought there were no coincidences in our business,' Gabriel said, a little petulantly.

'Well, this wouldn't be a coincidence, of course – it would just look like one.'

'Bit of a risk.'

'Worth the risk, wouldn't you say?' Belhaven interjected.

'I suppose so,' Gabriel said. 'But if Furlan is spooked then there's nothing we can do.'

He smiled faintly and looked at Faith again, taking in her cool beauty, as he saw it, her unfailing allure, pleased to be back in a room with her, in any event, a few feet away.

'Is there a washroom here?' Belhaven asked.

Faith gave him the directions and he left the room. Gabriel was pleased.

'What is this place?' he asked.

'One of our safe houses. Our "coops" we call them. Guaranteed bug-free.'

'I've missed you,' Gabriel said, quietly, reaching out his hand across the table. She didn't take it.

'Not now, Gabriel, if you don't mind.'

'Why didn't you make contact?'

'It's been a very difficult, not to say fraught, time for me.'

'What's happened to Ishbel Dunbar?'

'She's been posted to Lima, Peru. Out of the Institute for ever.'

'That's a victory, isn't it?'

Faith looked round to check that Belhaven wasn't returning.

'There's collateral damage. She had accused me of defecting—'

'You? How ridiculous!'

'Yes. It was brazen. Opportunistic. Exactly what I suspected – which is why I came to stay with you. To flush her out. But it stirred things up. These allegations tend to do that. Mud sticks, you know. I had to calm everything down. It wasn't easy.'

He felt for her, half-understanding the enormous pressures of her strange, unique job; her dangerous brinkmanship; the challenge of her five days' absence hiding out at Rose Cottage. Yet, she had won the day – or so it seemed.

Belhaven loped back into the room.

'The, ah, flush doesn't seem to be working on that toilet.'

'I'll make sure it's reported,' Faith said.

Belhaven sat down and turned to Gabriel.

'What do you say, Mr Dax?'

'Do I have a choice?'

'Of course you do,' Faith said. Of course I don't, Gabriel thought.

'All right, Berlin here I come.'

Belhaven visibly relaxed.

'Excellent. You'll liaise with Agent Baumgarten in Berlin. Parker Baumgarten. You'll have every resource that the Agency can offer.'

'Come by the Institute next week,' Faith said. 'Lee will call and give you the date and all the relevant information you'll need.'

Gabriel sat silent for a moment, feeling depressed. How had this happened to him? What did he have to do with threats to the safety of the President of the United States? Was he the only person in the world who knew Dean Furlan?

He stood up.

'Well, I'll wait to hear from Lee,' he said.

'We're very grateful, Mr Dax. This is important, significant work, believe me,' Belhaven said, rising to his feet. They shook hands again.

'I'll do what I can,' Gabriel said. 'Nothing ventured, and all that.'

Faith walked him to the door.

'I'll be in touch, Gabriel,' she said, and allowed her fingers to brush his knuckles. 'Well done.'

Well done what? he said to himself as he descended to Curzon Street in the lift. He felt the usual caul of irritating dissatisfaction enfold him, wondering once again how he could ever free himself from the Institute and its relentless grip. Yet the Institute had given him Faith Green. How could he let that go? Was it a price worth paying?

3.

Lorraine and Varvara

Harrison Lee handed Gabriel the now familiar document wallet.

'Everything's there,' Lee said. 'Tickets, vouchers. Travellers' cheques for supplementary expenses. Your cheque. Though you might want to encrypt some of the information.'

'Right. Will do.'

'Baumgarten's personal telephone number, for example.'

'I have done this before, Harry,' Gabriel said. 'Several times.'

'I know. I envy you.'

'What?'

'Agent in the field and all that. I'm stuck in an office in Covent Garden.'

'I'll gladly let you go in my place,' Gabriel said.

Lee laughed, genuinely.

'It all seems exciting. Derring-do.'

'It's not exciting. It's stressful, believe me. And if it's not stressful, it's boring.'

Gabriel looked through the various documents in the file.

'What hotel is Furlan in?'

'The Berlin Hilton near the Kurfürstendamm. A big hotel, over six hundred rooms. You should be as anonymous as you like. We've booked you a suite, by the way. You'll see the voucher – there it is.'

'Much appreciated.'

'We know how fussy you are about hotels, Gabriel.'

Gabriel smiled and slipped the file into his briefcase.

'Is Faith around?'

'She's not in today.'

'Right. I'd better get home and pack my bags.'

★

Gabriel thoroughly watered his Swiss cheese plant. It was parched, the leaves limp, and he hoped he'd saved it. Maybe house plants weren't the best idea, currently, given he was off to Berlin – and with no idea how long he'd be there. If the plant revived he should give it to Roland Rees, he thought.

There was a knock at the door. He opened it to find Corless with his usual salacious grin.

'More messages from your girlfriends, Mr Dax. Or should that be your harem?'

'Thank you, Mr Corless. Most amusing.'

He took the folded slips of paper from the man and closed the door on him. Three from Lorraine. Two from Varvara Suvorina. The message was the same: 'Please call me.'

Gabriel lit Lorraine's cigarette with his lighter and then lit his own. They were in the Goat and Crow. It was early evening, just after opening time, strong, angled May sunlight basted the street outside. Summer on the way.

'I can't believe it, Gabe,' Lorraine said, the hurt in her voice and expression very evident. 'I thought we were back on again.'

'But I met this woman, and something happened,' Gabriel said, trying to sound both calm and rueful. 'Something clicked. It was very intense. Very – you know – passionate. It's not something you can control – it's something that happens. Just like you and that Kevin bloke with the sandwich bar.'

'Ken.'

'Ken. It was you who broke up with me, remember.'

'I shouldn't ever have done that.'

'Look, Lorraine. We've always been honest with each other. I could string you along, tell you some elaborate story, but it wouldn't be fair. Better that we should face up to what's happened. Be honest with each other. No hard feelings.'

'But I love you, Gabriel.'

'No, you don't.' It was the first time she had ever made this declaration, he realized, with a little shock. 'You're wounded, you're hurting. You're in love with an "idea" of me. Not the real me.' The false me, he thought, not the true me.

She sipped at her Bacardi and Coke, thinking.

'Maybe you're right . . .'

She stubbed out her cigarette.

'Smoking too much, drinking too much. I don't know where I'm going, Gabe.'

'Look, I'm here. We're friends. I want to help, if I can.' He shrugged. 'But I'm off on my travels again.'

'Can I stay at your place? I got to get out of my mum's. She's driving me mental.'

Gabriel thought. It was an idea, a compromise that softened the blow, perhaps. But no. Not a good move.

'It would be great but it's complicated,' he said. 'The lease, all that. They're very fussy at the studios.'

'Yeah. Sure. Just an idea.'

They finished their drinks. They had another round, smoked another cigarette. Gabriel said he had to go – he was off in the next few days, he said. He'd let her know and maybe have a word with the caretaker, Mr Corless, but he wasn't hopeful. They hugged outside the pub; Lorraine tried to kiss him on the lips but he managed to gently deflect her. He wandered home to Ruskin Studios in a fug of indecision and frustration, a litany of complaints and dissatisfactions running through his head, as usual. What was going on with his life? And tomorrow he had to meet Varvara Suvorina. He was almost anxious to flee to Berlin.

He was the first at Dovehouse Gardens and sat on the bench, smoking a cigarette, looking at the vegetation, trying to empty his mind. It was warm and he took his jacket off and loosened his tie, watching a gardener digging in a border, suddenly wishing that was his job – simple physical exertion, the satisfaction of seeing plants grow, the seasons waxing and waning, time passing in an ordered, reassuringly boring fashion.

Varvara Suvorina appeared promptly. They shook hands and

she sat down beside him, taking out her American cigarettes from her bag and lighting up. She looked a bit wan and stressed, Gabriel thought.

'By the way, I have a drawing for Kit Caldwell,' he said.

'There is no urgency,' she said. 'We can wait for your visit to Moscow.' She blew a strong jet of smoke from the side of her mouth.

'There is urgency on another matter,' she said. 'We need your help to get information.'

'I'll do my best,' Gabriel said, feeling weary himself, all of a sudden.

'Have you had contact with this woman, Faith Green, recently?'

'No.'

'This woman, she disappeared for five days. Completely disappeared. Where was she? What was she doing? Can you find out for us?'

'How do you know she disappeared?' Gabriel asked, trying to seem only vaguely curious.

'We were informed.'

'May I ask who informed you?'

'This is classified, I'm sorry, I can't tell you.'

'Right. I'll see if I can find anything out.'

Gabriel's mind was working furiously. Ishbel Dunbar, he thought. It must have been Ishbel Dunbar, trying to amass damaging information about Faith. Or trying to implicate her, perhaps. Or was it something more covert? Was Ishbel Dunbar a termite? He saw a larger, more damaging plan: a termite at the head of the Institute. He thought further, saw how it could be ideal, super-valuable penetration . . . He had to tell Faith, he supposed. Or maybe not. Maybe she knew. Maybe she herself secretly informed the KGB as a way of implicating Ishbel Dunbar . . . He sensed the spy's disease – paranoia – begin to take him over, like a virus.

Varvara was saying something.

'Apologies,' Gabriel said. 'I was just thinking about this Faith Green.'

'No. I was saying it is my birthday on Saturday. Perhaps I could invite you for a supper. Just you and me – to get to know you better. You to get to know me. We can find a restaurant of your choice.'

'Unfortunately, I have to go to West Germany,' Gabriel said, instantly. 'For my new book. I leave tomorrow.'

'Maybe when you return, we can meet.'

'I'd like that very much.'

He smiled, but felt his shoulders stiffen with tension. This couldn't go on, he said to himself, this unlooked-for role as Caldwell's London go-between, Caldwell's 'man'. What would happen if they ever found out about Caldwell, what if he was exposed? What consequences would redound on Gabriel Dax? There had to be a way out. Faith had to finesse something – she had buried him in this hole, after all.

'Are you all right, Gabriel?'

'What? Yes. Though I think I may have a cold coming on.' He gave a sniff as if to prove the diagnosis.

Varvara gestured at the dappled sunlight.

'We have a saying in Russia: spring is here and so are the head colds. I make the bad translation.'

'I know what you mean.'

'I will leave you now,' she said. 'Please call me if you have the information. It's important to us.'

They both stood up and shook hands. Gabriel promised to do his best. Varvara squeezed his hand and smiled, then turned and walked away. Gabriel sat down. Berlin, paradoxically, was his lifeline, he thought. He couldn't wait to leave London.

4.

Berlin. Unreal City

Gabriel stood at the window of his suite in the Berlin Hilton, looking out over West Berlin as dusk arrived. Neon signs were going on everywhere, creating the luminous electric embroidery of a city as evening fell. It was strange being in this curious enclave of twentieth-century capitalism in a communist country. A capsule of hope in a sclerotic body, somebody had said. Who was it? Bertrand Russell, Thomas Mann, Arthur Koestler . . .?

The hotel, a stark, modern thirteen-storey rectangle with a chequerboard facade, was a perfect symbol of this Western material challenge, this confident affront to the East and the Soviets. Look what we can build, what luxury we can offer. He could just about see, in the gloaming, in the middle distance, the ruined tower of the Kaiser Wilhelm church. It looked like a hoary, blackened standing stone – a modern menhir – amidst all the glass and steel, the glitz and glitter, the swarming, honking traffic. A totemic memory of bad times past – bad times not so long ago, Gabriel thought. A good idea to leave it in place, he considered, a potent reminder of how easily things could go terribly wrong.

He had seen the famous pictures of Berlin in 1945 – the endless wasteland of rubble and the shattered hulks of buildings – and now the modern city was spread out before him, plate glass and aluminium, concrete and bitumen, automobiles and smartly dressed pedestrians. Unreal City, he said to himself – or rather, half an unreal city. There was the immutable division of the Wall – *die Mauer* – and beyond that the grim austerities of East Berlin.

All very bizarre, he thought, stepping back from the wide window and drawing the curtains. Somewhere in this huge hotel Dean Furlan was also staying, a fellow guest. Find out what he's up to in Berlin – what more vague and unachievable mission brief was there than that?

He poured himself a Scotch from the half-bottle he had brought with him from London and lit a cigarette. As far as he could figure out the key objective was to somehow initiate a 'casual', impromptu meeting with Dean Furlan. They would then renew their acquaintance and Furlan would obligingly tell him exactly what he was doing here in Berlin. Yeah, sure, Gabriel thought. First things first. He should meet up with his CIA contact, this Parker Baumgarten, and see what he had to say. Who was running this show, anyway? Belhaven? Faith? The CIA head of station in Berlin? He looked at the notes and contacts he'd been given – the man was called Peter Carlyle. He sipped at his Scotch, drew deeply on his Gitanes. At least he had a decent room.

They'll know when you've arrived, Harrison Lee had said. They'll make contact – discreetly. They don't want Furlan to have the slightest sniff of CIA involvement.

Great. Gabriel felt his anger rise in him again. Stop, he told himself. You can only do what is possible. If Furlan didn't want to engage with him he could go back home and resume his old life – he would do his best, what more could he offer?

He decided not to use the hotel lifts and took the stairs down to the lobby. If he spotted Furlan it would have to be handled very carefully. Imagine if the two of them stepped into a lift together. No, first he should explore the hotel and get his bearings. Maybe find out what Furlan's room number was. He wandered around the wide lobby and had an idea.

He went up to the reception desk, making sure his door key was visible in his hand.

'Hello. *Guten Abend*. I'm a guest in the hotel and I think my friend has just arrived. Mr Furlan. Room 325, I believe.'

The receptionist checked the hotel ledger.

'Ah . . . No. Mr Furlan is in 437.'

'Of course. My mistake. I'll call him later. *Danke*.'

It was that easy, Gabriel thought. Good artifice.

He then went and spoke to the concierge. There were three

restaurants in the Hilton – the Rotisserie in an inner courtyard, the grander Ambassador restaurant, and the Roof Garden on the top floor, open until 2 a.m. All had bars. He rather suspected Furlan would be drawn to the Roof Garden – more informal – with its terrace and the views of the city. Who knew? Maybe Furlan would stay in his room and order room service. Gabriel allowed a mood of fatalistic resignation to settle on him. *Que será, será*. He handed in his key and went for a walk. He was feeling hungry – some *Wurst* would do the trick, he reckoned.

When he returned and went to collect his key from reception there was a message for him. He stepped away from the desk and read it: 'Café Glücklich. 103 Kurfürstendamm. 10.30 a.m. Parker.' He went up to the Roof Garden and ordered a brandy and soda, casually scrutinizing the crowded terrace and dining area. No sign of Furlan – not surprisingly, he considered. He was pleased by the size of the hotel – and the number of guests. It was busy, almost full, the concierge had told him. The risk of a chance encounter was obviously slim. He smoked a cigarette and drank his brandy, analysing the complexities of the situation he found himself in. And yet there were some compensations, he had to admit. Money, for one – he had never been so solvent – and, more importantly, Faith. Those five nights they had spent together had changed everything. At least for him. He couldn't speak for her – the Sphinx of the Institute of Developmental Studies. He smiled at the appellation. He would call her that the next time they met – see if it annoyed her or made her laugh. He still had his jade love token from Guatemala – to be bestowed at some point, if that point ever arose again. He thought she would like it. And he would like to see it round her neck, caught in the small, shadowed hollow below her throat, between her collarbones. His stone on her flesh. He stopped himself. Concentrate on the matters in hand. Stop dreaming.

The Café Glücklich was a small, brightly lit coffee bar with aluminium chairs and red formica tables. Pop music was playing from a radio and the clientele was young. Gabriel found a seat by the window and watched the passers-by and the shiny cars whizzing up and down the boulevard. The sun was brightly glaring. Life was good in the capitalist West, even the sun agreed.

'Mr Dax?'

He turned, a strange feeling of déjà vu fleetingly overcoming him. A tall young woman stood there wearing sunglasses and a fawn leather jacket over a pink T-shirt.

'Yes?'

'I'm Parker Baumgarten. Pleased to meet you.'

She held out her hand and Gabriel shook it, trying not to seem nonplussed. So this is Parker Baumgarten. Agent Baumgarten.

She sat down opposite him and removed her sunglasses. She had modishly cut hair, dark brown, somehow layered short at the back so that the front and sides flopped over her forehead in a kind of heavy fringe, half-obscuring her eyes. She brushed the fringe aside with her fingers and smiled at him,

'I'm nearly finished *The Wine-Dark Sea*. Loving it.'

'Doing your research.'

'Yes. A fun bonus.'

She looked absurdly young, Gabriel thought, but she couldn't have been more than two or three years younger than he was, he assumed. Late twenties, thirty.

'Do you want to see my ID?'

'That's not required. You left a message at the hotel, and here we are.' He shrugged. 'Apologies if I looked a bit blank. It was the "Parker" that threw me.'

'Sometimes I wish my parents had called me Jane.' She folded up her sunglasses and slipped them into a pocket of her jacket.

'I could kill for a coffee,' she said. 'How about you?'

They ordered coffees. When they arrived, Gabriel offered her one of his French cigarettes and she accepted. A good sign, he thought. He reached forward with his lighter and lit her Gitanes. She took a deep drag and savoured the taste.

'Have you spotted Furlan?' she asked, picking a shred of tobacco from her slick pink tongue. 'French tobacco: yes, sir. Different hit.'

'No, not yet. I've looked. I do know he's in the hotel, however. Room 437.'

'We've been told to keep our distance,' she said. 'Leave everything up to Unit A.'

'Unit A?'

'That's you.' She smiled. There was a slight gap between her front two teeth, Gabriel noticed. 'We call freelancers "units",' she said. 'As opposed to agents.'

'Fair enough. Happy to be Unit A.'

'Actually, I think two puffs on this will do me,' she said, and stubbed out the Gitanes. 'No disrespect. I smoke menthol. Kools.'

'It's an acquired taste, French cigarettes,' Gabriel said. 'Misspent youth.' He stubbed his own cigarette out in solidarity. 'So, what's the plan?' he asked.

She paused, thinking. Pursed her lips and exhaled.

'You know that President Kennedy is coming to Berlin towards the end of June,' she said. 'This very month. For one day. June twenty-sixth to be precise.' She gestured vaguely, as if shaping a ball in the air. 'We think Furlan's presence here is not a coincidence. Worse: it's sinister. We hope to find out what he's up to and preempt him.'

'Why not just arrest him and deport him.'

'On what charge?'

'Do you people need a charge? It's never been a—'

'We could do that,' she interrupted, 'but he obviously won't be working alone. Furlan may be gone from Berlin but the problem remains. That's what we need Unit A to find out.'

'Jesus. Excuse me. Apologies.'

'No need to apologize. It's kind of down-to-the-wire time.' She shrugged off her leather jacket.

'Another coffee?'

Gabriel smiled and looked at her more closely as she hung her jacket on the back of her chair. There was something both gamine and brisk about her, he thought. It wasn't just her short hair – something also about the swift, no-nonsense way she moved enhanced the impression. She had blue eyes and tight, thin lips. No visible make-up. Almost a kind of asexual—

'Another coffee?' Parker repeated.

'What? Yes, please,' Gabriel said.

'You should meet Peter Carlyle. I'll set it up.'

Gabriel returned to the Hilton after his meeting with Parker Baumgarten. American mother, German father, she had briefly explained, hence the bi-national name. She was almost fluent in German as a result, she said; at home her father spoke German to her all the time. The lobby was busy – some large group of conventioneers seemed to have arrived, debouching from two coaches in front of the entrance. Then he saw Furlan, and froze. He was talking to one of the duty managers. He was looking dapper, in a dark suit, a younger man standing beside him also participating in the discussion. Gabriel walked by them, deliberately quite close, but it was immediately apparent Furlan hadn't registered his presence. He felt the inevitable adrenaline surge. Target identified. Now he had to somehow manufacture an 'innocent' encounter. He strode off to the stairway.

He sat in his room, pondering his next steps. The contact with Furlan had to be a priority – everything would be determined after that meeting.

He took a taxi to Checkpoint Charlie and had a good look at the Wall. It seemed fearsomely strong, he thought, rooted and solid with a strangely permanent aspect, even though it had been erected less than two years previously. It had the air, paradoxically, of a construction that had been there for all time. It was also an ongoing project, he knew, its fortification being ceaselessly refined and improved on; it had swiftly become as much a fixture in the geography of Berlin as the Brandenburg Gate. He wandered a few hundred metres along its length, noting the towers, the soldiers observing the West through their binoculars, the profusion of barbed wire, the star-shaped girders of the Czech hedgehog anti-tank obstructions. He could hear barking dogs beyond. A wall to keep people in, he thought, not a means to defend against hostile enemies. The graffiti on the Western side symbolized the affront. Here we are free to paint our slogans – over there, you aren't. He hailed a taxi and headed back to the Hilton, wondering what tiny footnote he might provide in divided Berlin's history. Or not, of course. It would all depend on the Furlan encounter, he suspected.

That evening he wandered over to the reception desk. Room key in hand.

'*Abend*,' he said to the receptionist. 'I'm dining with Herr Furlan tonight – room 437 – but I've forgotten which restaurant he chose.'

He lit a cigarette while the receptionist telephoned the Hilton's three restaurants and confirmed that Herr Furlan had indeed a reservation at the Roof Terrace. 8 p.m. Table for two. Gabriel expressed his gratitude.

At 9 p.m., Gabriel entered the restaurant and said he just wanted a drink at the bar. He found a seat at the corner near the maître d's lectern. Furlan could only exit this way, he noted – he'd pass within feet of Gabriel. Gabriel ordered a Scotch and soda and peered into the restaurant. Furlan – and the young man he'd been with in the lobby – were sitting at the rear. Gabriel took out his notebook and opened it. There was nothing like someone writing in a notebook to attract attention. Gabriel had noticed the effect before on his travels – it was a near-instant conversation starter. The key element in this would-be encounter was that Furlan should be the one who spotted him and initiated the meeting. Gabriel had to feign total surprise at the 'coincidence' and therefore diminish or cancel the manipulation. If Furlan didn't see him and renew their acquaintance then he'd have to try another manoeuvre.

Gabriel waited. He drank his Scotch and smoked. He ordered another drink. Then he spotted Furlan calling for the bill. He felt his tension levels rise and once again asked himself what in the name of reason he was doing playing these dangerous games in a foreign city at the behest of his puppet-mistress, Faith Green. Still, here Furlan was. In for a penny. He bent over his notebook and scribbled nonsense as Furlan and his companion ambled out of the restaurant.

'Oh, no! I don't fuckin' believe it. Who'd have thought?'

Gabriel looked round to see Furlan beaming at him. He was wearing a white shirt, tieless, the collar spread over the lapels of his black jacket.

'Gabriel Dax, as I live and breathe.'

Gabriel imitated total astonishment, stood and they shook hands warmly.

'My God, Dean. What the—'

'What're you doing in Berlin, my man?'

Gabriel gestured at his notebook.

'Writing my book on rivers. I'm doing the Spree. The river, here.'

Furlan turned to his companion.

'This is Mr Gabriel Dax, famous writer. We had a few adventures in Guatemala City, not so long ago. This is my kid brother, Matt.'

Gabriel shook hands with Matt. Furlan clapped Gabriel on the shoulder.

'I can't believe it! Incredible.'

'Can I buy you a drink?' Gabriel asked.

They opted for a couple of brandies and joined him at the bar. Furlan and Gabriel outlined their Guatemala City encounter to Matt. He was a slim, serious-looking young man, dark like Furlan, with shrewd eyes. He had softer, floppier hair, unlike his brother, and didn't say much, just nodded and smiled as he listened to them talk. Furlan was expansive, maybe a bit high, Gabriel sensed, super-genial. Matt Furlan, by contrast, seemed to be weighing him up, so Gabriel thought.

'What're you doing in Berlin?' Gabriel asked Furlan. 'Not buying coffee, I assume.'

'We're gonna open a pizza restaurant. Right here. Or two, or three. Clean up. All these American soldiers can't eat sausages all the time.'

They laughed. Very smart idea, Gabriel said. Matt, it turned out, was the managing director of the Furlan franchise in Buffalo. They were spending their days in Berlin looking at potential sites, trying to weigh up what was the best area in the West. Probably, obviously, the American sector, Furlan said.

They lit cigarettes, smoked, toasted each other, reminisced about the mayhem in Guatemala City.

'Oh, yeah,' Furlan said. 'How could I forget? How are you – after the attack?'

Gabriel felt a sudden alarming stillness bloom inside him. A chill.

'My God. How did you know about that?' he said, without thinking.

'The hotel. My cousin told me, remember?'

'Of course, of course. No, I'm fine. Bit of a scare, but no lasting damage.'

'I didn't know how to reach you. The police said you were in hospital. Someone else settled your bill. Gianfranco – my cousin – called me: hey, your friend was attacked. Where was it? Up the Hudson valley, wasn't it?'

Gabriel related the details of the attack for the benefit of Matt. Another side of his brain was working overtime.

Things fell squarely into place.

It was now immediately clear to him that it was Furlan who must have ordered the attack in New York – had ordered the hit to kill him. Gabriel registered that he'd checked into the very hotel in Manhattan that Furlan had recommended, for the sake of a discount, to be organized by his cousin, the manager. Bad procedure. But the fact that he was in Furlan's 'cousin's' hotel meant that he was under easy surveillance. Easy to follow. Easy name identification. Easy to make it look like a street robbery gone wrong.

Gabriel smiled and chatted, somewhat amazed that he could dissemble so well. Just a flesh wound, yes, all healed. Still – a deeply disturbing moment. And, yes, indeed, the world was full of insane, angry people – armed with knives, amongst other weapons.

'We have to have dinner,' Furlan said, looking at his watch. 'Tomorrow? How are you fixed? The next day?'

'Damn it, I'm off to Vienna tomorrow,' Gabriel lied.

He knew he had to put real physical distance between himself and Furlan, instantly. Furlan would have him killed in Berlin as easily as the Hudson valley.

'Too bad. Shit. But I come to London. Maybe we could meet there. We could open a pizza joint in London, Matt.'

'Not a bad idea,' Matt said, flatly, staring at Gabriel.

Gabriel tore a blank page out of his notebook and wrote down the wrong address and the wrong telephone number. Furlan handed him his business card once more. They shook hands again, enthusiastically looking forward to meeting up in the near future. What a coincidence! All smiles, they made their farewells and the Furlan brothers went to their rooms.

Gabriel packed up his belongings and made a reservation in a small hotel in Kreuzberg, the Alpina Hof. Eighty bedrooms, his guidebook said. His surveillance of Furlan would have to be from a distance. And maybe it would be an advantage if Furlan thought he had actually left the city, although – no doubt – alarm bells might be quietly ringing, all the same. Gabriel thought the 'coincidence' of their meeting in Berlin had seemed entirely random and natural but he knew that Furlan would be running through all the implications of the encounter. Innocent or suspicious? If he never saw Gabriel in Berlin again then that might make him relax.

As he packed his bag, thinking about the conversation, he realized – almost as a revelation – why Furlan would want him dead. Of course, one simple, overriding reason: Gabriel was a witness to the connection between Furlan and Canul. Perhaps the only witness. The man who had 'confessed' to being the killer of Padre Tiago had been seen with Dean Furlan – by Gabriel – on at least three separate occasions. It was enough grounds to have to eliminate the sole witness – Gabriel Dax. Keep everything neat and tidy. Stay at my cousin's hotel. You'll get a great discount. Gabriel felt a bit sick as he ran through the ramifications and his complacency. One thing was for sure – pizza restaurants were just a useful cover. Other business was afoot in Berlin.

Gabriel checked out of the Hilton at 6 a.m. the next morning and taxied over to Kreuzberg, thinking about the new problem that had arisen. He obviously couldn't shadow Furlan, but who could? Maybe Parker Baumgarten could come up with a solution.

His new hotel, the Alpina Hof, was cosy and comfortable – *gemütlich, behaglich* – and he immediately felt safer in its well-padded surroundings. His room was small but heavily cushioned – the bed, the armchair, even the lavatory seat. There were extra cushions available in the cupboard, had he an urge for further cushioning.

He had breakfast in the hotel dining room – breads, four types of ham, pickles, smoked fish – feeling pleased with himself at his quick thinking. A pleasure that was undermined, as he thought further, taking stock of Furlan's cold hypocrisy. If he was right about Furlan ordering his murder in New York, in Hyde Park, then the hail-fellow-well-met enthusiasm of their surprise re-encounter had been entirely convincing. Mind you, Gabriel told himself, his own dissembling had been fairly damn impressive also. Faith would have been proud of him. Anyway, he thought: Plan A abandoned – Plan B to be developed.

5.

Plan B

'Nice little hotel, this,' Tyrone said, tucking into his main course. Somewhat to Gabriel's astonishment Tyrone had ordered, seemingly at random, *Schleie in Dillsoße*, a white fish that Gabriel's pocket German–English dictionary identified as tench, served with a dill sauce. There was a side order of small white turnips. 'Very tasty' was Tyrone's verdict. Gabriel felt more at home with his *Wiener Schnitzel*. The restaurant in the Alpina Hof was small and dark with panelled walls boasting an array of embroidered samplers and many mounted heads of delicate-looking, horned deer. The helpings were on the generous size. Gabriel's cucumber salad that accompanied his *Schnitzel* would have easily served four. As long as Tyrone was happy, he thought.

Gabriel had called Parker Baumgarten and they had met again at the Café Glücklich. He told her that he felt sure that Furlan suspected him and recounted the story he had spun – that he was leaving Berlin the next day, heading for Vienna. He needed someone anonymous to follow Furlan, he said. Parker replied that they had any number of 'units' who could do the job but there were problems with security – the key thing was to keep all CIA involvement at maximum distance from Furlan. Nothing must spook him, she said, thinking: maybe the answer was a private detective . . .

Then the solution came to Gabriel with a flash of insight. I can have somebody come over from London who will do the job, he said, done to perfection. Someone I can trust absolutely. He told her about Tyrone. Sounds ideal, Parker said, adding that she needed to consult Peter Carlyle. She called Gabriel that evening at the hotel. Tyrone Rogan was approved. Unit B could move into action.

Gabriel telephoned Tyrone in London. A job to be done in Berlin, he said, similar to the job he'd done for him before when he'd followed Faith Green and found out where she lived. 'Berlin?' Tyrone said – Gabriel could tell from his tone of voice he was intrigued. There was some fraught negotiation over his fee. All expenses paid and £50 per day was the sum they settled on. Gabriel decided to clear it later with Faith. He had considerable funds at his disposal himself, everything could be covered and he knew Tyrone would want some of the money in advance.

Two days later he met Tyrone at Tempelhof airport and drove him to the Alpina Hof in a newly rented Ford Taunus 12M. Once Tyrone had checked into the hotel, he paid him £100 up front and asked him to keep all receipts for any purchases he made while he was following the target.

'Who is this geezer, anyway?' Tyrone asked.

'An American. He knows who I am so I have to keep out of sight.'

Gabriel gave Tyrone a photograph of Furlan and a miniature camera, a Minolta 16. Both had been provided by Parker.

'We'll rent you a scooter. Just follow him as best you can. I don't think he'll be suspecting anything. Keep a note of where he goes and, if you can, photograph anyone he meets.'

'It's not dangerous, is it?' Tyrone asked.

'No. Keep your distance. He mustn't spot you, that's all. He thinks I'm in Vienna so he shouldn't be on his guard – particularly.'

'I don't like that "particularly", Gabe.'

'Just take your usual precautions. He's with his brother, his younger brother, so there may be two of them. I just need to know where he's going.'

And so the next morning they waited outside the Hilton, parked with a view of the main entrance. One hour, two hours went by. They smoked cigarettes and drank coffee from a flask provided by the hotel. Tyrone's scooter – a Vespa – sat behind the Taunus while they waited for a sighting.

'What're you actually up to, Gabriel?' Tyrone said. 'Be honest. I mean, you're a travel writer, for fuck's sake. This ain't got nothing to do with travel writing.'

'Well, it has, in a peripheral way.'

'Peripheral?'

'Loosely connected. This Furlan man was someone I met when I was . . .' He stopped himself. 'It's a criminal issue.'

'What's it got to do with you, then?'

Gabriel thought fast.

'He's an art thief. He stole several paintings from my uncle, very cleverly. My uncle's an art dealer. We're trying to gather evidence against this man.'

'I knew it! I fucking knew it. I said to Lorraine: there's something moody going on with Gabriel. An art thief? You're not joking me, are you?'

'No. I'm sort of reluctantly involved, to be fair. I'd rather not be. But I happened to have got to know Furlan. My uncle thought that would be very useful – turns out it isn't. Seeing me made Furlan suspicious. Still, we need to know what he's up to in Berlin. Which is why I called on you.'

Tyrone exhaled and shook his head.

'I'll do my best. Jesus.' He looked back at Gabriel, and wagged a finger at him. 'You're a bit of a dark horse, Gabe.'

'It's confidential. Strictly. Don't tell Lorraine.'

'You might have told me.'

'Look, I'm being honest with you. And you're being well paid. Better than burgling. Or locksmithing.'

'Who told you about burgling? Lorraine?'

'Come on, Tyrone. You've practically told me yourself.'

'I don't do it no more. I shouldn't have did what I done.'

'Shouldn't have done what I did.'

Tyrone looked at him, not amused.

'You can be a bit of an arse, you know, Gabriel.'

'Sorry, sorry. I can't help myself. Here he is!'

Gabriel pointed out Furlan and his brother exiting the hotel, heading for the taxi rank.

'Right. Off you go. Keep your distance.'

Tyrone slipped out of the car. In the rear-view mirror Gabriel saw him kick the engine of the Vespa into life and pull away slowly from the kerb. The Furlan taxi exited from the Hilton forecourt and turned right. Tyrone took up a position a couple of cars behind and they motored away out of view, aiming for the Kurfürstendamm. Fingers crossed, Gabriel thought. He started the Taunus and drove back to the hotel. Tyrone would report to him at the end of the day or whenever the Furlans returned to the Hilton. Gabriel had an idea that he might explore more of the length of *die Mauer*, in the meantime. The Berlin Wall might make a good chapter for *On the Beaten Path*, he considered. Waste not, want not, and so forth.

'It's incredibly boring following people,' Tyrone said, gulping at his beer. 'I want you to know that.'

'I'm not asking you to do it for nothing. You've earned fifty quid today.'

They were sitting in the Alpina's tiny bar. Three tables and a grandfather clock with a loud minatory tick to it. The bar itself was like a pulpit, stuck in the corner, with just room for the barman behind.

'Right.' Tyrone took a small notebook out of his pocket and began to read.

'They went to a place called Schöneberg. In a café they met this bloke – obvious estate agent. Showed them brochures. Then they went and visited about six restaurants in the area. I took a photograph of the estate agent, if you want it. Then they all had lunch. And then went to another four or five restaurants. Then Furlan and the other bloke went back to the Hilton.'

'Hmmm,' Gabriel said to himself. 'All very above board.' He smiled at Tyrone. 'Thanks, Tyrone. Good work. Let's see what tomorrow brings.'

'What's on the cards for tonight, me old chum?' Tyrone said.

'Find a restaurant, have some supper, I suppose.'

'I talked to the geezer at reception. He says there's a club nearby. Live music.'

'Sounds great,' Gabriel said.

'We'll have a bite to eat then hit the town,' Tyrone said, with a grin. 'Maybe meet some nice Berlin babes, yeah, Gabriel? Can I have another beer?'

★

Gabriel's mouth was freakishly parched, he thought, as if he hadn't drunk water for forty-eight hours, and his headache pulsed at his right temple, conjoined with his heartbeat.

He and Tyrone were standing outside the Alpina – it was 7 a.m. Gabriel calculated that he'd had three hours' sleep. Medically speaking he was still drunk, he supposed – this hangover he was experiencing was merely the prelude to the proper hangover that was heading his way.

'Leave it to me, Gabe,' Tyrone said. He seemed annoyingly chipper and on form. 'I know what the bloke looks like. I'll just hang around outside the hotel. Catch you later.'

He flung a leg over his Vespa, kick-started it and roared off, leaving a grey spoor of exhaust smoke. Gabriel turned back and entered the hotel, thinking: breakfast, yes, a large breakfast, then a sleep, then a hot bath, and maybe another breakfast. He stacked his plate at the buffet in the dining room and ordered some scrambled eggs. He asked for a pot of black coffee and tried to remember what he could of the night.

The club was called Das Kino and was indeed a disused cinema with the seats removed. Around the impromptu dance floor was a ring of assorted tables. There was a leather-clad band that played cover versions of American and British rock 'n' roll hits. Young people danced where the cinema seats had been. There was a bar at the back of the room and Gabriel thought it would be wiser to restrict himself to beer, forgetting just how intoxicating beer could be. Tyrone roved about the place, chatting to girls, and brought two back to their table – Hetti and Irmgard, as far as Gabriel could remember. One blonde, the other – that was Irmgard, he thought – a redhead. It all became something of a blur. He danced with Irmgard – who spoke good English – then Tyrone said he was going back to the hotel with Hetti. Then Irmgard left in a huff and Gabriel stayed on drinking beer and smoking, wondering yet again why his life had veered off its perfectly satisfying straightforward course and had left him stranded in this position. He got into a long conversation with some young people who seemed interested in him when he said he was a writer. Then, somehow, he had wandered back to the hotel.

His scrambled eggs arrived and he added several types of ham to his plate and two bread rolls. He ate very quickly, like a refugee, he thought, or a prisoner, as if someone was going to snatch his food away before he finished. He pushed his empty plate aside and reached for his cigarettes, looking up to see a young blonde woman whom he vaguely recognized wander into the dining room. Ah, yes, it was Hetti. She waved at him and joined him for breakfast, asking where Tyrone was. At work, Gabriel said. He'll be back this evening. She ate well, also ordering scrambled eggs, adding smoked salmon and herring to the mix. Gabriel waited until she'd finished then they each smoked a cigarette and drank more coffee. Gabriel's headache was in some sort of retreat, his desert thirst calmed by the food and the many cups of coffee. Hetti's grasp of English was rudimentary so they abandoned conversation for their respective thoughts. He closed his eyes for a moment, registering the absurdity of the situation. Such was the life of a spy, he said to himself: hungover, mutely breakfasting with the one-night stand of his colleague. Faith Green would not be impressed or amused, he thought.

But the day – spent mainly in sleepy repose in his room – brought a late dividend. Tyrone returned and they met in the bar for a cocktail. Gabriel was feeling more like himself. He had a cautious Dubonnet and soda. Tyrone asked for whisky. He seemed animated, pleased with himself.

'It started off just like yesterday,' he said. 'Same estate agent, more visits to crap restaurants.' Then they had lunch, he continued, and then the brother went off with the estate agent, Furlan staying behind. After about half an hour he was joined by this weird-looking young guy. A weedy bloke, Tyrone said, blonde hair parted in the middle, a pathetic moustache. About twenty-something years old.

'And I knew, Gabe, that this was nothing to do with pizza restaurants.'

'Did you get a photograph?'

'Yes, I did, Gabriel.' Tyrone seemed irritated by the question. He shoved the Minolta across the table.

'Well done,' Gabriel said, pocketing it. 'What happened?'

'They talked,' Tyrone said. 'Quite intense, like. Then Furlan passed him something in a bag, quite heavy. I don't know what – and the odd-bod left.'

'Is that it?'

'Let me finish, will you?'

'Apologies. Go on.'

'Before he headed off I walked by the table, dead casual, you know, like I was going to the khazi. Close enough to hear them talking. And I got a name. Hendrik.'

'Excellent. Hendrik. That'll help.'

Gabriel called for more drinks. Tyrone was thinking.

'It was odd, you know. Your man, Furlan, sitting there all smart and rich in his snazzy silk suit talking to this man who was – you know – shabby, sad, like a vagrant. What's that all about, Gabe, eh?'

'With a bit of luck, we'll find out. By the way, Hetti left a message for you at reception. I think she's keen to reunite.'

6.

Vollmöller

Parker Baumgarten came to the hotel with the developed stills from Tyrone's camera. She and Gabriel sat in a lounge area and she spread them out on the table between them.

'Good job,' she said. 'These, plus his name – it took about five minutes to identify him. Hendrik Vollmöller, minor criminal, fascist, troublemaker, would-be psychopath.'

'That was fast,' he said.

'We have our people in the Berlin police.'

'Very useful.'

'I should introduce you to our principal guy, Ödön Hempel. He'll help in any way.'

She lit a Kool and pushed a photo towards Gabriel.

'Why would Furlan meet a deranged minor criminal like Vollmöller?' she asked.

Gabriel looked at the photograph. Slightly blurry but distinct enough to make the individual recognizable. A thin nose and large ears, fair hair combed over his forehead then parted in the middle, a weedy moustache, a slightly thrusting, full lower lip. Unmemorable, unattractive, a face in the crowd. Well done, Tyrone, Gabriel thought.

'I'll have a think,' Gabriel said.

'The Berlin police have a small dossier on him,' Parker continued. 'Vollmöller claims to have been in the Hitler Youth during the fall of Berlin in '45. He brags about it. A lie. He was six years old – not even the Hitler Youth would recruit kids that young. He's been arrested a few times – selling amphetamines, fights in bars, drunk and disorderly – he was caught painting a Swastika on a travel agency offering tours to Israel. Then a hammer and sickle on a government building. You know: angry, incoherent, thought-disordered.'

Gabriel was thinking.

'Furlan has led us to Vollmöller,' he said, slowly, remembering Denilson Canul and what he had missed there. 'Something tells me that's who we should concentrate on now.'

'We?'

'You and me, Parker. Tyrone's done his job, I would say. Vollmöller will unlock this, if we go carefully.'

He had a thought.

'Are your people keeping a tab on Furlan? Do you know when he comes and goes?'

'Yes, of course,' Parker said. 'We have units in the hotel. We log him in and out. Why?'

'I'd like to have a look in his room, when he's out for the day. Might be some clues there.'

'I'll let you know.'

He smiled at her, thinking suddenly: what was going on here? What was going on with himself, more to the point? Why was he acting like this? Agent Dax. It was almost as if some sort of spying demon had infiltrated his body, he reflected, and was taking over – he had to resist, take stock, remember, hold on to his old persona. But how? Here he was in Berlin at Faith's behest. Unit A liaising with the CIA, following suspects, trying to second-guess their motives, their objectives.

'Are you OK, Gabriel?' Parker asked.

'What? Yes, just – you know – just thinking. Always thinking.'

He met Tyrone in the bar and bought him yet another drink.

'Everyone's very pleased with your photography.'

'Happy to be of service, Gabe. As I told you once before – I could've been a detective.'

'I'm sure you could. Talking of crime and detection – did you happen to bring your special equipment with you?'

'What would that be?' Tyrone asked, sipping at his beer.

'Your skeleton keys.'

'I don't use skeleton keys. Old school. I – being a locksmith, Gabriel – use lock-picks. And I never travel without them.'

'Good news. I have need of your special talents.'

The next morning, Parker telephoned with the information that Furlan had left the Hilton. Gabriel and Tyrone drove over there in the Taunus. At reception, Gabriel booked a room for two days hence. A booking gave respectability. He asked to see a typical double room and was duly presented with one on the second floor by an under-manager. Gabriel professed himself pleased. He then asked to be shown to the bar and the under-manager left them there as they ordered coffees.

'What is all this about, Gabe?' Tyrone asked.

'We're in the hotel. We're potential clients who've made a booking. No suspicion. We haven't just wandered in off the streets.'

'Right. Yeah. I'll take a note of that. Good point.'

They finished their coffees and then headed for the stairway and climbed to the fourth floor where Furlan's room was. Number 437. It took Tyrone less than three seconds to pick the lock and they stepped quickly inside. Gabriel hung a 'Do Not Disturb / *Bitte Nicht Stören*' notice on the door handle.

'These hotel locks are a disgrace,' Tyrone said. 'I mean, a child could get into these rooms. Any idiot thief.'

Gabriel looked around while Tyrone fulminated.

Housekeeping had yet to tidy and clean the place. The bed was unmade and the remains of a room-service breakfast trolley were waiting to be cleared away. Tyrone helped himself to a leftover rasher of bacon and munched at it.

'Don't steal anything, Tyrone. And if you pick anything up replace it exactly.'

'What the fuck's going on, Gabe? You're a travel writer. What's happening?'

'I told you. I'm trying to gather evidence about an art theft.'

'Is it anything to do with that woman I followed, last year? The one I found out where she lived?'

'Ah. No. That's another story altogether.'

'Right. Up to you, Gabe. I'll ask you no more questions. You're the boss.'

Gabriel wandered around. On the coffee table between the sofa and two armchairs was a stack of estate agents' brochures and cyclostyled information sheets on various properties that Furlan was interested in or had visited, it seemed.

Gabriel carefully shuffled through them. They were nearly all restaurants or cafés of one sort or another – though there were quite a few apartments as well, he noticed. All of them on the main square of Schöneberg. Rudolph Wilde Platz.

'Did he look at any apartments when you followed him?' Gabriel asked.

Tyrone was leafing through a copy of *Playboy* that was on the bedside table.

'What? No. Just restaurants.' Tyrone thought. 'But if he's gonna open a restaurant in Berlin he might need somewhere to live.'

'True,' Gabriel said and carefully repositioned the brochures.

He walked into the en-suite bathroom. Shaving kit. An expensive bathrobe. A lingering smell of a pungent aftershave. Nothing out of the ordinary, he supposed.

Back in the main room he opened drawers, looked in the cup-boards, searched Furlan's empty suitcases. There was nothing, he conceded, that didn't fit Furlan's profile as a restaurant-entrepreneur looking for new Berlin pizza franchises. He felt a slight irritation at his presumption: what did he think he was going to find here that would be somehow incriminating?

'Let's go,' he said to Tyrone. 'I've seen everything I need.'

They stepped out of the room, carefully checking the corridor was clear, Gabriel rehanging the 'Do Not Disturb' sign on the inside door handle. They headed for the lifts.

As they waited, Gabriel realized Tyrone's usefulness to him was at an end. Vollmöller was the key now, not Furlan.

'You can go back to London, Tyrone,' he said. 'I'm really grateful.'

'OK. I'm grateful too, Gabe. I like West Berlin. It's a strange place, well different. I'll be back. Thanks, man.'

There was a ping and the lift doors opened.

Matt Furlan stepped out.

Gabriel was amazed at his self-control. He could see that Matt Furlan was surprised, not to say shocked, to see him.

'Hey, Matt, how are you?'

They shook hands. Furlan was wearing a tan suede blouson jacket and jeans. Gabriel kept talking.

'This is a friend of mine, Denis Ritter. Matt Furlan.'

Tyrone and Furlan shook hands.

'We were just looking at a suite,' Gabriel continued. 'Not for you, I feel, right, Denis?'

'Not at those prices,' Tyrone said. 'It's a joke.'

Matt Furlan laughed faintly.

'I thought you were in Vienna,' he said to Gabriel.

'Just back,' Gabriel said. Tyrone was holding the lift doors open. 'Better run. Tell Dean I'll give him a call. Maybe we can get together.'

'That would be great,' Matt Furlan said, and raised his hand in farewell as the lift doors closed.

'Fuck,' Gabriel said. 'Fuck.'

'Denis Ritter?' Tyrone said. 'Do I look like a Denis Ritter?'

'Better than I should give him your real name.'

'Yeah. Suppose so. Quick thinking, Gabe. Who's he, that geezer? He was always with Furlan.'

'I told you. He's Furlan's brother. Matt.'

'Shit. Lucky he didn't see us coming out the room, then.'

'Yeah. But – that was still bad luck. Grade-two bad luck. It'll have consequences.'

'Furlan and his brother have left Berlin,' Parker Baumgarten told him. 'Flight to Paris last night from Tegel.'

'Right,' Gabriel said carefully. He had decided not to tell her about his encounter with Matt Furlan. 'Maybe he really was looking for a restaurant.'

'Did you find anything significant in Furlan's room?'

'No,' he said. 'Nothing out of the ordinary.'

They were sitting in the small bar of the Alpina Hof, Gabriel drinking beer, Parker a Coca-Cola. This modest hotel had become the informal hub of this MI6/CIA collaboration, Gabriel thought, oddly enough. But maybe that was good, he reasoned, the circle was small, the shared information was confined. And there I go again, he admitted, thinking like a spy.

He took out his cigarettes and offered one to Parker.

'I'll stick to my Kools, if you don't mind,' she said.

They both lit up and smoked for a few moments, reflecting. Parker was gazing into the middle distance and Gabriel took the opportunity to study her more closely. The adolescent boy's hairstyle didn't suit her, he thought. She would look better with something freer and shaggier. He could see her hair was thick and glossy. She had a pretty face. Severity wasn't doing her any—

'What is it?'

'What? Sorry,' Gabriel said. 'I was in a kind of brain fug. Wondering where we might go next.'

'We initiated a twenty-four-hour watch on Hendrik Vollmöller. Nothing significant. Maybe give it one more day now that the Furlans have left town.'

'Yes . . .' He thought. 'I suppose Vollmöller is our only lead.'

'Shall I pick you up tomorrow? Six a.m.?'

'I'll be there, ready and waiting.'

7.

The Vollmöller Surveillance

Gabriel sat beside Parker in her silver-grey Volkswagen Type 3 outside Vollmöller's shabby apartment block in Kreuzberg. It was 6.30 a.m., the third day that Vollmöller had been subject to twenty-four-hour scrutiny. Gabriel felt hungry and thirsty. A quick coffee and a cigarette in the hotel hadn't really set him up for the day. He felt a bit scratchy and grubby and wished he'd had time to shave. Parker, on the other hand, seemed bright and full of vim and vigour. Scrubbed and glowing, he thought. She should definitely let her hair grow longer, he found himself speculating. Everything would be different about—

'Here he is,' Parker said. 'Same time every morning. Mr Punctuality.'

Gabriel peered through the windscreen, interested at seeing Vollmöller in the flesh. A medium-sized, untidy-looking young man, a little on the plump side, with a near-invisible blonde moustache. His shirt tail had not been properly tucked into the back of his trousers. He was wearing a peaked black forage cap that made him look vaguely Russian, Gabriel thought, watching Vollmöller straddle his motorbike and kick it into life. He gunned the motor and sped off. Parker started the Volkswagen and headed after him.

'Don't worry,' she said. 'We know exactly where he's going. He works for a small printing firm.'

She followed him – an accomplished driver, Gabriel noted – as Vollmöller made his way from Kreuzberg to Neukölln, near Tempelhof airport, where Kestner Verlag, Industriedrucker had their small printing factory. Vollmöller parked his bike on the pavement outside and walked in, greeting a few colleagues as he did so.

'What could be more normal?' Gabriel said, trying to keep the frustration from his voice. 'Why would Dean Furlan meet someone like him? Hendrik Vollmöller? What's he got to do with a pizza restaurant?'

'They have a cafeteria inside the works,' Parker said. 'He won't emerge until six p.m. And then he'll go home.' She shrugged. 'He's a very lowly employee. Sweeps the floor. Oils the presses. A man of regular habits.'

'Mystery piles on mystery,' Gabriel said. 'I think I'll head back to the hotel – Tyrone is leaving for London.'

Tyrone handed him two lock-picks.

'What you have here, Gabriel, is a hook-pick and a rake-pick,' Tyrone said. 'In my brief experience here in Berlin, trying out things as an experiment, like, these picks will allow you to open ninety per cent of the locks here. If they don't work, then you'll just have to kick the door in.'

Gabriel looked at the picks. Slim, dark, long-handled pieces of metal with a unique, tiny angled turn at the end. Like incredibly thin daggers, vaguely reminiscent of the keys with which one opened a tin of sardines or anchovies. Or more like dental implements . . .

'Stick the rake-pick in the lock,' Tyrone said. 'Whip it out – that may do the business. If not, then test the pins inside one by one. Very gently. Some will give, some won't. Turn the pick when you feel the pin give. Work down the pins. The lock will open.'

'Right,' Gabriel said. 'I think I've grasped the principle.'

'Practice makes perfect,' Tyrone said. 'Try it out on a few locks. Get a feel for it. My gift to you. A present from Denis Ritter.'

Gabriel opened his wallet and paid Tyrone in pounds what he was still due for his Berlin sojourn.

'What about the taxi to the airport?' Tyrone said.

Gabriel added some Deutschmarks.

'Keep the change,' he said.

They wandered out to the front of the hotel where the taxi was waiting and shook hands.

'I still don't know what the fuck you're really up to here in Berlin, Gabriel,' Tyrone said, sincerely. 'I smell a rat. But mind how you go – yeah? Look after yourself.'

'I'll take every precaution,' Gabriel said. 'Don't worry. Safe journey home. Give my love to Lorraine.'

He waved vaguely at the taxi as it turned out of the hotel parking area and wandered back inside, looking at the two picks in his hand. He was fairly sure he would have no need of them – but you never knew, he told himself. Tyrone's legacy.

He went to the hotel bar and ordered a *kühles Blondes*, a Berlin *Weißbier* with a shot of raspberry juice, a drink that Tyrone had recommended. He sat in the bar drinking his beer – perfectly agreeable – and registered the strange fact that he rather missed Tyrone, his good companion. He had done well, Tyrone – more than well – but to what effect? Furlan had met Vollmöller and had given him something. Vollmöller had been identified. That was all that they had verifiably achieved. What did that mean in the scheme of things? And Tyrone, of course, had been more than well recompensed for this paltry return.

Still, he felt a thin shroud of melancholy descend on him, like a kind of mental drizzle. The Furlans had gone, Tyrone had now gone. Parker had called off Vollmöller's surveillance. Vollmöller appeared to live a life of diurnal rectitude. He went to work at the printer's six days a week. On the way home he might shop, go to a café, visit a small bar and then return to his flat, from which he promptly emerged early the next morning. There was absolutely nothing out of the ordinary. Hence his own melancholic mood, Gabriel realized. What exactly had he contributed during all these days in Berlin? What exactly was the point of all this effortful subterfuge? Then he had an idea. Sunday, he said to himself. Sunday was the day after tomorrow. On a Sunday – a day off work for Vollmöller – everything might change.

Gabriel decided to follow Vollmöller himself. There was nothing to be gained by alerting Parker to his hunch and obliging her to re-engage the CIA surveillance team.

Consequently, he found himself across the street from Vollmöller's apartment block at 6 a.m. on Sunday morning, sheltered by a bus stop and a privet hedge with a good oblique view of the entrance to the building. It was a cloudy but warm day, strangely humid, giving the atmosphere an untypical tropical feel for mid-June in Berlin. He had chosen to use Tyrone's scooter rather than the Taunus – easier to follow Vollmöller's motorbike should the man venture forth. He had an apple in his pocket and a full pack of Gitanes. Let's see if anything might unfold, he speculated, trying to gee himself up. Maybe he'd get lucky.

By midday, he had eaten the apple, smoked six cigarettes and was hungry again; and there was no sign of Vollmöller, who was doubtless enjoying a well-earned long lie-in, he supposed, on his day of rest. He wondered if he should abandon his stake-out and return to the hotel for some lunch. Then, just as he was preparing to leave, Vollmöller appeared. He was wearing a black leather jacket and had a rucksack on his back. He mounted his motorbike and kicked it into noisy life. Gabriel was on his tail seconds later as they motored on in a westerly direction on quiet Sunday streets.

Vollmöller seemed to be taking no precautions – Gabriel never saw him look around once – but he kept a careful distance all the same. They whizzed through Schöneberg and Schmargendorf and eventually arrived at the edge of West Berlin's own forest, the fifteen square miles of the Grunewald.

Vollmöller seemed to know where he was going, heading down narrow paved roads through the forest of pines, beeches and birches towards the artificial hill, the Teufelsberg, constructed from the millions of tons of rubble that the bombed and flattened city provided in 1945. Now capped with fat white towers surmounted by geodesic golf-ball domes packed with listening devices, Teufelsberg was the eyes and ears of the Allied forces' interception of East German radio traffic. A hill built from rubble created by Allied bombing now had become the highest point in West Berlin – perfect positioning to listen in to the chatter on the other side of the Wall. There were too many ironies to list, Gabriel thought, following Vollmöller as he skirted the artificial hill. It was enough to recognize the facts.

Vollmöller parked his bike by some waterworks next to a small lake and headed off at a brisk pace down a gravelled roadway that led deeper into the forest. Gabriel dutifully kept a careful distance, fifty yards back, concentrating on Vollmöller's striding figure, his bouncing rucksack a helpful visual aid. The park was busy. Families wandering around, picnicking, couples sunbathing, people playing games, throwing balls and quoits at each other, children running after dogs – the place was thronged with Berliners enjoying the last clement hours of the weekend.

It was apparent, as they progressed, that Vollmöller was going as deep as he could into the forest, leaving the idling Berliners to their pastimes and heading down ever-narrowing tracks and footpaths. He strode around a small swampy lake and took what looked like a deer-path that disappeared into a dense stand of alders.

Gabriel paused. It might be tricky to follow him now, he thought. The path was too singular, and too narrow. And if Vollmöller was waiting . . . He stepped a few yards to his right and pushed through the screen of alders. He followed a parallel route, making his way through bracken and undergrowth, on what he assumed was Vollmöller's trajectory. The early-afternoon sun slanted dustily through the foliage and the setting, he thought, was ideally bucolic, though he quickly realized, to his frustration, that in fact he now had no real idea where Vollmöller was. He was lost in the Grunewald. He paused by an ancient oak, hearing only birdsong, feeling the wind-pulse of a breeze on his face, listening intently. He assumed this must be a rendezvous of some sort – Vollmöller meeting someone in a secret place they shared in the forest. For some reason he imagined the encounter would have a dubious sexual content to it . . . Who knew what someone like Vollmöller got up to on his Sunday off?

Perhaps he should go back to the track, he thought, then simply follow the deer-path and see where it led him. Vollmöller had no idea who he was – even if they bumped into each other it needn't necessarily seem suspicious: just another nature-lover out for a ramble. A *'Guten Tag'*, a smile, a tip of the hat, as it were. But how to rediscover the deer-path? He turned through 360 degrees. He had no idea what direction to go in. Fuck and shit.

Then he heard someone sneeze – three times.

Gabriel headed carefully in the direction of the sneezer. Obligingly, the person sneezed again, twice. Gabriel pushed around the side of a willow – and then drew back. He had a view of a sizeable clearing, about fifty feet wide, with an old beech tree right in the middle and surrounded on three sides by a line of Douglas firs. Vollmöller was standing there, jacket off, rucksack at his feet, blowing his nose vigorously. Thank the Lord for hay fever, Gabriel thought, carefully edging round to a small clump of young, dense robinias. He crouched down, watching. Vollmöller was about ten yards away from him, he calculated, happily unaware that he was being watched, and, indeed, giving the impression of a man entirely confident in his absolute solitude.

Vollmöller took a sheet of paper from his rucksack and a hammer and, Gabriel supposed, a nail. He then paced out the distance from his rucksack to the beech tree – about ten long strides – and proceeded to nail the sheet of paper to the trunk. He then walked stiffly back to the rucksack, still counting, his lips moving. He dropped the hammer, cracked his knuckles, inhaled, exhaled, flexed his shoulders and stooped to remove something from the rucksack.

It was a piece of wood, oddly shaped, like a haunch of meat. Then Gabriel saw Vollmöller open the end of the wooden container and remove a gun – an automatic weapon of some sort. He saw a heavy pistol with a drop-down magazine in front of the trigger. It had a long barrel. More intriguingly the wooden holster was then fitted by Vollmöller to the grip of the gun to form a stock, like a small rifle. The word 'Mauser' came into Gabriel's head for some reason. He had seen films in which such guns were used, he was sure.

Vollmöller braced himself, spreading his legs, and took aim at the target he'd nailed to the beech tree. Gabriel held his breath. Why had he not brought Tyrone's Minolta camera? Because it had been returned to Parker Baumgarten, of course. However, here he was, a witness, and his eyes would have to record everything.

Vollmöller fired three times in quick succession. *Blam! Blam! Blam!* Flat retorts, not particularly loud, the surrounding vegetation acting as an efficient damper to the percussion.

Gabriel heard birds squawking and the flutter of panicked wings. It suddenly became very quiet. Gabriel saw Vollmöller step forward and advance to the beech tree where he inspected the success of his target practice.

Then Vollmöller visibly froze. The sound of children's voices singing – boys' voices, treble voices – carried through the trees, gaining in volume, voices singing a song that Gabriel knew intimately, a song he had heard many times on the radio: 'The Happy Wanderer'. The voices, the song, grew louder – maybe twenty or thirty singing, Gabriel thought – and beneath the melody the sound of tramping feet.

Mein Vater war ein Wandersmann,
Und mir steckt's auch im Blut;
Drum wandr' ich froh, so lang ich kann,
Und schwenke meinen Hut.

Faleri,
Falera,
Faleri,
Falera ha ha ha ha ha ha,
Faleri,
Falera,
Und schwenke meinen Hut.

The singing immediately spooked Vollmöller. He rushed back to his rucksack, broke the gun into stock and weapon and thrust the two pieces inside. He picked up his jacket and the rucksack and blundered quickly out of the clearing, racing back down the deer-path.

Gabriel stayed, not moving, letting the singing die away. 'I love to be a wanderer,' he reflected: it could be my theme song, soundtrack to my life. He stood and stepped carefully into the clearing. Who could have been singing? he thought. A troop of young boy Scouts, he supposed, or some similar children's organization. Berlin kids at a weekend camp in the Grunewald, out for a day's rambling . . .

He crossed the clearing towards the great tree. Vollmöller had forgotten to remove his target and Gabriel was curious to see how accurate he had been.

He paused in front of the beech tree, with its wide, pale grey trunk, and looked at Vollmöller's target, feeling his throat thicken with tension and alarm.

It was a picture of a smiling John Fitzgerald Kennedy, thirty-fifth President of the United States of America. Three small, ragged bullet holes punctured his face.

8.

The JFK Predicament

Gabriel pushed Vollmöller's bullet-riddled JFK target across the desk towards Peter Carlyle. Parker Baumgarten was sitting on Carlyle's side of the table – a small symbolic illustration of the power balance in this encounter, Gabriel thought.

Carlyle looked at the punctured image, and ran his fingertips over the tears.

'I guess this is evidence of some sort,' he said.

'Pretty hard evidence of some sort,' Gabriel said, adding diplomatically: 'I'd have to say.'

'Well done, Gabriel,' Parker said. Then turned to Carlyle. 'We'd ceased surveillance on Vollmöller. Gabriel took up the tail on his own initiative.'

Loyal Parker, Gabriel thought, shooting her a quick smile of thanks.

'What's your take?' Carlyle said. He was sweating. He mopped his brow with his handkerchief. 'Haven't they heard of air conditioning in West Germany?' he added, vaguely, waving a hand in front of his face as if to generate a breeze.

'My take,' Gabriel said, 'is that Hendrik Vollmöller will try to assassinate President Kennedy when he comes to Berlin. When exactly is that, again?'

'June twenty-six,' Parker said. 'He's here just for the day – not even staying a night.'

'Do you have a complete itinerary of his visit?' Gabriel asked.

'That's classified,' Carlyle said.

'Sir, Gabriel is assigned to the Agency,' Parker interjected. 'We wouldn't know about Vollmöller without him. We wouldn't know the Furlan connection.'

'Where is Furlan, anyway?' Carlyle said, almost as if irritated.

'We haven't any recent information.'

'Well, he's not in Berlin,' Carlyle said. 'That's a plus, I guess.'

'But Vollmöller is,' Parker said.

'OK.' Carlyle paused. 'Let's bring him in. Reduce the threat to zero. Who's our guy in the Berlin police? Heinrich?'

'Ödön Hempel,' Parker said.

'Hempel, that's it. Get Hempel to bring in Vollmöller on some charge. Keep him under lock and key until after June twenty-sixth. Problem solved.'

'I'll set things in motion,' Parker said. 'The sooner the better.'

The meeting was over. Gabriel and Parker left Carlyle's office and walked down the corridor towards hers.

'He looks, forgive me, a bit like a man out of his depth,' Gabriel said, quietly.

'He's under a lot of pressure,' Parker said. 'The US President visits Berlin. It's a global news event. Eyes of the world on the place. Cold War brinkmanship, et cetera.' She shrugged, opening the door to her office. 'You could be right. Maybe Carlyle is out of his depth. What's that British saying? "People rise to the level of their incompetence." I've always liked that.'

Gabriel sat down opposite her.

'Good for you, Gabriel,' she said, leaning across her desk. 'I thought Vollmöller was a dead end.'

'I think I was just bored, you know,' Gabriel said, with false modesty. 'Nothing else to do on a Sunday in Berlin.'

'Do you want to come on the raid? Five a.m. tomorrow morning, I'd say. I'll get Hempel and his team on it.'

'Wouldn't miss it for the world,' Gabriel said. They both took out their cigarettes and lit up. The mood was mildly jubilant, Gabriel reckoned. Something had happened. There was a plan.

And in that moment of jubilation, he noted, something suddenly changed in his relationship with Parker. Or, rather, hers with him.

'Hey,' she said. 'Here's an idea. Why don't you come and have supper at my place tonight? I found a German butcher who can cut a decent T-bone. And I've a good bottle of Valpolicella.'

'Sounds great,' Gabriel said, managing what he hoped was a sincere smile. For some reason, he wasn't sure if he was ready for a *diner à deux* with Parker Baumgarten. Still, needs must. 'Needs Must', he thought – maybe that should be carved on my tombstone.

'I'll get you Kennedy's itinerary,' Parker said. 'Don't worry. Carlyle doesn't need to know.'

'I have a feeling that'll be very useful,' Gabriel said. 'Where exactly in Berlin do you live?'

Parker Baumgarten's apartment was in the Westend district of Charlottenburg in a quiet street off Branitzer Platz. On the way there in his taxi, Gabriel looked at the swarming shoppers on the Kurfürstendamm and the neon glowing in the advancing dusk. People were streaming out of cinemas and the café terraces were full. When he wound down the window of the taxi he could hear pop music coming from the bars – reputedly over a hundred of them up and down the wide thoroughfare. As ever, it was hard to remind oneself that this was an island of freedom, commerce and capitalism in a dour communist country. This was new Berlin – but the old, grey, unsmiling one surrounded it on all sides. It was easy to forget – but forgetting was a mistake in this city, he was coming to realize.

Parker lived in a modern 1950s building and her apartment was on the top floor. Gabriel rang the bell and a buzzer admitted him. The lift in the foyer took him up to the fifth floor. He had brought a small bunch of flowers as a token, ranunculus, and a bottle of Montepulciano, should the Valpolicella run out. He felt oddly nervous, as if he were on a first date. We're colleagues, he told himself – this is only a way of getting to know each other better, not a prelude to some romance.

Parker opened the door. She was wearing a pale blue shirt and black pedal-pusher trousers. It was odd to see her made up, Gabriel thought, lipstick and mascara – suddenly the efficient CIA operative no longer firmly in view. She led him into the sitting room with its floor-to-ceiling plate-glass windows. She gestured westwards.

'Apparently you could see the Olympic Stadium from here – before they built that office block,' she said. 'Thank you for the flowers and the wine. Give me one minute and I'll be back. I have to check on the potatoes.'

Gabriel looked around the room in some amazement once she had slipped into the kitchen. There was a bold checked rug – yellow and green – on the parquet floor. Two leather-and-chrome armchairs faced a daybed covered in a red throw and piled multi-coloured cushions. The coffee table between them was made of glass and had some low stacks of books on it and a flat black wooden bowl filled to the brim with lemons. There was a large TV set on a trolley and on a wall span of irregular shelves and stor-age cabinets facing the tall windows he noticed a turntable and an amplifier, wires leading to two separate speakers. Stereo, my God, he thought. On the walls were abstract prints and film posters. He felt he was in the home of some young artist or designer. Parker Baumgarten had surprised him. He thought of his own home – his shabby, chintzy, over-crowded cottage with its second-hand furni-ture, decorated in a style that wouldn't have been out of place in the 1920s. It was stimulating to see how Parker lived. He wondered if he could give number 3 Ruskin Studios a more modern 1960s spin. Maybe he'd ask her advice.

She offered him the choice of a bourbon on the rocks or a dry martini and he opted for the bourbon. Then she passed him a plate of small cheese squares pronged with toothpicks. The bourbon and the cheese went very well together, he said, and complimented her on her taste in interior decoration.

They ate their T-bone steaks and *pommes dauphinoises* in the kit-chen, seated opposite each other at a perspex-and-aluminium table. They finished the bottle of Valpolicella and opened the Montepul-ciano. After the steaks they paused for a cigarette and then Parker produced some kind of sweet flat almond cake with cream – a *Sand-torte*, she said.

During the dinner she told him more about herself. Born and raised in Cincinnati – a city with a large German immigrant popu-lation, she informed him. Her father, Ernst Baumgarten, had gone there, fleeing Nazi Germany in 1933, married a local girl and joined the police force, eventually becoming a detective.

'So I always knew I wanted to be a cop,' Parker said, with a shrug. 'Of some sort.' After college, she had applied to join the FBI but was headhunted and diverted to the CIA. Two years in Paris and two years – and counting – in Berlin.

'That's my story,' she said. 'What about you? You're a writer. What're you doing in MI6?'

'Good question,' he said. 'It's a long, complicated business – to do with my brother, my late brother, and some serious trouble he got me in. Somehow, I found myself working – part-time – for MI6. But then part-time became more and more full-time. It's rather overtaken my old life.' He paused, feeling sorry for himself, as usual. 'I am writing another book, if you can believe it, but I see my old life sort of disappearing into the distance and I find myself wondering if I'll ever get it back – or am I in too deep?'

'Well, at least it's in a good cause,' Parker said, almost apologetically.

'That's what everybody tells me,' Gabriel said, petulantly. 'But this life – this spying, covert life – isn't something I chose, unlike you. It was kind of thrust upon me.' He paused again. 'Or, rather, it's like quicksand, sucking me down.'

'What do you say to a schnapps?' Parker asked, clearing away the plates.

'Hello, schnapps. Yes, please.'

Gabriel lit another cigarette while she went in search of the bottle and two small glasses, almost like thimbles on squat orange stems. They moved back into the sitting area.

'Sorry to talk shop,' Gabriel said. 'But what's happening with the Vollmöller raid?'

'There's a delay. Day after tomorrow,' Parker said. 'Hempel can't get a team together before then.'

'Just as well,' Gabriel said, raising his tiny glass. 'In that case I'll have another schnapps, if I may, Agent Baumgarten.'

She laughed and topped up their glasses. The mood was definitely mellowing, having been a little stiff and shyly formal at the start of the evening. Gabriel wondered if he was becoming a little drunk. That would be a bad idea, he realized.

They talked about themselves again. Parker confessed she had been engaged – a Frenchman she'd known in Paris – but had broken it off when she was posted to Berlin.

'It would never have worked. Funny how you know that, instinctively.'

'Trust your instincts.'

'What about you, Gabriel?'

'Well, I am in a relationship, I think. Of sorts. But it's very complicated.' He managed a smile, thinking fiercely – almost tearfully, all of a sudden – of Faith, recalling their days at the cottage in Claverleigh. 'It blows hot and cold. In a maddening, compulsive way.' He cleared his throat, exhaled. 'She's quite a bit older than me – not that I'm bothered about that,' he added.

He looked at Parker and smiled at her. She was twenty-eight or twenty-nine, he had calculated. This was the sort of person who should be commanding, driving his emotional expectations, not Faith Green. Parker was attractive, lively, clever, accomplished – and lived in some style, a style that reflected her interesting, unique personality. He felt a weight descend on him, sensing that parallel life flash by him, feeling the sharp, poignant stab of missed opportunities, the wrong road taken. What was that word? *Anomie?* Was that right? *Taedium vitae?* There should be a word for that feeling – a deep soulful ruefulness that your life has not gone according to plan. There was probably a precise German compound noun for that state of being: heart-aching-ruefulness. *Herzschmerzreue* . . . Would that work?

'Are you OK, Gabriel?'

'Yes, yes. I was just thinking about something.' He clenched his fists. 'My sad, stupid brother and the unwanted legacy he left me. I should probably go,' he said abruptly and stood up.

He thanked Parker for the delicious meal – the best steak he'd ever eaten – her excellent company, a wonderful few hours, just what he'd needed.

She walked him to the door and Gabriel knew there would be a farewell kiss, after so much shared over the evening, such honesty. And there would be, he knew, the unspoken option of more.

He leant forward to kiss her farewell, taking the initiative, thanking her once again, and angled his head so she couldn't kiss his lips. She got close, kissing the corner of his mouth, and Gabriel, noting the extra impress of her lips, received the implicit message. He stepped back quickly, seeing her momentary quizzical look, as she wondered how she had somehow misinterpreted the signals, the moment. She smiled brightly. All forgotten. No matter.

Gabriel walked through Westend for a while, heading for the bright lights of the Kurfürstendamm, knowing there would be plenty of taxis there to carry him back to his hotel. The night had cooled and the cloudy sky reflected West Berlin's raucous neon glow – like a burnished yellow sodium shield above his head – a nightly visual rebuke to the cowed brethren in the dark East. He felt disquieted. Perhaps he and Parker should have kissed, fully – and, granted, maybe not have slept together that first night, but initiated the possibility of an affair – a proper, passionate, adult relationship kindled. Maybe he was being a fool. Too late now, fool. What could be more agreeable than to kiss a young woman like Parker and hold her slim, tall body in his arms? He kicked angrily at a pebble and it flew into the side of a parked car with a sharp ping. Shit. What did she make of him? he wondered. Perhaps she would be grateful, as she readied herself for bed, thinking back, that nothing more sensual had ensued. Dodged a bullet, as the saying went. Who wanted to be in a relationship with a tormented, unhappy, fucked-up writer? Conceivably, he had done her a favour.

9.

The Raid

It was still dark at 5 a.m. Still night, effectively, though there was the faintest glimmering of light creeping onwards, infusing the dark – not illuminating, exactly, Gabriel thought, but just about allowing you to see more clearly: buildings, cars, people, taking on their shapes.

He was standing behind an unmarked police van about fifty yards down the street from Vollmöller's apartment block. There were six uniformed police officers and the detective, Ödön Hempel. He and Parker were talking quietly to each other in German.

Gabriel reached inside his jacket and touched his shoulder holster. It was odd being armed, he felt, but Parker had insisted he be issued with the weapon. He had signed a chit for the holster, the gun and its several clips of ammunition. They were both carrying the same handgun – a High Standard HDM, as it was called. It was a .22 ten-round pistol with a fixed silencer, or 'suppressor'. Quite a heavy weapon with a long barrel but incredibly quiet, so Parker had told him. The noise of its firing was no louder than clicking your fingers, she said. He eased his shoulders, feeling the belt and braces of the holster tight around his body. He wondered what his editor, Inigo Marcher, would think of his author: armed, standing with police in a Berlin street before dawn, about to raid the flat of a suspect? He realized he had to stop this persistent rail, this plaint. These rhetorical questions he kept asking himself were beginning to drive him a little insane.

He glanced over at Parker. She was in a one-piece navy overall with a blue windcheater with 'CIA' on the back. Gabriel was wearing a long brown tweed deer-stalking jacket in a red check and with big flap pockets. The collar was lined with leather and there were leather patches on the elbows. He had never been deer-stalking in his life but this jacket had travelled the world with him. And here it was having an outing in Berlin.

Parker wandered over.

'We'll go in five minutes,' she said, with a smile. 'This is thanks to you, Gabriel.'

'I just feel a bit odd, that's all. What with this gun, et cetera.'

'Vollmöller has a gun. So should we.'

'True.'

'I assume you've had weapons training,' she said.

'Yes. Sort of. A while ago,' Gabriel replied, thinking back to the brief target practice he'd had at the former chicken farm in Leyton. At least he wasn't lying.

He was relieved that there had been no perceptible fallout from the supper they had shared together. Parker's attitude to him seemed unchanged. Perhaps it was only he who was aware of the supposed undercurrents flowing, he wondered. Over-analysing, over-sensitive, second-guessing, as per usual.

The detective, Ödön Hempel, approached. He and Gabriel had been introduced earlier. Hempel was a stocky, blonde-haired young man, with an eager, infectious manner. He was a CIA agent in the Berlin police force, earning two salaries. He spoke good English and was clearly curious about Gabriel.

'You come in last, Mr Dax. Agreed? We all go first.'

'I won't argue with that. Please call me Gabriel.'

'I am Ödön.'

'You just tell me where to stand, Ödön. I'll happily leave every-thing up to you and Parker here.'

Hempel looked at his watch.

'OK. Let's go.' He issued instructions to the policemen and they set off at a slow jog up the street towards the apartment block. Two of the men, Gabriel noticed, were carrying sledgehammers. Another man had a three-foot-long jemmy. They all had holstered automatics and truncheons at their belts. Gabriel strode after them.

The front door caved in after three sledgehammer blows and the team raced inside, heading up to the second floor where Vollmöller had his room. There were agitated shouts from the other tenants as they realized something untoward was going on in their building. A man appeared in his nightshirt on the stairs and was shoved brusquely aside by a policeman. He began to yell imprecations. Gabriel stepped carefully around him and followed the others up the stairs. He arrived as the policeman with the jemmy wrenched open the door of Vollmöller's room, 210, with one swift, wood-splintering heave. The police thundered in, guns drawn, shouting. And then quickly stopped shouting. Gabriel peered over their shoulders. No Vollmöller.

Gabriel and Parker stood in Vollmöller's rank room, looking around. Down below, Ödön Hempel and his team were remonstrating loudly with the inhabitants of the building. A faint smoke-grey light crept in through the window. Dawn was upon them.

There had been a quick search but there was no sign of the Mauser pistol. Gabriel noted that some aspects of Vollmöller's lair met the clichéd expectations. The bed was filthy, the sheets a greasy saffron, sebaciously shiny from the weeks and months of contact with Vollmöller's unwashed naked torso. A small Primus stove on a rickety table, a blackened saucepan and opened tin cans were testimony to his limited short-term culinary needs. No nude pin-up pictures, however. Taped images of German footballers filled half a wall – Borussia Dortmund seemed the favoured club.

It was the smell – or, rather, the smells – that Gabriel noticed more than anything. The lingering whiff of fatty-spicy cooking, underlaid by cigarette smoke, underlaid by sour body odour, under-laid by human effluvia. The sickle-edge of a chamber pot poked out from beneath the bed. The universal smell of poverty, Gabriel recognized, observing that Parker had covered her nose with a handkerchief. It triggered something in his memory. Where had he smelt that same fetid pungency before? He remembered: in Lucian Applegate's filthy cottage, thinking that tense visit now seemed a lifetime ago.

They stepped out on to the landing where the air was clearer.

Things seemed calmer downstairs – the residents retreating to their rooms.

'Can you believe this loser wants to assassinate the President of the United States? Has the gall? The presumption?' Parker asked. She seemed genuinely offended.

'Loser' in this context was not a familiar term to Gabriel, though, having seen Vollmöller's desperate pit of a room, he understood the implications of the word immediately.

'Aren't they always "losers", in that sense?' Gabriel said. 'Starting with John Wilkes Booth.'

Parker lit a Kool, thinking.

'I just don't get it,' Parker said. 'Where the heck is he? How did we miss him?'

'He knew we were coming for him,' Gabriel said. 'So somebody must have tipped him off.'

'That's not possible.'

Gabriel looked at her and shrugged.

'It's the only explanation.'

10.

The Itinerary

The next morning, Gabriel was in his hotel bathroom, shaving, when he heard the telephone ring. He quickly wiped his face and picked up the phone.

'Morning, Gabriel, it's Parker. I'm downstairs.'

'Give me five minutes,' Gabriel said.

He found her waiting for him in the lounge. She looked a bit abashed.

'I still can't get over the Vollmöller fiasco,' she said. 'Furlan's gone, his brother is gone – and now Vollmöller's disappeared. Do you think this is an abort of some kind?'

'It looks like it,' Gabriel said. 'But my hunch would be that's exactly what they want it to look like.'

'Interesting point. Yeah.'

They ordered some coffee.

'There was a meeting yesterday,' Parker went on. 'A debrief after the Vollmöller raid. There was a top-brass CIA man there, Frank Sartorius, over from the States – he said he knew you.'

'Yes, we met in Guatemala,' Gabriel said, trying to look unperturbed.

'And someone from MI6, British, called Faith Green. She said she knew you as well.'

Gabriel took a sip of his coffee. So Faith was in Berlin. He felt the usual sudden agitation – a little depth charge of emotion detonating inside him – and told himself to calm down.

'Yes, I do know her, also,' he said, in as throwaway a manner as possible.

'Kennedy will be in the British sector for a while, at the Branden-burg Gate, hence MI6, I guess.'

'Makes sense,' Gabriel said, though his mind was active. Faith would make contact if she wanted, he realized. There was nothing for him to do. Just wait.

'So, the upshot of this meeting we had,' Parker continued, 'was that we should form a sort of Vollmöller cadre, within the general security operation around the President. You, me, Hempel – and Hempel's police team – overseen by Frank Sartorius, focusing on the Vollmöller threat.'

'Let me know what you want me to do,' he said.

Parker handed him a document.

'That's JFK's itinerary,' she said. 'It all starts on Sunday twenty-third, when he flies into Cologne.'

Gabriel studied the schedule, and was immediately impressed at how demanding it was. Sunday in Cologne, then everybody moves to Bonn. Speeches, receptions, a meeting with Chancellor Adenauer, a dinner, more meetings. Monday picks up again in Bonn. Lunch and a brief address. Adenauer once again. Then another press conference, then a meeting with the Mayor of West Berlin, Willy Brandt, the day concluding with a dinner at the American embassy.

Tuesday 25 June, it all kicks off anew, he saw, no respite. Meetings, then a helicopter to Hanau. Speech to the US 3rd Army division. Lunch, then by car to Frankfurt.

Gabriel looked at Parker.

'I'm already exhausted and this is only the third day.'

'It's insane, I know. But it's what they do.'

Frankfurt – another speech. Then helicopter to Wiesbaden. Another meeting, another reception.

'Cologne, Bonn, Hanau, Frankfurt, Wiesbaden. Then Berlin,' Gabriel said. 'On Wednesday. Just here for the day.'

'And what a day.'

'My God.'

'Yes. Air Force One should arrive just before ten a.m.'

Gabriel looked at the Berlin itinerary.

'Wow. Crowded,' he said.

'Sartorius would like to meet you. Monday morning, eleven a.m.'

'Of course. Where?'

'We'll let you know in good time.'

They chatted on for a while, then Parker left. Gabriel felt unsettled, not only because he knew that Faith was now in Berlin but because Frank Sartorius was back in his life as well, a re-encounter imminent. He thought back to Guatemala and the comings and goings in the Alcázar-Plaza. What, if any, was the connection between Sartorius and Furlan? Furlan had only said he knew 'of' Frank Sartorius and that might well be true, Gabriel supposed. They had been together in the same hotel but he had no evidence of any other significant contact between them, apart from seeing them chatting briefly in the lobby, just the once. Maybe that was unsurprising, maybe not. Guatemala City was not Berlin. It was a much smaller metropolis and the forces that ran the place, the country, were fairly obvious, clearly defined. And then Furlan had come to Berlin – and had now left, apparently. But now Sartorius was in town.

He decided to go for a stroll to clear his brain, try to distract his mind from the ongoing situation. Shut your thoughts off, he told himself, just wander, be a *flâneur* in this strange city, look around you.

He sauntered out into Kreuzberg with no sense of a destination. He would just let the phenomena of the daily life of the city wash over him – and stimulate him, maybe – and allow chance to haphazardly direct his aimless wanderings. He might stop for a beer, a coffee, a bite of lunch. He had a feeling that once Kennedy arrived in Berlin on Wednesday life would be as fraught and tense as it could be. Relax, enjoy yourself, he thought, trying to inject some *joie de vivre* into his day. Make the most of it, he encouraged, *carpe diem*.

He had no real idea where he was headed. On his right-hand side he could see the planes coming in to land at Tempelhof airport, a fact that positioned him somewhat and meant that he was heading eastward. So be it, that was all he needed to know. He took a left turn and then a right turn and found himself in a small parade of shops at a busy intersection around a small park, many roads running off the junction that the park afforded. The day was warm enough to sit outside and he found a café with some pavement tables and ordered a *Milchkaffee*.

He lit a cigarette and attempted to switch his mind off. Easier said than done. He found himself watching the traffic as it moved around the small central island opposite him with its little copse of trees and bushes. Vans and trucks, cars and lorries, he saw, all proclaiming the services and wares they provided, circled the roundabout: plumbers and electricians, florists and builders, decorators and removal men, dry-cleaners and TV installers. All these jobs, all these trades, all these people busy. Not to mention, he thought, the passers-by, all of whom would have professions, great and small, themselves: civil servants and nannies, cleaners and postmen, bricklayers and psychiatrists. This is what the witnessed life of a city offered you, he said to himself, every city, often unremarked: the omnipresent world of work, the relentless buzz of people going about their business, their daily occupations – how they made ends meet, put food on the table, paid the rent. And this was just one city in Germany, one city in Europe, one city in the world. Multiply the effect in Valparaíso, Shanghai, Turin, Cape Town, Bordeaux, Sydney, Cairo, Buenos Aires, Lagos, San Francisco – to name just a few. The world and its work; the world at its unending business, dizzying, universal, he reflected . . .

The idea came to him in an instant: another excellent idea for a book. Take three emblematic professions – he thought fast – butcher, hairdresser, taxi driver. Perfect. Go to ten cities around the world and look at these professions and how the different cultures, customs, climate, geography, politics and religion affect these simple universal jobs. There are hairdressers in Ulan Bator, he told himself; taxi drivers in São Paulo, butchers in Karachi. Title: *The Job*. His next book after *On the Beaten Path* . . .

Gabriel smiled. He could practically sense Inigo Marcher's glee. And he himself felt charged, exhilarated that his semi-conscious mind was still operating as he sat at this unremarkable corner of Kreuzberg drinking his *Milchkaffee*. Maybe there was a life to be led once he had rid himself of this burden of espionage. He left a few coins on the table and wandered off, thinking further, excited: at least one city in each continent, he thought, make the concept truly global . . . A lot of travelling, research, a good two years' work, he reckoned.

He turned a corner by a narrow canal and found himself face to face with the Wall. *Die Mauer.* Somehow the German made it more potently symbolic – but it was an undeniably shabby one in this context. A seven-foot, eight-foot-high edifice of thick, dirty breeze blocks, sun-wilted weeds sprouting at its base, surmounted by metal Y-brackets with rusty barbed wire tangled around them. On the other side, he knew, there was a raked, sandy no-go area, more wire and bricked-up empty buildings, all overlooked by watch-towers with searchlights and machine guns, patrolled by guards with attack dogs. He turned his head and saw such a tower, not far off. A guard was looking at him through binoculars and Gabriel gave him a wave.

Suddenly, he saw the scene as a surreal tableau. Himself, alone at this seedy angle of the Wall, with its smirched blocks of concrete, its brambly, rusted coils of barbed wire, standing in the lukewarm sun-shine of a June day, the narrow green gloomy canal in front of him, a scent of meadowsweet from somewhere, thistle-floss drifting, the East German soldier in his tower, binoculars focused, the Westerner raising his arm in comradely greeting. Click. The decisive moment captured.

Gabriel gave the soldier a thumbs-up, turned and headed back to his hotel. He walked home with more confidence, remember-ing his moment of inspiration, refining his new idea, thinking he'd draw up a list of twenty or thirty cities and whittle it down to the ideal ten. For a few minutes he had forgotten about Parker and Faith, Sartorius and Vollmöller, and the upcoming visit of the President of the United States to Berlin. His Kreuzberg stroll had been a necessary stimulus, a reminder of the person he was – his 'true self', as Katerina would have put it. He felt better prepared, all of a sudden.

Back at the Alpina, as he picked up his key from reception, the clerk handed him a message. He opened it.

'Kempinski. Room 387. Dinner at eight. Sunday.'

Faith. He had been summoned.

II.

Faith in Berlin

Gabriel sat in the wide marbled lobby of the Kempinski waiting for Faith. He had announced himself at reception and they had telephoned up to her room. He was wearing his dark blue linen suit and a peach-coloured tie and had shaved very closely. He checked his fingernails, the shine of his shoes, eased his collar. He was going to be calm, he told himself, thoughtful and intelligent. Nothing rash or spontaneous – even though he could sense the heart-thrum of anticipation at seeing her, feel the sweat moisture gathering in his armpits. We have a brain, he told himself, true – but fundamentally we are animals and the animal body will simply ignore the brain if it feels like it.

He saw her step out of the lift and look for him. He raised his hand and stood with a lurch, trying to breathe normally. She crossed the lobby towards him, smiling. She was wearing a suit of black-and-white pebbled tweed with over-sized black buttons and a white silk blouse and looked very glamorous, he thought, already a little overwhelmed, though she was still eight feet away from him. She held out both her hands, her smile constant, and Gabriel took them, feeling his throat tighten. She leant forward and kissed his cheek, whispering, 'You look very handsome, Gabriel. Berlin is obviously your kind of city.'

What the hell does that mean? Gabriel wondered, silently accepting the compliment.

'You look wonderful yourself,' he said. 'Very *soignée*.'

She closed her eyes tightly and froze for a moment. Irritation? Boredom? Duty? Gabriel wondered. She was so hard to read.

'Shall we go straight in to the dining room?' she said. 'We can have our drinks there.'

'Of course.'

They made their way to the Grill-Room restaurant and were directed to a corner booth. The place was gratifyingly dark, Gabriel thought, and began to relax. Faith ordered a Dubonnet with ice. He asked for a whisky. A waiter brought huge menus with tassels. Pale shelled almonds and green gherkins in little bowls were provided.

'Let's take our time,' she said. 'No hurry. It's so lovely to see you.'

'Great,' Gabriel said and took a huge gulp of his whisky. For some reason he felt like getting very drunk. Was that happiness? Or madness?

'They're very pleased with you, here, the CIA,' she said, lowering her voice, though there was nobody within hearing range, their booth ideally discreet.

'Oh. Good.'

'The Vollmöller identification. They would never have found him without you, they acknowledge that.'

'Well, now he's disappeared.'

Faith frowned.

'I know,' she said. 'Annoying.'

Then she smiled.

'How have you been, my Gabriel?'

He moaned a bit about Berlin, this role he had, how it was messing up his life, interfering with his writing. She nodded, commiserated, reminded him about the complex times we were all living in, how Berlin was the focal point of the Cold War and how crucial Kennedy's visit was.

'Imagine if some deranged creature like Vollmöller had his way. That's why you're here. By chance, you seem to be at the . . .' She searched for the word. 'The . . . The "nexus" of this conspiracy. Is that the right word?'

'It is – but the word I'm interested in is "conspiracy". Who's conspiring?'

She spread her hands, confessing.

'I don't know. It's an American thing.'

They were interrupted by a waiter and they ordered their food.

Faith opted for *Brathecht mit Specksalat* – fried pike with bacon salad – and Gabriel chose his usual *Wiener Schnitzel*.

'That's not very adventurous,' Faith said.

'To tell the truth I'm not that hungry,' Gabriel said. 'Maybe I'll have an adventurous pudding.'

'I want to know all about your new book,' Faith said, handing him the wine list. 'I can't wait. You choose the wine, money no object.'

Gabriel ordered an expensive bottle of Grüner Veltliner and told her about *On the Beaten Path*.

'What a very clever idea,' she said. 'I predict a huge success.'

Gabriel let her insincerity wash over him. He didn't care. He was simply enjoying being in her company again, he acknowledged, with all the sparks and kicks and swerves and percussions that implied. He realized, somewhat to his astonishment, that he felt he knew her well now. Those five days, five nights, at Rose Cottage had changed everything. She was as much a familiar to him as anyone else he had been involved with, not counting her maddening evasions and shifts of mood.

They finished the Grüner. They both ordered *Spritzkuchen* – a sweet fritter, speciality of the Kempinski – washed down with a small vintage schnapps with their coffees.

'What a lovely meal,' Faith said and reached for his hand, rubbing a fingertip over his knuckles. 'Shall we go upstairs?'

Gabriel looked into Faith's eyes. They were lying in her bed in room 387, naked beneath the tangled sheet, facing each other.

'That was nice,' Faith said. 'I've missed you.'

Gabriel inched closer and kissed her gently on the lips.

'I think I may be falling in love with you,' he said, suddenly wondering why he had spontaneously made this declaration. Just to push her, he supposed, see what she said in return.

She smiled.

'Only "think"?'

'It's something that dawns on you, bit by bit,' he said. 'In my limited experience, anyway. Not a blinding revelation. What about you?'

She frowned, thinking.

'I do know I love being with you . . . But that's not quite the same thing, I suppose. Is it?'

She reached down and took his cock loosely in her hand, feeling it thicken.

'Bit by bit,' Gabriel said.

'Well, let's wait and see, then.'

He pulled back the sheet from her breasts, kissed her small dark nipples, kissed the little white dots of her burn scars, her 'leopard spots' as she called them. He rolled on top of her and her legs parted as she drew up her knees.

'Shall I stay the night?'

'Not a good idea, I have to leave for Bonn at the crack of dawn.'

'I'd better not waste any time, then,' he said and bent to kiss her lips again.

PART SIX

Berlin
East Sussex

24–27 June 1963

Monday 24 June 1963

Gabriel stood in the wide square opposite the town hall – the Rathaus – in Schöneberg, looking at the final touches being made to the high, long podium that had been attached on to the facade of the building. Teams of workmen were installing vast, swagged red-white-and-blue banners behind it. Directly opposite was a wide TV-camera platform, still under construction, the sound of multiple hammers coming from beneath shrouding tarpaulins.

Gabriel wandered around Rudolph Wilde Platz. This was where Furlan had met Vollmöller, he reminded himself. All of Furlan's café and restaurant sites had been on this square or just nearby. Everything told him that Schöneberg should be the Vollmöller cadre's focus. The square was in fact a wide, huge, extended rectangle, he saw. A few trees planted within grass borders were dotted around, here and there. Just as well, he thought, an enormous crowd was expected for Kennedy's speech, predicted at 200,000 – or more. What did 200,000 people gathered in one place look like? he asked himself. No stadium on earth held that number. He wandered off to a taxi rank – it was time for his meeting with Frank Sartorius.

The meeting was taking place in a rented office in a building in Schmargendorf, off Kissinger Platz. The room was basic. A trestle table with six chairs, carpet tiles and shabby vertical blinds at the windows. There was a large map of West Berlin on an easel showing the Allied sectors and the meandering course of the Wall. A chrome thermos of coffee and some styrofoam cups were set out on a trolley. There were two telephones on the table.

When Gabriel arrived, early, only Ödön Hempel was there, sipping coffee. They shook hands and talked about the failure of the

Vollmöller raid. He was a cheerful fellow, Gabriel thought, Herr Hempel. He didn't seem that put out by the setback.

'We will catch him,' he said. 'Vollmöller is essentially a stupid person – like many criminals. That's why they're criminals. That's why we catch them.'

'But even a stupid criminal can evade capture if he's being helped from the inside,' Gabriel said. 'How did he know about the raid?'

'He didn't know,' Hempel said. 'It was his good luck, our bad luck.' He shrugged. 'We will get him, don't worry, Mr Dax. We have even contacted his parents. They are – what is the word? – strangers?'

'Estranged.'

'*Exact.* They will tell us if he tries to make contact.'

Then Parker arrived with Frank Sartorius and an aide who was introduced simply as Walcott. He was carrying two bulging briefcases.

Sartorius seemed pleased to see Gabriel. He was in his usual pale blue seersucker suit. His moustache seemed denser but his geniality was unchanged. They reminisced about Guatemala City.

'Some change of scene, huh?' Sartorius said.

He then went to make a phone call, picking up the phone with its long extension cord and going to stand in a corner while Walcott laid out sheets of paper and files.

Gabriel poured Parker a coffee and one for himself.

'How was your weekend?' Parker asked.

'Not bad. I went for a walk and thought up an idea for a new book.'

'So your trip to Berlin hasn't been entirely wasted.'

'Well, I've got to know you as well.'

To his surprise he saw a blush redden her cheeks.

'Nearly over,' she said. 'Just got to get through Wednesday.'

Sartorius finished his phone call and everyone sat down. Walcott was taking notes.

To Gabriel's surprise, Sartorius told him that he wanted Gabriel to join the press corps at Tegel airport and to follow the motorcade in one of the many buses laid on for journalists.

Walcott interjected.

'You'll see you have a press pass among your papers, sir,' he said.

Gabriel opened up the file in front of him and saw an oval lapel badge with a string attached. It had 'PRESSE' printed on it and his name and a number: '18'.

'You'll be in the first bus,' Sartorius said. 'Right behind the President's limousine and the Secret Service car.'

'May I ask why?' Gabriel said.

'We had some intel that maybe there was a threat – someone might be posing as a journalist or a photographer,' Sartorius said.

'Furlan?'

'Maybe. You know what he looks like so we figured that was the best place for you to be. Scrutinize the pack.'

Gabriel picked up another lapel badge with string attached. It was larger, the size of a postcard. It had a crest on it, a stamp and another number: '223'.

'What's this?'

'It's your CIA accreditation,' Parker said. 'Keep it in your pocket. Then put it on when you join us here in Schöneberg.'

Sartorius explained further. There would be a command post in three vehicles at the southern edge of the town hall square.

'Inspector Hempel and his team will be based there,' Sartorius said. 'That's where we'll coordinate the search for Vollmöller.'

'They're talking about two hundred thousand people being in that square,' Gabriel said. 'How're you going to find one man?'

Hempel held up his hand.

'Thanks to you, Mr Dax, we know that Vollmöller's weapon is a Mauser C96. He will have to be closer than ten metres to the podium to guarantee any kind of accurate shot. Our men will be in the crowd at the very front. We will all have walkie-talkies. And . . .'

He searched the papers in front of him.

'We have your excellent photograph.' He held up Tyrone's photograph of Vollmöller. 'All our men will be issued with this photograph. He's not a difficult fellow to spot, I would say.'

Gabriel gave a slight smile. Tyrone would be pleased to learn how his handiwork was being employed. Gabriel looked at Parker, she was studying the photograph. Sartorius was talking quietly to

Walcott. There was something wrong, Gabriel said to himself. The mood was calm, confident. Shouldn't there be more tension and worry . . . ?

Parker took over.

'After the visit to Checkpoint Charlie the motorcade will come to the rear of the town hall. I'll meet you there,' she said. 'That's when you change into CIA mode.'

'Right,' Gabriel said, feeling relieved.

'You have your weapon,' Parker confirmed.

'Yes.'

'You should be armed. On the day.'

'OK.'

They went through a few more details, giving an estimation of the time Kennedy would be in Schöneberg, and a vague approximation of the length of his speech. After Schöneberg he was visiting a US Army base.

'At that point we can relax,' Sartorius said.

'If anything's going to happen it'll be in Schöneberg,' Gabriel said. 'I'm convinced.'

'You know, Gabriel,' Sartorius said, a little condescendingly, Gabriel thought, 'I've been coordinating security for US Presidents since Harry Truman. We prepare for the worst – but usually absolutely nothing happens. Absolutely nothing. That's our job, if you will, dealing with non-existent worst-case scenarios.' He reached across the table and shook Gabriel's hand. 'However, we're very grateful for your contribution. Invaluable.'

The meeting broke up. Sartorius and Walcott went into a huddle. Gabriel and Parker lit cigarettes while Hempel searched his pockets and took out a small cigarillo with a plastic filter. Gabriel offered him his lighter.

Then Gabriel saw that Sartorius was about to leave. He wandered over and caught him at the door.

'Frank, can I have a quick word?'

'Sure.'

Walcott slid by with his briefcases and waited outside on the landing.

'Did you ever meet Dean Furlan in Guatemala City? By any chance?'

'No. That's why you were – are – so valuable.'

'It's just that he was always in the Alcázar. I wondered if your paths had crossed there.'

'No.'

'He seemed to know who you were, that's the only thing.'

'Everybody knew who I was in Guatemala City. It's a small town. When you're CIA head of station you're in the spotlight, like it or not.'

'Right,' Gabriel said. 'Of course. See you on Wednesday.'

He went back to rejoin Parker and Hempel. Something at the back of his mind was worrying him, but he couldn't be precise – couldn't nail down what it was.

'We have a Berlin-wide search on for Vollmöller,' Hempel said. 'Every hostel, poor people's refuge, cheap hotels. He can't hide for long.'

'Well,' Gabriel said. 'He just has to hide until Wednesday, I suppose.'

Hempel smiled his unperturbed smile. And offered his hand to shake.

'I see you on Wednesday at the Rathaus,' he said.

They shook hands, then Hempel shook Parker's hand and left.

Gabriel looked at his watch: 12.45. 'Fancy a spot of lunch?' he said.

'Thought you'd never ask.'

2.

Tuesday 25 June 1963

Gabriel shot the clip out of his High Standard automatic and counted the ten bullets. Then shoved it back into the grip. He wondered why he'd done this. Perhaps, as ever, to underscore the incongruity of the situation he found himself in. He slid the gun back into the shoulder holster and laid it down on the bed alongside his press credentials and his CIA pass. He was looking forward to leaving this life behind him, yet again, to such an extent that he had booked a plane ticket from Berlin to London on Thursday – maybe a bit precipitate, he was aware, but he wanted his old life to resume as soon as possible.

Still, there had been that night with Faith in compensation. He thought again of their warm, accomplished lovemaking, both familiar with each other's bodies as well as showing genuine affection and pleasure in each other's company, he sensed. And there was his almost-declaration of love. He wondered why he had felt moved to say what he had. It was a kind of spontaneous, gentle provocation, he thought – to force her to confront the reality of their relationship, however strange and unlikely it was, and its curious, sporadic nature. He brought her naked body to mind and felt himself stirred, aroused. But it was more complicated than that, he knew: it wasn't just a man and a woman who were physically attracted to each other, no, there were power relationships in play, also. Power relationships that favoured her, he considered, ruefully. Yet when she had suddenly needed refuge and security she had turned to him and the balance slightly shifted.

God, he thought, stop. Stop thinking about her. What would happen when Berlin was over? He didn't like to consider it. There was Varvara Suvorina to deal with. And Kit Caldwell in Moscow. How to evade those two unwelcome obligations? Faith Green's various snares still held him tight in their annoying grasp.

He put his gun and his ID passes away in a drawer that had a lock and turned the key. Time for breakfast.

Later that morning, something drew him back to Rudolph Wilde Platz. He stood in the middle of the wide square in front of Schöneberg's town hall. Loudspeakers were being fitted to lamp posts. There were more police there today, he noticed, standing around, chatting, and he saw a dog-handler with an Alsatian leading the sniffing beast over the planted garden areas. He wandered back to the café where Furlan had met Vollmöller, and where Tyrone had taken his now emblematic photograph, sat down on the terrace and ordered a coffee. It was a breezy day but the sun was shining between the flotillas of clouds that scudded overhead. He wondered if there was any clue in the various catering premises that Furlan had visited. What sort of clue? he asked himself. Whatever his motives, Furlan had doggedly been going through the studied motions of a man looking for a site for his pizza restaurant.

He thought on. The Schöneberg town hall was the seat of government in West Berlin – hence Kennedy visiting it, hence the significance of the keynote speech and the huge crowds that would be attending. That made him concerned – Rudolph Wilde Platz was also the perfect place for an assassination attempt. The symbolic vision of American support for 'freedom' dashed and destroyed . . .

Something was still nagging at him. It was Sartorius's monosyllabic declaration that he hadn't ever met Dean Furlan. He thought back to another moment in the hotel in Guatemala City. Furlan had been smoking a cigar on the terrace. He, Gabriel, had been talking to Sartorius in the bar. But he was almost a hundred per cent sure that when Furlan entered and crossed the bar to the foyer and looked over towards them, he had seemed about to raise a hand in semi-covert greeting. To Sartorius? Or someone sitting beyond them? Or was he going to scratch the back of his neck? And then that glimpse of them in the foyer – talking. Perhaps they were just exchanging views on the day's weather. It was the slimmest evidence. But then Furlan had asked him if he knew Sartorius. Yet Sartorius had that covered as well, claiming everyone in Guatemala City knew who he was.

He exhaled, ordered another coffee and lit a Gitanes. It was a lovely summer's day: enjoy it – tomorrow would be complicated, to put it mildly. He should switch off, he told himself, try to stop the whirring, noisy machinery of his brain.

He thought back to his lunch, yesterday, with Parker. They had found a small café round the corner from the meeting place with a few outside seats under some bright umbrellas advertising something called SPEZI. They ordered beers and *Wurst*.

'When in West Berlin . . .' Gabriel said, spooning some mustard on to his plate. What was it about German mustard? An entirely delicious variant on an old familiar.

They sat and chatted, ordered another beer and smoked their cigarettes. Then Parker reached into her handbag and drew out a paperback copy of *The Wine-Dark Sea*, and asked if he would be so kind as to dedicate it to her.

He took out his pen and wrote: 'For Parker, comrade in arms, affectionately, Gabriel Dax.' He thought that struck the right tone and noted her pleasure as she read the inscription, thinking again that this was the type of young woman he should be wooing – with a view to marriage and a family, even – but knowing at the same time that he was in thrall to someone altogether more disturbing, compelling and alluring. Why was that? What was it about Faith Green that set his senses into action, his pulse quickening, his pheromones agitating? There was no logical explanation, he realized: it was just the random conjunction of two people that somehow triggered this reaction.

He closed his eyes for a second and called Faith to mind – her sly smile, her long face, her absolute self-confidence. Fate, he decided. There was nothing one could do.

'Shall we have a coffee?' he asked Parker.

'I'd better go,' she said.

They stood and, after a small pause, kissed each other goodbye.

'Bad procedure, I know,' Gabriel said, smiling. 'Who cares? And, anyway, I'm only a unit.'

'We'll forgive you, Unit A. See you tomorrow,' she said. 'Fingers crossed.'

3.

Wednesday 26 June 1963

Gabriel waited with the gathered journalists and photographers as Air Force One – a Boeing 707 – pulled into its parking area at Tegel airport and cut its engines. Out on the apron was the welcome committee: Chancellor Adenauer; Willy Brandt, Mayor of West Berlin; a French general whose name he had forgotten; and other dignitaries, as well as a guard of honour and a band.

Gabriel eased his shoulders, aware of the holster and its straps attached around his upper body. He was wearing his dark charcoal-grey suit with a sleeveless maroon cardigan, a white shirt and a black knitted tie with cream bands. The cardigan was there to – he hoped – disguise the bulk of the High Standard automatic he was carrying. The cardboard oval of his 'PRESSE' pass dangled from his lapel button, his name inscribed on it and a unique number below.

The door opened and John Fitzgerald Kennedy stepped into view and gave a brief wave. He was wearing a mid-grey suit, a white shirt and a navy-blue tie, and was carrying a homburg hat in his hand. Why the hat? Gabriel wondered. It was a blustery day – maybe it was part of the accoutrements required by a visiting head of state.

Gabriel turned away and headed back to the buses, all labelled 'PRESS POOL'. He was indeed in the first bus, he was glad to see, the number on his pass granting him this privilege. He climbed aboard and was swiftly joined by other journalists from the world's media. He found a seat behind the driver and felt a thud as another journalist sat heavily beside him. He looked round. He was a solid-looking older man with an unruly shock of grey hair and a dense near-white moustache, tinged brown with nicotine. His badge said: 'Sam M. Goodforth'. Gabriel offered his hand and they shook.

'*Gainesville Daily Register*,' Goodforth said with a pronounced Texas accident.

'*New Interzonal Review*,' Gabriel replied.

'And what might that be, sir?'

'Political monthly. Published in London.'

'Pleased to meet you . . .' He peered at Gabriel's pass. 'Mr Dax.' He tugged at his tie. 'Last time I was in Germany was 1945 – a dog-soldier in the US Army. I'm not totally at ease, if you get my meaning.'

'Everything's different in West Berlin,' Gabriel said. 'The natives are very friendly now.'

'Are we allowed a smoke in this here bus?' Goodforth said.

'I think so,' Gabriel said.

Goodforth took out a soft pack of cigarettes and offered one to Gabriel. Picayune was the brand.

'I only smoke French cigarettes,' Gabriel said, showing him his Gitanes.

'You must be a true-blue intellectual, then, Mr Dax,' Goodforth said, and seemed to find his observation amusing, embarking on a slow wheezing laugh as he lit up his Picayune.

More journalists joined as the motorcade began to take shape, as far as could be discerned from the Press Pool bus. There was an initial arrowhead of white-jacketed, white-helmeted motorcycle policemen, then a curious-looking truck with a high-raked row of wooden benches on the rear designed to hold some two dozen photographers, all with a view back to the huge Lincoln Continental open-topped limousine that held Kennedy, Brandt and Adenauer, in that order, all able to stand and wave at the crowds that lined the road leading out of the airport. Secret servicemen stood on little platforms that were pulled out from the chassis of the Continental. Then there was another limousine filled with secret servicemen in their dark suits and sunglasses and then Gabriel's 'Press Pool' bus. And beyond that more buses and cars transporting the huge entourage that a travelling President of the United States required.

Gabriel looked out of the window. On either side of the motorcade there were more white-jacketed motorcycle cops. It was quite a show – the finale of Kennedy's triumphant visit to West Germany. Gabriel swallowed. He hoped it wouldn't end in bitter, shocked tears.

He stayed on the bus at the first stop. Kennedy was giving a short speech to trade unionists at the Congress Hall, the *Kongresshalle*, a dramatic modern building with a sweeping, undulating roof like a collapsed pancake. He stepped out as the journalists returned for the resumption of the journey. He quickly scanned faces to see if there was anyone who resembled Furlan or Vollmöller but almost instantly realized that it was most unlikely that they could have inveigled their way into this highly vetted throng. He took his seat beside Goodforth again as the convoy moved on to the Branden-burg Gate in the British sector. There were to be no more speeches until they arrived at the town hall in Schöneberg.

At the Brandenburg Gate another platform had been erected to give the President a view of the Wall and this totemic monument now just in East Berlin by a few yards. Great red curtains had been hung within the gate between its tall columns to block the view down Unter der Linden, and a long rambling message in English on a giant poster in front of the building reminded the President of unfulfilled pledges made by the Allies at the Yalta and Potsdam conferences.

Gabriel joined the assembled journalists and watched as Kennedy looked out over the wall. Here, it was only breeze blocks, Gabriel noted, with no barbed wire. It looked like something one could shin over in seconds.

Then it was on to Checkpoint Charlie in the American sector. Gabriel looked at his watch: midday. The Schöneberg speech was scheduled for 1 p.m. They were running a bit late, he noted.

The Checkpoint Charlie podium afforded more of a view of East Berlin. In fact, there were East Berliners standing at their apart-ment windows, waving and cheering, as Kennedy – now noticeably serious-looking, Gabriel thought – stared out, wordless, over the crossing point. Here there was barbed wire, and the so-called 'kill zone' flanked with its steel-girder tank traps.

Then Kennedy spontaneously moved into the crowd, shaking

hands, smiling, talking. Gabriel thought that this was foolhardy – and the agitation amongst the secret servicemen bore this out. The crowd were adoring, rapt, cheering, screaming, but there was no doubt that this moment on the carefully choreographed procession presented Kennedy at his most vulnerable. He was gently ushered away to the Lincoln Continental. Gabriel, for some reason, noted the huge car's number: GG 300.

The motorcade drove on through a blizzard of ticker tape towards Schöneberg. Gabriel felt weary: they had been under way for three hours. Yet Kennedy had been on the go for three days and showed no sign of flagging. He wondered what special fuel these politicians ran on. Goodforth was nodding, head slumped forward. Gabriel took some deep breaths. Now they were entering the most dangerous and crucial hours of the day.

Parker was waiting for him beside the rear entrance of the Rathaus. He swapped his press badge for his CIA identification and she led him up a back stairway into a wide lobby area. Refreshments were being served to the dignitaries – coffee and sandwiches. Dozens of people milled around. The large windows gave on to Rudolph Wilde Platz, now totally crammed with West Berliners. Gabriel wandered over to the windows and looked at the vast crowd. He had never seen so many people together in one place – people standing, patiently waiting – it was almost disturbing.

'They reckon there may be four hundred thousand out there,' Parker said, joining him. She was wearing a black trouser suit and had fastened her hair back from her forehead with a couple of tortoiseshell clips.

'Are you ready?' she asked.

'Apologies, but I need to pee,' Gabriel confessed. 'It's been a long morning. Excuse me.'

He was directed to the lavatories at the far end of the lobby. Gabriel went in and did his business and washed his hands. As he emerged he saw Kennedy himself step out of a toilet – guarded by a secret serviceman. Yes, we are all human beings, Gabriel thought, and we all need a piss from time to time. He watched the President wander over to a window that overlooked the square, reading small index cards held in his hand. The secret serviceman was keeping a discreet distance as Kennedy was clearly preparing for the defining speech of his one-day visit. Gabriel rejoined Parker and indicated Kennedy by the window.

'The man himself,' Gabriel said, inclining his head. They were only ten yards apart and he looked closely at him. Kennedy was tall – six foot, a bit over, maybe, about my height, Gabriel thought – and very thin. Almost buttock-less, Gabriel saw, judging by the slack fabric of his trousers at his backside. He was tanned and his reddish-brown hair was densely thick, severely parted on the left with a kind of bouffant quiff that seemed almost rigidly held in place.

Then an aide came to fetch him and he turned and crossed the floor towards a meeting room on the other side of the wide foyer where he was clearly expected, Willy Brandt waiting at the door. As Kennedy passed, Parker saluted, the gesture making Kennedy look round and smile at them both. He raised his hand.

'Thank you,' he said. And strode on.

'Well, that was something,' Gabriel said.

To his vague astonishment, he saw that Parker had tears in her eyes.

'I will never forget that,' she said, fiercely. 'Never in my entire life.'

Gabriel was about to remonstrate – a man passing by had merely said, 'Thank you' – but decided against.

'Shall we go and join the Vollmöller cadre?' he said.

The Vollmöller cadre was to be found at the southern edge of the square and consisted of three police vans tightly parked. Now he was out in the square the presence of the hundreds of thousands of people was even more tangible – individual and generic. Close by, he could see identifiable men, women and children – and then beyond them the people became a crowd, a vast amorphous mass of human beings, occupying the entire space of the square and beyond – waiting. It was destabilizing, he thought, even though the mood was buoyant and expectant. What was disturbing was that the crowd, filling the square, filling the streets that led into it, was so closely packed. People were standing shoulder to shoulder – so close they were touching – far too many people to be policed or controlled. One panic would let loose terrible, fatal mayhem. Panic stimulated by a shot being fired, for instance, he thought, suddenly confronting the seriousness of the business before them.

Sartorius was there in a CIA windcheater, with Ödön Hempel and some ten policemen. They were all given the Tyrone photograph of Vollmöller and a small walkie-talkie. They checked their channels were all working.

'Move close to the front,' Sartorius said. 'Right under the podium. If he's here that's where he'll be.'

He paused as huge cheers erupted.

Kennedy, Brandt and Adenauer had climbed up to the podium, followed by the entourage, German and American, and were waving to the crowd. Another man stepped up to the microphone.

'Who's he?' Gabriel asked.

'He's called Otto Bach,' Hempel said. 'President of the West Berlin parliament. A very boring man.'

Bach began to speak – his amplified voice booming out from the loudspeakers positioned throughout the square – and Hempel said to his team, '*Auf geht's*,' whereupon they all moved off into the crowd. Gabriel and Parker followed and quickly split up. Sartorius remained behind.

Gabriel found it surprisingly easy to move through the packed crowd. He held up his CIA accreditation and people willingly stepped back and made space for him, smiling and polite. He soon found himself at the base of the podium in a scrum of press photographers, all taking endless pictures of the speaker and the key individuals behind.

Gabriel turned his back on the podium and began to scan the faces in front of him: men and women – young men and women. Berlin was a city of young people, these days. Hatless in the main, their faces were full of joy and vivid expectation. The mood was infectious, Gabriel thought, these people sensing what Kennedy's actual presence was bringing to this unique city, how history was being made in front of their eyes. Vollmöller mustn't be allowed to spoil it, he thought. No. He imagined the catastrophe of shots being fired, the charismatic President falling, mortally wounded.

He clicked on his walkie-talkie.

'Come in, Parker,' he said.

'Copy.'

'How's it looking?'

'We're all spread out. We've got it covered as best as possible, I'd say.'

Gabriel stared around him. He would know Vollmöller – he had covertly been a long time in his company, unlike the others – and he sensed he would instantly recognize him. He looked at the faces around him, five deep, deliberately keeping his gaze within Mauser range, as he termed it – no point in searching beyond the close perimeter to the podium. And it wouldn't be an easy shot, he thought – aiming upwards, trying to find an angle where the lectern and the microphones weren't in the way.

He felt a slight panic overwhelm him and once again, for the umpteenth time, cursed the circumstances that had conspired to put him in this position. But, then – maybe the anger and the panic sharpening his vision – he saw Vollmöller.

The man had shaved his head and his fair moustache – he was completely bald – and he was wearing a short-sleeved sky-blue shirt with a red tie. But nothing could disguise the protruding lower lip or the permanent hangdog, resentful nature of his expression. He had a Lufthansa Airlines bag over his shoulder, Gabriel saw, no doubt containing the Mauser.

He calculated, quickly. Vollmöller was about fifteen yards away from him. A lot of people in the way, there had to be someone closer.

He called up Parker – opened all the channels on his walkie-talkie.

'I've seen him. Shaven head, pale-blue shirt with red tie, Lufthansa bag, standing to the left of the podium. Very close in.'

'Copy that,' Parker said and then translated everything into German.

Otto Bach finished speaking and Chancellor Adenauer stepped up to the microphones. More cheers from the crowd.

Gabriel saw two of Hempel's men steadily making their way through the press of people towards Vollmöller. They separated and approached him from either side. A gun was discreetly drawn, pressed into his back, and both of Vollmöller's arms were grasped. Words were whispered in his ear. He seemed to slump for a moment, tried ineffectively to shrug off the grip on him and then surrendered once more. The Lufthansa bag was removed from his shoulder. He was led away, swiftly. The crowd, gazing at the podium, waiting for Kennedy, seemed not to notice the small disturbance.

'Got him!' Parker said, gleefully. 'Well done, Unit A.'

Back at the cadre base Gabriel watched Vollmöller being cuffed and shoved in the back of one of the vans. Hempel's men were exuberant – grinning, shaking hands and slapping shoulders. Mission accomplished – Vollmöller in custody. Hempel had removed the Mauser from the Lufthansa bag and was showing it to Sartorius. Gabriel looked at him as he examined the gun. His mood wasn't even remotely exultant, strangely; not even pleased – it was more calm, more comprehending. Sartorius beckoned Parker over and started issuing instructions. Gabriel stepped away and looked back at the podium.

Adenauer finished speaking and gestured for Kennedy to take his place; he did so, followed by his interpreter. The ecstatic din that greeted him was enormous. A collective spontaneous effusion of – what? – love, gratitude, hope, adoration. It was as if he was the most famous person in the world – and he probably was, Gabriel thought, but he was worried. Kennedy stood there, smiling widely, a bit overwhelmed, waiting for the cheering and the screaming to die down.

Gabriel looked across the square. There were two six-storey 1950s blocks of apartments facing the town hall. Every apartment had a balcony and every balcony was filled with spectators, glad to have this privileged view. Except one. Top floor on the very left. There was no one on the balcony and Gabriel could see that, above it, there was an open widow, a net curtain billowing from it. Then a hidden hand grasped the curtain and pulled it in. Gabriel strained his eyes. There was a sign on the balcony railings, but it was too far away to be read. He looked around and spotted a policeman with a pair of binoculars hanging from a short cord around his neck. Gabriel made his way towards him and showed him his CIA accreditation. He pointed at the binoculars.

'*Darf ich?*'

The policeman unslung his binoculars and handed them over. Gabriel focused on the balcony. The blurred sign sharpened through the lens. '*VERKAUFT* '. Sold . . .

His mind went into overdrive as he handed back the binoculars – thinking almost manically. Furlan, yes, of course. Furlan had been looking for restaurant premises but when Tyrone and he had searched Furlan's hotel room there were lots of agents' brochures advertising apartments around Rudolph Wilde Platz as well. He felt a sudden nausea as he understood what was happening. Apartments. Furlan had bought an apartment on the square.

He called Parker on his walkie-talkie.

'Parker, follow me. The apartment block on the left opposite the Rathaus. Top floor, left-hand side. I'm going there now.'

'What? What's going on? I've got to go to—'

'Follow me.'

Gabriel realized he couldn't traverse the square with the crowd pressing forward as Kennedy was about to speak. He ran down a side street into a little park. This was the edge, the fringe of the huge crowd on the square. Here he could make his way faster. He ran around the back of the crowd, and then up Belziger Straße, looking for the rear entrance to the apartment block.

He heard Kennedy begin to speak – the flat Bostonian vowels ringing out through the loudspeakers. Then Kennedy paused to let his interpreter render his words into German.

Gabriel ran on, panting. He passed the rear of the first apartment block and turned left down Meininger Straße. Here was a side entry to the second building, the one he was interested in. He pushed open the doors into a small lobby area. The place was empty – everyone out on the square in front of the town hall. He began to race up the stairs, deliberately not taking the lift – these were fire stairs, service stairs, he supposed – counting the floors as he went. He reached the top, paused, leant forward, hands on knees, inhaling great draughts of air. He had to get fitter, he admonished himself, cut down on the cigarettes.

He straightened up, equilibrium of sorts returning. The last apartment on the left, he recalled, recalibrating his position within the block, pushing open a door that led to a corridor servicing the top-floor apartments. Empty. He took a few paces, still trying to calm his breathing. There it was: Apartment 601.

He listened. There was a TV set on inside, very loud. He could hear Kennedy's voice as he launched into his speech once more.

Gabriel reached into his jacket and removed Tyrone's lock-picks. Blessed good fortune, he said to himself. He inserted the rake-pick into the keyway of the door lock, trying to find the pins to flip up above the shear-line in the cylinder. He wished that he had listened more attentively to Tyrone's instructions and advice and had prac-tised more. He whipped the rake-pin out and listened for the pins clicking back into place. Nothing. He tried the hook-pick. Same result. He felt a sob in his chest. He'd have to shoulder or kick the door down. So be it. He grasped the doorknob and braced himself. The knob turned and the door opened. It wasn't locked.

He stepped inside. He left the door very slightly ajar behind him, hoping Parker was on her way.

The TV volume was very loud. He moved forward. This was a sitting room with the empty balcony giving on to the square. A duplex apartment – there were stairs to an upper floor. The TV was showing Kennedy on the podium talking, pausing, then the German translation. The place was full of cardboard boxes and packing cases. The former owner moving out, he assumed.

There was a woman lying on the floor amongst the boxes. Dead – he sensed instantly. He stooped over her. She had a bloodied bruise on her forehead but it was the unnatural position of her head related to her torso that told him her neck had been broken. He looked around – there was a small brown paper parcel tied with string on the floor beside her. She had wiry, dyed fair hair and looked to be in her fifties, he thought. Who had killed her?

He reached into his jacket and removed his automatic from the shoulder holster, checking that the safety catch was off. He began to climb the stairs as quietly as possible, relieved that the TV was blaring.

The door to the bedroom upstairs was ajar. Gabriel paused on the landing, holding back, and peered in cautiously. A table had been pushed close to the window and a man was sitting on a chair behind it. A rifle with a telescopic sight was resting on two pillows placed on the table, pointing out towards the town hall. The man was wearing some sort of uniform suit, navy blue. There was a large black leather shoulder bag on the floor beside the table. A peaked cap was placed on it.

Gabriel kicked the door open, levelled his automatic.

'Stand up, step back, and kneel down,' Gabriel said.

The man froze. Gave a slight shudder.

'I can shoot you in the back, if you prefer,' Gabriel said. 'Move away from the rifle – now. Raise your hands.'

The man stood, raised his hands and stepped back. Then he turned.

It was Matt Furlan.

There was an embroidered badge high on the sleeve of his jacket – a bugle in a circle. He was wearing a grey shirt with a blue tie. A postman's uniform. Gabriel recognized the logo of Deutsche Bundespost.

'Kneel down. Hands behind your head.'

Matt Furlan slowly complied.

'You,' he said, staring at Gabriel. 'Fuck me.'

'No, thanks.'

He stared at Gabriel intently, as if the force of his gaze could disarm me, Gabriel thought.

'Keep your hands behind your head,' Gabriel told him, hoping that Parker was on her way. He was holding the gun, his grip tight, with his arm fully extended, aware of the High Standard's unusual weight, the muzzle trembling slightly from the effort of keeping it trained on Furlan. Then Furlan spat at him, the blob of spittle falling short on the floor.

'I should've killed you for smashing my cousin's nose in,' he said. 'He has to breathe through his mouth for the rest of his life.'

'My condolences.'

Furlan nodded to himself, as if he'd just realized something.

'Mr Dax, please listen to me. I warn you. There will be serious consequences. Think about it. There is a way out of this situation.'

'Yes, there is. My way. I assume you were the man who killed Padre Tiago. Is that right? You're the crack-shot in the family, yeah?'

'I don't know what you're talking about. Listen, Dax, don't be a fool.'

'Stop talking.'

Gabriel glanced out of the window. There was the town hall, the podium, President Kennedy at the bank of microphones about two hundred yards away. So easy.

Furlan dropped his right hand and reached behind him, searching for a back pocket.

Gabriel shot him twice in the chest, the High Standard making barely a noise: like clicking your fingers, Gabriel remembered.

Furlan went down very quickly – the proverbial sack of potatoes, Gabriel thought. A puppet with its strings suddenly cut. Thump.

Gabriel bowed his head. Exhaled. He felt a tremor shudder through his body.

Parker Baumgarten came into the room. Breathing heavily from the stairs. Her gun in her hand.

They looked at each other. Then Parker looked at Furlan, face down on the floor, the sniper rifle resting on its pillows. The room with a view.

'Fuck,' she said. 'Just in time.' She holstered her High Standard. Gabriel did the same.

'Why did you shoot him?' she asked.

Gabriel hunched his shoulders.

'I assumed he was going for a gun. So I took no chances.'

'Right thing to do. Who is this guy?'

'Matt Furlan, Furlan's brother.'

'Jesus.'

'Yeah. I'd met him a couple of times.'

Parker went over to the body, turned it slightly and removed a small automatic pistol from Furlan's back pocket.

'Just as well. A Beretta 950, if I'm not mistaken.' She showed it to him. 'Neat little killer.'

She put the gun in her pocket and stepped over Furlan's body to look more closely at the sniper rifle.

'Oh, shit,' she said.

'What?'

'This is US Army issue.' She pointed to a serial number on the side by the trigger. 'It's a modified M1D Garand with a folding stock.' She picked it up and folded the metal stock back against the barrel, shortening the gun dramatically. 'Handy. Used by special forces, paratroopers, you know.' She paused. 'And assassins.'

She picked up the postman's bag from the floor and slid the rifle into it.

'Neat,' Parker said. 'Postman knocks on the door. Parcel for delivery . . . The lady downstairs opens the door. Sees the postman, smiling. A parcel for me? *Wunderbar.*'

Gabriel saw how everything must have panned out. Why hadn't Furlan locked the door behind him? Maybe the woman struggled, was harder to kill. Maybe he was running late, the speeches had started and he had to make sure he was properly set up.

'What do we do now?' Gabriel said.

'Leave him there.'

Parker closed the windows, moved the table to the side, carefully put the pillows back on the bed. The place had returned to being a bedroom once again – with a dead postman on the floor.

Gabriel followed Parker down the stairs. She put the bag with the rifle on a sofa and, glancing at the dead woman, walked out to the balcony. Kennedy's speech was still under way. Gabriel turned the volume down on the television and joined her.

The view from the top-floor balcony was spectacular. Kennedy was speaking to the enormous, rapt, silent crowd, apparently without notes, the huge red-white-and-blue banners behind him shifting busily in the stiffish breeze. His amplified words boomed out through the speakers.

'All free men, wherever they may live, are citizens of Berlin, and, therefore, as a free man, I take pride in the words, "*Ich bin ein Berliner*."'

Then there was huge applause from the crowd and a chant began: 'Kenn-ed-y, Kenn-ed-y!' Kennedy acknowledged the ovation, making little chopping gestures, a kind of wave with his right hand. He stepped back, smiling, from the microphones and Willy Brandt took his place, ready to make his speech.

Parker frowned.

'It should be "*Ich bin Berliner*",' she said. Then thought: 'No, I guess it kind of works.'

She went back inside. Gabriel followed and closed the glass doors to the balcony. Parker took the Beretta from her pocket and wiped it down with a handkerchief, then placed it in the right hand of the dead woman.

'A thief disguised as a postman is shot by the flat-owner before being killed herself.' She shrugged. 'It's a story, of sorts. Maybe Hempel can make it stick.'

'Can he do that?'

'Anything will do for a while as long as it's not a failed assassination attempt. Give me your gun.'

Gabriel took out his High Standard and gave it to her; Parker handed him hers.

'Let's say I shot Furlan. It makes everything simpler.' She gave an ironic smile. 'It's something I'm allowed to do, after all.'

'Can I give you a piece of advice?'

'Of course, Gabriel. You've done an incredible thing here. Incredible.'

'Don't tell Sartorius. Tell Peter Carlyle.'

'Why?'

'Just a hunch.'

'I don't get it.' She frowned. 'Sartorius will find out.'

'Yeah. But not yet. It's important that Carlyle knows. First.'

'OK. We'll do it your way.'

They had a final look around. Willy Brandt was now winding up his speech. He called for a moment's silence. The huge crowd went quiet and the so-called 'Freedom Bell' in the Rathaus's high tower began to toll. Gabriel shivered as goose-pimples erupted over his body. He held his hands out in front of him – they were shaking slightly, strengthless, he felt. He sensed the tremor spread through his being again as he thought about what he had just done. He tried to close his mind down. Concentrate on the here and now, he told himself.

'Shall we go?' he said.

'Yeah. We're all through here.' Parker lifted the receiver off the telephone and placed it on the tabletop. 'Phone engaged. Might buy us a bit more time.'

They left the TV set playing and closed the door quietly behind them. There was no one in the corridor and they took the stairs down to Meininger Straße, now busy with people wandering away from the square, the great day over, history made.

Parker slung the leather postbag over her shoulder and they joined the elated spectators for a minute or so before peeling off and cutting round to meet the others at the Vollmöller cadre.

As they approached, they could see an ambulance backing up to the three police vans at the edge of the square, beacon lights flashing. The square was emptying remarkably quickly. The podium was deserted, everyone back inside the town hall.

Gabriel and Parker increased their pace. They found Hempel standing behind the police vans looking a bit shocked. Two ambulance men were zipping Vollmöller's corpse into a black plastic body bag.

'My God. What happened?' Parker said.

Gabriel saw Vollmöller's slack, blunt face for a second before the zipped-up sides of the bag covered it. The bag was heaved on to a gurney and wheeled off to the ambulance.

'We were just transferring him,' Hempel said, still looking a bit shaken. 'I was covering him and he went for my gun. I had no choice.' He opened his jacket to show his own High Standard, back in its holster.

'I thought he was cuffed,' Gabriel said.

'We uncuffed him for the transfer.' Hempel wiped his face with a handkerchief. 'My mistake. He was a maniac. I had to stop him.'

Snap, snap, Gabriel thought: no one would have heard a thing.

'Where's Sartorius?' Gabriel said.

'He left earlier. They're having a banquet in the town hall. He was invited.'

So Sartorius didn't witness Vollmöller's shooting, Gabriel realized. How convenient.

The ambulance drove away, no siren – this was not an emergency, after all. The three of them watched as it sped off down Dominicus Straße.

'*Mein Gott! Scheiße,*' Hempel said, fiercely, seemingly very aggrieved. 'Just when you think you can congratulate yourself, you know, everything goes wrong.'

'Such is life,' Gabriel said.

'What about you two? Anything interesting?'

Gabriel threw a warning glance at Parker.

'No,' he said. 'False alarm.'

4.

Thursday 27 June 1963

It was early evening when the taxi dropped Gabriel on Offham Lane outside Rose Cottage. He stood by the gate for a moment, after the taxi had driven away, taking time to survey his familiar surroundings after his Berlin absence. It was a balmy evening, the light thickening. Rooks were cawing in the elms that fringed the big field opposite – their harsh half-laughs, half-coughs filling the air. A hint of summer's warmth remained despite the cooler breezes of the evening arriving from the north. Deepest England, Gabriel thought, hoping to be reassured now he was back home. 'Home', he considered – that most elusive and potent of concepts. All the same, he felt a near-tearful mood of affirmation and completion settle on him as he pushed his way through the gate and searched for his keys in his pocket. The clematis over the door had lost almost all its flowers and the garden looked uncared-for – the lawn thick, the herbaceous borders unpruned and rampant. Good, he thought, lots of work to be done – physical, distracting.

He opened the door, dumped his suitcase and grip in the hall, and wandered into the sitting room, switching on lights. There was a small odour of neglect: cold ash from the fire, ancient cigarette smoke and that faint, drainy undercurrent of ancient, semi-efficient pipework – not recently flushed through – that old buildings had. He looked at his watch – too late for shopping: it would have to be whisky and cigarettes for this evening – and whatever tins might be in the kitchen cupboard – before he could replenish supplies.

On the plane from Berlin to London airport he had written up an account of his Berlin stay and, more importantly, the events of President Kennedy's visit to the city. He had decided to be unequivo-cally contentious. He alleged that the Berlin attempt on Kennedy's life had been a joint operation between rogue elements in the CIA and their Mafia conspirators. He named Frank Sartorius, and Dean 'Dino' Furlan and his brother Matt 'Matteo' Furlan. Elements of the Berlin police were also part of the conspiracy, namely Kriminal-hauptkommisar Ödön Hempel.

The pattern was classic, he outlined. A lone, unstable gunman was the scapegoat, the 'patsy', in this case a deluded young man called Hendrik Vollmöller. Vollmöller, armed, was present in Rudolph Wilde Platz just before Kennedy's speech and was appre-hended. The threat seemingly averted. This was irrelevant as there was another key shooter present, a sniper in a nearby apartment block, in an apartment bought by Dean Furlan. This gunman, Matt Furlan, was discovered and killed by CIA agent Parker Baumgar-ten. Gabriel thought it was safe to specify – now that their guns had been swapped – and Parker would have told Peter Carlyle their new version of events. In the meantime, Vollmöller – who would have been an invaluable, not to say revelatory, source of information about the conspiracy – was also shot and killed by KHK Hempel. Again the established pattern: the 'lone gunman' is always elimin-ated. Case closed. He ended his report with the warning that it was only through sheer good fortune that President Kennedy was not assassinated in Berlin.

He lit a small fire, even though it was late June. The play of the flames and the crackle of dry wood was comforting. He poured himself a whisky, lit a Gitanes and set about typing up his report, adding a carbon copy for himself. It didn't take him long. He slipped the pages into an envelope and addressed it to Faith Green, Institute of Developmental Studies. He would post it to her tomor-row: she could make of it what she wanted. His task was over, he considered.

He switched on the television, searching for something mind-lessly diverting, and found a talent show. He topped up his whisky and lit another cigarette, urging his brain to slow down, to stall, go inert. He was trying not to remember the fatal confrontation with Matt Furlan. The second man he had killed in his life. The second man he had shot. Good Christ, he thought, feeling a bit shaken.

How deeply integrated was he in his parallel world now? He felt very insecure.

Then he heard a noise in the kitchen and stiffened, before realizing it was just the click-clack of the cat-flap operating. He looked around and saw the Cat pace softly into the room. It came close and sniffed at the cuffs of Gabriel's trousers. Gabriel sat very still. Then, to his astonishment, the Cat sprang on to his knees and stared at him, eye to eye, for a few seconds, before curling itself comfortably into his lap.

Bloody hell, Gabriel thought, almost about to stroke the Cat but deciding against it. One step at a time. He must have missed me, he realized. He sat there, sipping whisky, smoking, watching his talent show, the Cat warming his thighs, until the telephone rang.

'Sorry,' he said, sliding the Cat to the floor. It stalked off, tail high, clearly very irritated. Gabriel picked up the phone.

'Hello?'

Silence.

'Hello?' More silence. He waited a couple of seconds.

'Yes, it's me,' he said. 'I'm back.'

Hampstead, London

Friday 22 November 1963

Gabriel walked briskly to Frognal Way from Hampstead Tube. It was a cold, dark night with a brisk, surging wind and he was glad of his tweed coat and scarf – and wished he'd worn a hat. This was the latest appointment he'd ever had with Katerina Haas – 7 p.m. She was off to Vienna the next day, her receptionist had said, and this was the only opportunity available.

He had spent the night in his flat in Ruskin Studios – his first time there in weeks. Corless had handed him a strange note from Varvara: 'I am going back home. Can we meet? Varvara'. He assumed 'home' was Moscow. So, she was being recalled. That was quick, he thought – she had only been in London a few months. He wondered what the reason might be and also how it would affect his long-overdue encounter with Kit Caldwell. Perhaps it was a stroke of good fortune, he told himself – a delay would be inevitable and he wouldn't be complaining, that was for sure. He would meet Varvara if he could but it would have to wait. He too was off on his travels, once again. Happily, his own priorities seemed to have resumed their usual place in his life.

He pushed through the gate that led to Katerina's elegant house, keen to speak to her and tell her what was on his mind. This seemed to be the role she now had in his life – mother-confessor rather than psychoanalyst. He was happy to pay for the strange ease that confessing to her gave him.

He handed his cheque to Katerina's plump, smiling receptionist, Donalda – always payment in advance *chez* Haas – and was shown into the empty, panelled waiting room with its four chairs. Sitting there, waiting to be summoned, he could hear faint music. He assumed it was Donalda's little transistor radio that he'd spotted next to the telephone on her desk. What was that song? So catchy. He had heard it everywhere since he'd returned to England from his travels. Did she love me? he thought of Faith. Yeah, yeah, yeah.

Katerina appeared at the door to her consulting room. She was wearing a rich chestnut-coloured cowl-neck jumper with a long cream pleated skirt and tan Cuban-heeled boots. Her grey hair seemed much shorter, spikier. They kissed and she led him into the room and they took their seats. The oatmeal curtains were pulled to and the lights were low.

'I haven't seen you for ages,' she said. 'How are you?'

'Fairly OK.'

'That seems a bit considered.'

'I'm busy on a new book. I've been travelling for weeks, months – Paris, Rome, Cairo, Gibraltar. Off to Japan tomorrow. But I felt I wanted to see you before I left. Things on my mind. I've had some stressful times.'

'And I'm going to Vienna,' she said. 'Family matters. I'd rather be flying off to Japan with you.'

They looked at each other, smiling. There had been so many sessions together, he thought, though she was still a puzzling, half-known figure to him. Almost emblematic, he considered: his own Delphic Oracle, his personal Pythia. He knew so little about her – and yet she knew almost everything about Gabriel Dax. Maybe that was how things were meant to be. Maybe that was how this process worked.

'Shall we begin?'

She stood and switched on the tape recorder.

EXTRACTS FROM THE TRANSCRIPTION
OF SESSION 15

GABRIEL DAX: Earlier this year, in the summer, after our last meeting, I went to Berlin – on one of my 'assignments'.

DR HAAS: Oh, yes, your 'missions'. I seem to remember you

254

telling me you were going to Berlin. A most interesting city. I remember it well – before the war, of course. Why were you there?

GABRIEL DAX: It was to do with President Kennedy's visit to the city – in June.

DR HAAS: I remember. A triumphant success, no?

GABRIEL DAX: In almost every degree. But I was there because of a suspected plot against his life. A potential assassination.

DR HAAS: My Lord! But what had you to do with this?

GABRIEL DAX: I knew a man – a man I had met in Guatemala – who was suspicious. And because I knew him I was asked to go to Berlin to see if I could discover what he was up to.

DR HAAS: Who asked you?

GABRIEL DAX: The same woman – Faith Green.

DR HAAS: Ah, Faith Green. The Mata Hari in your life.

GABRIEL DAX: More like the Jocasta.

[SILENCE]

DR HAAS: I'll have to think about that. Are you sure?

GABRIEL DAX: In a way. I'm no Oedipus – look, we're not related – but there is something, I don't know, something fateful about our encounters. I saw her in Berlin, on this last trip, for one night.

DR HAAS: Did you have sexual relations?

GABRIEL DAX: Yes. And, ah, I have to say that they were very warm and fulfilling. Yes. In fact, I almost declared my love for her. That was a mistake, I think. I feel she still wants to keep a kind of distance between us. She always reminds me – you are 'my spy', she says.

DR HAAS: That maintains the power structure between you, of course.

GABRIEL DAX: I can see that. But at the same time, I feel a sort of helplessness when I'm with her, I have to admit.

DR HAAS: That's because all the feeling, all the 'love', is coming from you. No reciprocation.

GABRIEL DAX: There is some reciprocation, now. I do believe that. [Pause] I didn't particularly want to talk about Faith Green tonight. There's something else I need to tell you.

DR HAAS: Of course, please. Do continue.

GABRIEL DAX: These assignments I'm sent on – they're complicated, and sometimes dangerous. On two occasions they have been very dangerous indeed – and I've had to defend myself. [Pause] I have had to kill two men.

DR HAAS: *Verdammt noch mal!* Are you serious?

GABRIEL DAX: Yes. It was me or them. Self-defence. If I hadn't killed them I would be dead myself.

DR HAAS: My God . . . This is shocking, shocking. [Pause] But, you know, now I think about it, it seems to me that you should feel no guilt, Gabriel. I mean it. What were you meant to do? Anyone in your position would have to do the same—

GABRIEL DAX: But I've killed two people, Katerina. Me. Gabriel Dax. How did this happen in my life? How do I cope with this?

DR HAAS: How *do* you cope with it? How have these killings affected you?

[THE SESSION WAS INTERRUPTED AT THIS POINT]

Katerina Haas frowned and held up her hand. They could both hear the sound of sobbing. Out of control.

'It must be Donalda,' Katerina said and jumped up, alarmed. Gabriel followed her out into reception. It was indeed Donalda, the receptionist, her cheeks shiny with tears, her eyes red and bruised. She pointed at her now silent transistor radio.

'He's dead,' she choked. 'President Kennedy's been shot.'

Upstairs in Katerina's sitting room they watched an announcer on television confirm the news. President Kennedy, shot dead in Dallas, Texas. Three bullets, as the motorcade drove through Dealey Plaza.

Katerina watched with her hand to her mouth.

Gabriel felt a weight descend on him, as if his limbs were suddenly concrete and his spine was bending under the pressure.

'How awful,' Katerina said, a quiver in her voice. 'How absolutely terrible.'

'I'd better go,' Gabriel said.

He kissed her goodbye and headed downstairs, collected his coat and scarf and stepped out through the side entrance. Donalda had gone. He stood on the gravel path and lit a cigarette, gathering himself, thinking about Berlin and that short encounter with the man. The raised hand, the smile, the thanks. He felt a bit sick, in fact, a dry sour taste in his mouth. He threw away his cigarette.

He walked out on to Frognal Way. A wind had got up and the trees were thrashing about, autumn leaves being sent cantering through the silver pools of light cast from the lamp standards. A parked car flashed its headlights. A Mercedes-Benz 190 SL. Faith. How did she know where he was . . .? He stopped himself. Silly question.

He walked towards the car, opened the door and slid into the passenger seat. Faith was wearing a thick cable-knit cream cardigan and had a cream scarf loose around her neck.

'They got him,' Gabriel said. 'Finally.'

'I know.'

'Jesus fucking Christ . . .'

'There's already a suspect,' she said. 'A man called Oswald.'

'How do you know all this?'

'Austin Belhaven just told me.'

'Let me guess: a "lone gunman".'

'So it seems.'

'Well, he'll be dead soon,' Gabriel said and gave a dry little laugh. 'I'll give him twenty-four hours. Case closed.'

'Dean Furlan was spotted in Dallas,' she said. 'Yesterday.'

'Long gone by now. And Sartorius?'

'He was there. Coordinating security with the Dallas police.'

'Whose brilliant idea was that?' Gabriel shook his head incredulously.

'I don't know. Someone high up in the Company.'

'Didn't anyone read my report about Berlin?'

257

'I did. Its conclusions were quietly circulated.'

'To no avail, clearly.'

They sat in silence for a while.

'Furlan doesn't know you killed his brother,' Faith said. 'You're safe.'

'I wouldn't be too sure.'

'Parker Baumgarten got a medal. For bravery.'

'That won't protect her.' Gabriel inhaled, suddenly feeling small tears salt in his eye. 'What a mess,' he said.

Faith reached out and touched his face, his cheek, with her fingertips.

'It's awful, I know,' she said, 'But, look – remember – you saved him once.'

'I suppose so.'

He took her hand and kissed her knuckles.

'We're on the same side, Gabriel.'

'I know.'

'Can I drive you home?'

He looked at her.

'Thank you. That would be kind.' He suddenly remembered. 'I've got a present for you at the studio.'

'A present for me? Something from Berlin?'

'No. From Guatemala.'

She smiled at him and shook her head.

'Guatemala. Gabriel Dax. Incorrigible.'

She started the engine and the car headed off, powerfully, down Frognal Way and left into Frognal, making for the Finchley Road and Swiss Cottage. He had a strong feeling that Faith would stay the night. They both needed one another's company, needed to hold each other close. The thought reassured him as a bitter silt of sadness about Kennedy coursed through him again.

He turned his head and looked out of the window at the city as it flashed by, soft beads of white and yellow light climbing the dark glass, travelling over the contours of his reflected face like lucent, benign jewels bestowed on him.

Or burns that didn't burn.

Books by Gabriel Dax

The Wine-Dark Sea

Travels without Maps

Dictatorland

Rivers

On the Beaten Path (in preparation)

DISCOVER THE FIRST NOVEL
STARRING GABRIEL DAX

GABRIEL'S MOON

**An accidental spy. A web of betrayals.
A mystery that will take you around
the world . . .**

Gabriel Dax is a young man haunted by the memories of a tragedy: every night, when sleep finally comes, he dreams about his childhood home in flames. His days are spent on the move as an acclaimed travel writer, capturing changing landscapes in the grip of the Cold War. When he's offered the chance to interview a political figure, his ambition leads him unwittingly into the shadows of espionage.

As Gabriel's reluctant initiation takes hold, he is drawn deeper into duplicity. Falling under the spell of Faith Green, an enigmatic and ruthless MI6 handler, he becomes 'her spy', unable to resist her demands. But amid the peril, paranoia and passion consuming Gabriel's new covert life, it will be the revelations closer to home that change the rest of his story . . .

'A cinematic tale of globe-trotting adventure'
Guardian

AVAILABLE TO ORDER NOW